SAUL AND MORRIS, WORLDS APART

By the same author

SAUL
AND
MORRIS,
WORLDS
APART

A NOVEL BY

JAMES YAFFE

Holt, Rinehart and Winston
New York

Library of Congress Cataloging in Publication Data
Yaffe, James, 1927–
Saul and Morris, worlds apart.
I. Title.
PS3547.A16S28   813'.54   81-13304   AACR2
ISBN: 0-03-059432-4

First Edition

Designer: Margaret M. Wagner
Printed in the United States of America
1 3 5 7 9 10 8 6 4 2

ISBN 0-03-059432-4

THIS ONE IS OWED TO MY SON
GIDEON,
WITH ALL MY LOVE

According to Euclid, whose geometrical propositions we all live by, parallel lines can never meet. By definition they are equidistant at every point. Though they may come within sight and hearing of one another, they are bound to travel forever in their separate orbits.

Saul Glazer and Morris Unger had known each other for years. They were almost the same age, had been born and brought up in the same city, went to the same family parties, and looked back in their seventies on the same events of a disastrous century. But the truth was, they couldn't have been more different. Saul was a businessman; Morris was an artist. Saul had been married to one woman for fifty years; Morris was a confirmed bachelor. Saul lived in a penthouse on Park Avenue in New York; Morris lived in a studio on the Left Bank in Paris. Saul got a new overcoat every winter; Morris went on wearing his shabby old overcoat with the frayed velvet collar, which he threw over his shoulders like a cape. The two old men, in everything that mattered to either of them, were worlds apart.

And then, one night in November 1970, they defied the laws of Euclidean geometry. For just a few minutes they met.

MOVING

M O R R I S

At around two o'clock that afternoon Morris Unger left the office of his doctor, Artie Boroff. He had come all the way from Paris to New York to consult Artie, and afterward the specialist Artie had recommended. For the last half-hour he had listened to Artie explaining the specialist's findings. They didn't upset Morris very much. It could have been a lot worse.

Now, opening the outer door of the waiting room, he found himself face-to-face with his cousin Ruth Glazer, who was just coming in. A truly embarrassing moment. He hadn't told her or anybody else in the family that he was in New York. He had hoped to slip in and out without anybody knowing, because he didn't want people fussing over him, asking him a lot of questions about his health.

He apologized to Ruth, and she forgave him. "But only on one condition," she said. "You have to come to the party Saul and I are giving tonight. Seven o'clock, at our place, the whole family's invited. It's in honor of Jeffrey, he's just been promoted to full professor."

Morris vaguely remembered that her son was teaching at a college somewhere. He hadn't seen the boy in years. Skinny, with pimples and thick glasses, wasn't he?

He accepted the invitation. He wasn't really in the mood, but he couldn't hurt her feelings, could he?

He left the building and walked up to Central Park, to do what he had been planning. He sat on a bench at one of his favorite spots, the little lake near Sixtieth Street. He put his sketch pad on his lap and reached for the drawing pencil in the inside pocket of his jacket.

But he didn't bring it out. He blinked around at the trees and up at the sky. . . .

What's on my mind, for heaven's sake? My usual bench, this nice little lake in Central Park, my sketch pad on my lap—why don't I open it, take out my pencil, start doing what I came out here this afternoon to do?

Am I still thinking about what happened at the museum yesterday? Or that woman at the gallery this morning who wouldn't buy anything? No, that couldn't be it. I got used to that sort of thing years ago.

So get to work, will you? It's after three, the light won't be good much longer. Sad blue New York light, so different from dancing pink Paris light. Sun glinting off the water. Rocks reflected below. Maybe, if I'm lucky, a swan will come along. I could use a swan for the background of my girl in blue. Back home, sitting on the easel. Neck stretching out lazily, like a swan's neck. Her hair isn't right yet though. Too blotchy, the highlights need softening. So why don't you take out your pencil?

Dear God, what *is* the matter with me anyway? Is it running into Ruth Glazer, being invited to her party? Knowing I'll be seeing Saul again, those other businessman types like him: overbearing. Yes, I did tell myself I'd avoid all that for this trip. All right, I can't. Is that any reason to let them interfere with my work? They've been trying to do that for years, haven't they? Never let them pull me off the track before. No, not even a fraction of an inch. Straight ahead, in my own direction, that's how it's always been with me. That's been the basis of my career.

Not a bad career either, as these things go. All right, I'm not Picasso—world-famous, millionaire, reproductions hanging in every middle-class hallway and hotel room. Wonder how he felt about that, the way he hated the middle classes. But I'm not a complete unknown either. Done better than *most* painters do. People liked my work enough to pay money for it—earned my living by it since I was a boy, though no doubt it isn't what Saul Glazer and that businessman crowd would call a living. When Rembrandt died, he was poverty-stricken and forgotten.

And I've had other things in my life too. Love. No wife, no family—true enough—but that doesn't mean I haven't known love.

Really known it—which, if the truth were told, is more than the businessmen, giving mink coats to their wives, expensive cars to their children, can claim.

And freedom. Yes, I've known freedom. Wasn't handed to me on a silver platter when I was born. Had to earn it. Fought for it. Reached out and took it for myself. I was born in prison—so was my father, my mother, everyone else I grew up with. *They* couldn't even see it was a prison. *I* saw. Knew there was a world outside, a beautiful world—broke through the bars to get at it. Never looked back since then. Can Saul Glazer say as much, with all his tailor-made suits and his big cigars? He's in the prison still, I'm the one who got out. . . .

Even when I was a boy I wanted to be a painter. Very peculiar. Nobody else in my family ever did anything like that. In the old-country village, where my parents lived before they came to America, there was a superstition: good Jews didn't draw pictures of people, animals, or things; it was breaking the law against graven images. Nothing allowed but abstract designs. Maybe that explains some of the crazy painters nowadays, with their smears and their squiggles; it's their Orthodox Jewish ancestors coming out in them.

I can't remember when I didn't want to do it. Drew a picture of the rabbi during Yom Kippur service—in the old synagogue, when we lived on Delancey Street. His beard was flying in all directions, I had to get that down on paper. Drew him on the back of the hymnbook, my grandfather saw it. He would have killed me if my father didn't stop him. How old was I then? Ten, eleven years?

Four years later—or was it five?—an even bigger scandal. That little girl who lived on the floor below us—she was a year younger than me—they caught her in my room with her clothes off. I tried to explain. I was only drawing her: how else could I get a nude model? I did love the curve around her buttocks. Lovely half-moon dimple. Used that curve many times since then, still using it in my latest things. I'm not sure which explanation was more shocking to my family, the true one or the one they wanted to believe. My grandfather was dead then—my mother kept thanking God for that. A year before, when he died, she criticized God for taking him. People can be very odd. I've never been able to understand people.

My father protected me, but he looked sad. For weeks he gave me sad looks. He loved me—he knew I would turn out badly. I was sorry to make him feel that way. Never intended to hurt him. What could I do? I couldn't stop seeing things and wanting to draw them.

Maybe I didn't hurt him as much as I thought. My father was a timid little man, short and thin, round shoulders, bald spot on his head. Gray cheeks, gray clothes, gray fringes of hair—study in gray—Whistler. He never had any success in his life. A stationery store—that was his business downtown, also later when we moved up to 128th Street. It was no way to get rich. He didn't. Nobody ever paid attention to him. If he expressed an opinion, people ignored it or contradicted it. My mother especially. He didn't express many opinions. Maybe, in his heart, he was glad to have a son who had talent, loved beauty, might be an artist someday. Maybe, since there was nothing special *he* could do, he got some pleasure from knowing there was something special his son could do.

Maybe. I don't know. We didn't talk much.

I was eighteen, just out of high school. What I wanted more than anything was to go to art school, to study painting. There was the Art Students League, just opened on Fifty-Seventh Street. What was the year, 1915? If I was eighteen, that had to be the year. It cost very little to go there in those days. More than I could afford though—I had no money at all. It was my intention to ask my father for it. He would ask my mother, she was the one who kept hold of the money in our family. Ordinarily my father wasn't good at fighting for things. When they were for me, he got better at it.

I never asked him. The car hit him early in the morning, he was crossing the street to open the store. He died very quickly, he didn't suffer.

Now I had to ask my mother. Decided to do it right away. If she was still feeling the grief and shock from my father's death, maybe she wouldn't be in the mood to turn me down.

I knew it wouldn't work, of course. She was a stingy woman, my mother. Money meant more to her than anything else in life, she hated to let any of it slip through her fingers. She wasn't going to throw it away on art lessons for me. Besides, she was taking over my father's stationery store, she needed me to work in it. I had no brothers or sisters, there was only me to save her hiring an assistant. Yes, if I mentioned the Art Students League to her, there would be an uproar. I hated uproars, still hate them. People yelling, saying nasty things. I want them to be nice and quiet and leave me alone. I want them to let me get on with my work. Even so, I had to ask my mother about this. Even knowing I would get nothing out of it except the pains in my stomach. It was so important to me. It was everything to me.

I came out with it at breakfast. As early in the morning as possible, because her temper got worse as the day went on. "I won't be in the store till after lunch today," I said. "I have to go downtown to take care of something."

Her head was up right away at that. Chin quivering, eyes glittering like little beads. A very small woman, smaller than anyone else I knew, bony arms and wrists and fingers. Not gray though—red. Spots of red in her cheeks, red little tongue flickering, flecks of red in her eyes. You found out soon enough how tough she was. Like a stalk of grass, still standing after a thunderstorm, though the trees around it were knocked down.

"What something? What something?" Her voice was shrill and sharp. "Something is more important than working, bringing in the money? You're a Park Avenue playboy, you don't have to work for money?" As always, when she was angry or excited, she brought out the rest of her speech in Yiddish. She didn't know enough insults in English.

I couldn't understand her words. My Yiddish was terrible then— today it doesn't even exist. But I knew what she was saying to me. Nobody could have any doubts about that.

When she finally got tired enough to stop yelling, I said, "I have to go to the Art Students League. It's registration week. The courses don't start till next month, but this week I have to register."

"What is it? What is it? What are you talking about?"

"The Art Students League—it's an art school, the best one in the city. I want to take the courses in painting and drawing."

"What, what? I didn't hear you."

She had her hand cupped to her ear. She wasn't fifty yet, she was going deaf. It made me impatient and irritated with her. I've been paying for that a long time. I think of her when I see the impatience and irritation on people's faces.

"I'll be back at lunchtime," I said, raising my voice. "I'll be in the store the whole afternoon, I'll keep it open an hour later than usual. And when my classes start, I'll still give the store all my free time."

I knew, while I said this, that I wasn't being honest. I didn't intend to *have* much free time, away from the Art Students League. They gave you an easel and space to put it, you could go there when you weren't actually in class, you could work on your own.

"Free time!" The screech in her voice set my teeth on edge. "You've got no free time! You're working for your mother! You don't desert your mother! Your father isn't cold in his grave yet, already you're deserting your mother!"

"I'm not deserting you. Painting is my whole life—"

"Painting, painting! You'll make a living with painting? You'll eat paint? Bum! Bum!" She was off with the Yiddish again. Louder and louder. My stomach pains were terrible, I knew I could stop her by telling her I wouldn't go to the art school. It's a miracle I didn't do it.

In the middle of the Yiddish I saw a little gleam in her eyes. Shrewd, calculating, it knew exactly what was going on, it didn't have one bit of anger or hysterics in it. "And money?" she said, very clearly, in English. "To go to this art school, it costs money, no? To sleep here in your nice room, to have scrambled eggs and coffee, like you're doing now, in this nice kitchen—you think it comes for nothing? God drops it down from heaven, like the manna? You live here, you pay your share. You work in the store, or some other job that pays money. Otherwise—out!"

I slammed down my coffee cup. I shouted at her that I was going down to register for the art school, there was no way she could stop me. If she kicked me out of the apartment, I would find a place of my own, I would get along very nicely.

I could lose my temper too, in those days. When you're young, you're hotheaded. I learned to hold it in since then. It's too much of a strain. It makes your stomach hurt. Not too many things are worth it.

Riding in the subway, I was full of plans. Leaving the apartment, finding a little room downtown—with a skylight so I could paint. Full of plans.

I got off the subway, I was calm and cool again. I was using my head. I wasn't going to leave home. If I had no money to live with my mother, how should I have money to set up on my own? Why register for those classes this morning? What chance was there I could ever take them? My mother knew it too. That gleam in her eye was from knowing she had the upper hand.

It filled me with bitterness. I'm not a bitter man. I've gone beyond that. I learned a long time ago to accept what happens to me. Take life as it comes, be content. I was very young then, that's my only excuse. Money was what I needed. Not much, just a little. For all the chance I had of getting it, it could have been a million dollars.

In my bed that night I prayed to God. Very odd, as I think back on it. I don't believe in God—I didn't then either. No, I do believe in God. There *is* somebody or something who created all this—who made sunrises, light glancing off an apple, women's thighs. None of us could make any of those things ourselves. How stupid though to say prayers to Him. He isn't listening. He doesn't care what happens to us. Why should He? He goes His way, we have to go ours. While we can.

That night I prayed. For money. For a miracle, so I could go to the Art Students League.

I got my miracle—yes, amazing. A week later the letter came, very thick, important looking, from the insurance company. My father had taken out a policy on his life. Years earlier, and he kept up the premiums. It paid double if he died in an accident. I was the beneficiary.

He had never mentioned it to anyone. My mother was furious about this. Especially because he wasn't there to listen to the tongue-lashing she wanted to give him. It was cowardly of him not to be there.

I knew why he did it, made me the beneficiary instead of her. It was his way of telling me he wanted me to be an artist. He wasn't going to let her spoil it for me. He was still protecting me.

I did what my father wanted for me—I went down to the Art Students League and signed up. . . .

S A U L

Saul Glazer found out about the invitation to Morris an hour after Ruth issued it.

He was in his office, with a pile of letters on his desk. He'd been meaning to get to them all day, but one thing or another kept interfering. And right now, just as he was about to buzz for the secretary, his phone rang.

It was Ruth, reminding him to buy the cigars for tonight's party. He knew she would've been glad to do it herself, but he never let her. God knows what she might come home with, horse manure wrapped in toilet paper most likely! She finished reminding him, and then she told him she had a big surprise. He'd never guess who was in New York unexpectedly, who she had run into and invited to the party.

"Queen Elizabeth of England," he said. "She says she'll come, providing she can find a sitter for the princes and princesses."

"Now that's ridiculous, dear," Ruth said. "If Queen Elizabeth were in New York, don't you think it would be in the papers?"

Then she broke it to him that the big surprise was her cousin Morris Unger, the painter. He had nothing on for tonight, so he had accepted the invitation.

"Did he ever turn down a free dinner in his whole life?" Saul asked.

This was the type of remark that could always be counted on to get a rise out of Ruth. Sure enough he heard her squealing angrily at the other end, as he hung up the phone.

All right, he told himself, no more delaying tactics. He positively had to polish off this stack of mail before the end of the day. So he reached again for the buzzer.

He didn't buzz. Instead he leaned back in his chair and gave a sigh, and passed his hand over his eyes. . . .

What's eating me anyway? Look at this pile of letters. I should answer them before I leave the office today; I should call in the secretary right now. So why don't I make a move?

Is it on account of Jeffrey's nonsense these last few days? Positively not. I stopped paying attention to that son of mine years ago. So I'm upset maybe because Ruth's cousin, the crazy painter, is coming to the party tonight? Foolishness! Morris Unger isn't my favorite person in the world, I wouldn't deny it. An oddball, an impractical dreamer—who knows what goes on inside such a head? But he sure as hell isn't important enough to get upset over.

Certainly not for *me* to get upset over. Impractical is one thing even my worst enemies never called me. I'm a successful established businessman. I've always stood on my own two feet, earned my own way with brains and hard work. Anybody that ever did business with me would have to admit it: Saul Glazer is at the top of the industry. All the big department stores and specialty shops carry my line: Je

Suis Belle, Incorporated, ladies' negligees and nightwear—if you're a female, you have to be familiar with it.

And another thing they'll have to admit about me in the industry: my product has always been first class. Not like those shlock houses that sprang up during the war, when the demand was so high any Mongolian idiot could make a fortune. Personally I'd be ashamed to put my name on some of those rags. Though no doubt the artistic types, the Morris Unger types, wouldn't believe me if I told them this.

And another thing about me—for the benefit of the artists and the intellectuals and the so-called liberals that like to look down their noses at us businessmen—the way I've always treated my people, the people that work for me, has always been fair. Wasn't I paying the highest wages in the industry, long before the goddamned unions moved in and the government came along and told a man how to run his own business?

And one last thing the Morris Ungers should know about me. I gave a lot of money to charity in my day, and I'm still giving. Not only to the charities that get all the publicity—UJA, Federation, cancer—and most of it you can write off your income tax anyway. I also give in private, people with hard luck that need a helping hand, friends from the old days or poor relations. And that means Ruth's side of the family too, not just blood.

So the point is, no crazy artist or anybody else like that has any right to look down on me and call me some kind of money-grubber or pushcart peddler. I'm ready to stack *my* life against *his* any day of the week. My life is just as good, in fact it's a lot better, and what's more it always *has* been. . . .

I was nine years old when Mama died, and Papa brought us all up, me and my three sisters—they came into the world at year-and-a-half intervals after me. Papa sacrificed a lot for us, and I'm grateful, but I'm not going to lie about him either and pretend he was different from what he was. He was a typical immigrant from the old

country. He was born in a village somewhere in Russia or Poland—
who knows which? The people living there didn't even know.

Everybody is familiar with the kind of ignorant superstitious old-
country place I'm talking about. Mud and huts and goats, little boys
running around with ear curls and black hats, old men with long
beards reading Hebrew. Papa's father was a rabbi in the shul, and he
wanted his son to be the same, but Papa couldn't see it so he ran
away from home and came to America when he was sixteen. He
never learned to talk English without an accent. He lived on the
Lower East Side, with the pushcarts and the kosher butchers and the
Orthodox yeshivas and such.

As a matter of fact, that's where I was born and brought up.

One thing about Papa was unusual. Even though he had his own
store—cut-rate jewelry, for people who couldn't afford the good
stuff—what he *really* cared about in life was opera. God knows where
he got this taste from, how he ever found out there was such a thing
as opera in the first place. But from a young age he started collecting
records: Caruso, Tetrazzini, Chaliapin, all the big names—those
scratchy old records, you listen to them now they sound like they
were made by retarded children. But till the day he died what Papa
loved most was to sit in his chair in the living room and listen to
those opera singers on the phonograph.

Opera or no opera, though, he had all the typical immigrant ideas,
and one of them he held on to the hardest, you couldn't knock it out
of his head with an atomic bomb: his son, meaning me, should someday become a doctor. That's right, "my son the doctor." It's the
corniest old expression in the world, but for Papa it was real and
important. I never could figure out why. Maybe because everybody
he knew felt the same way, maybe because Mama used to talk about
it when she was alive. One thing is for sure—whenever he tried to
explain the importance of it to me, he got all tied up in knots, he
couldn't keep from contradicting himself.

"To be a doctor is the greatest thing in the world," Papa would

say, with a light on his face, like some religious old lady looking at
the Torah in synagogue. "He saves people's lives—he relieves pain and
suffering—he's a humanitarian, a saint. Also, he's educated, he's been
to college and medical school: he's a man of learning. Also, he never
has to worry about money. Walk uptown, Park Avenue, all those
fancy streets. The doorways are full of doctors' names. Even in hard
times people don't stop getting sick."

Since I was a little kid, as far back as I can remember, Papa fed me
this propaganda. For a while it sounded pretty good, but when I got
to be fourteen, fifteen, I started *thinking* about it. Even then I was the
logical, practical type, so I could see that it didn't make sense. "If
money is what matters, Papa," I'd say, "why don't you tell me to
go into business? In America it's the businessmen who make the
big money."

"Businessmen!" You should have seen Papa's face when he spit out
this word—like somebody who just realized that the egg he's chewing
is rotten. "All they do is look out for themselves, thinking all day
long only about their profits! No learning, nothing for humanity!"

"So make up your mind, Papa. Do you want me to be rich, or do
you want me to be a saint?"

"You couldn't be both? There's a law somewhere, a saint has to be
a good-for-nothing that can't earn a decent living?"

That's what Papa was like: no logic! The immigrant mentality!

As for my own feelings—all the time I was going to high school,
while Papa talked about this doctor business, I knew it wasn't for me.
College and medical school, that's a long time, you're close to thirty
before you start making a penny. I couldn't wait that long. I was in a
hurry to do something with my life. That's why the day finally
came—April 1915, a couple of months before my high school gradua-
tion—when I got myself a job.

And then I had to tell Papa about it.

All right, so what? He was a weak skinny man, and shorter than
me. How could he hurt me? What was there for me to be scared of?

I'm a decisive type of person. If you've got a dirty piece of work to do, what I always say is, do it quick so it's over with and behind you. That's what I was like even then, at the age of seventeen.

Just the same, it took me the whole afternoon to get up the nerve to break my news to Papa. Finally it was early evening, the sky was getting gray outside, my sisters were in the kitchen fixing dinner. Papa was alone in the living room, sitting in his big old easychair, which had been cleaned and patched a hundred times, so the blue color was all washed out. This was practically the earliest memory I had, Papa sitting in that chair, with the curtains pulled and most of the lights turned out, because he needed darkness to put him in the right mood. And on the table next to him was his phonograph, the old crank-up kind, with some opera singer blasting out of it to an accompaniment of scratches and squeaks. I came up to him now, just as he was about to put a record on the machine, and I spoke up quick, knowing that once Caruso or Tetrazzini started in, Papa would be lost to the world.

"I settled it this morning, Papa," I said. "I took a job."

He put the record down slowly and gave me a few blinks, like I was talking to him in a foreign language. "Job? What job?"

"It's in an advertising company. A man is in business, he hires this company to write his advertising for him."

"He couldn't write it himself? He never learned how to read and write? I told you, didn't I, businessmen are ignoramuses?"

"Businesses are getting so big these days they don't have time to do such things for themselves. Anyway, I'll go there Saturdays for the next couple months, just to familiarize myself."

"You'll work on the Sabbath? Very nice!"

"It's the only time I've got, Papa. As soon as school is over, I'll start in on a permanent basis."

"For the summer, you mean—until college opens?"

That was the question I was afraid of hearing, I admit it. But I'll give myself credit, I answered him in a calm natural voice, with nothing on my face to give away what I was feeling. Seventeen years old, and already I knew how to act like a businessman. "I've taken this job on a permanent basis, Papa. I won't be going to college."

"How will you be a doctor, if you don't go to—"

"I don't *want* to be a doctor."

"You always said—"

"*You* always said. I want to be a businessman, a business of my own. That's why this advertising job is such a good opportunity. I'll meet a lot of people in a lot of different industries, I'll keep my eyes open. Sooner or later I'll spot some promising company, not too expensive, that I can buy into. And then I'll be on my way."

It was out now, and I stopped talking. I don't know how I expected Papa to react exactly. Some kind of big explosion maybe. What I didn't expect was that his face wouldn't change, his voice wouldn't get any louder, nothing at all would happen to him—on the surface anyway. Except that somehow, I don't know how to explain this in words, he would suddenly seem to be a little whiter and a little smaller than he had been a minute earlier. But that, I decided right away, was strictly my imagination.

I was silent and he was silent, and pretty soon I couldn't stand that goddamned silence anymore, so I spoke up. "I know you've been saving up since I was born, Papa. I know the money is in the bank, and what a disappointment this is. But once you understand—"

Now he spoke—still not very loud, but there was something in his voice that made me shut up quick. "I understand fine. I understand you're going to be a millionaire and get fat from eating steaks and artichokes. I understand you're throwing away your brains and your abilities and your chances to do something good with your life, because you prefer to be a pushcart peddler."

Such a speech, if he had yelled at me, with his arms over his head—like one of those prophets out of the Bible, with a long white beard—probably wouldn't have upset me half as much as it did. Because he *still* didn't raise his voice, he still talked like this was an ordinary unimportant conversation. This quietness of his made me mad, in fact. "You're not being fair to me. After all, I'm a grown man!"

"Seventeen years—grown!" He gave one of his grunts.

This got me madder. "You were younger than that when you ran away from home back in the old country! Because you didn't like the future your father had picked out for you! So why is it any different for *me*? Why don't *I* have a right to lead my own life?"

Maybe I shouldn't have said those things to him. I was a pretty dumb kid, with all my smartness. I didn't know yet that some people, when they're old, don't like to have their younger days thrown up at them. His eyes tightened a little, and even though I was all wound up in my anger, I had an understanding somewhere deep down inside of me that he was in pain. He turned his head away from me and lifted the phonograph record again. "Good—wonderful," he said. "So suit yourself, big shot, go make your million dollars. Right now I'm planning to crank up this phonograph machine and listen to Caruso, so this conversation is over."

All of a sudden, I was desperate. Which is very peculiar, when you come to think of it. I was the winner. I was going to do what I wanted to do, and there was no way he could stop me. So what was I feeling desperate about? Why did I have to go on arguing? It's one of the few times in my life that I actually caught myself being illogical and impractical.

"Don't be like that, Papa," I said, aggravated with myself because I could hear my voice positively pleading with him.

"Be like what? I'm not allowed to listen to Caruso? I'm a grown man, no? Don't I have a right to lead my own life?" Then he put on Caruso, and who could get a word in after that?

So I was left with his last words, very soft, cutting through me. People have told me I can be nasty and sarcastic. Ruth is always saying so, and incidentally I don't necessarily take it as an insult. But if it's true about me, I've inherited it honestly. From old Aaron Glazer, my papa, the master himself.

As a matter of fact, he never really got over this decision of mine. For thirty years afterward, whenever Ruth or Jeffrey or I got sick and I had to call the doctor, Papa would give one of his sarcastic grunts and say, "If you'd listened to your father, you could be saving the money for this visit."

All right, I just had to live with it. There are things in this world you have to live with.

The following Saturday I went to work. . . .

M O R R I S

. . . I did what my father wanted for me—I went down to the Art Students League and signed up.

The Art Students League, old dirty-brown building, high ceilings, long corridors echoing with shadows. Not very nice looking really. Beautiful in my eyes. Six years I studied there. Learned valuable techniques, how to save time and unnecessary effort. It made me a professional.

My mother hated my being there, never got over it that I wouldn't give up my life to the store. "So how's the painter? Did you sell any paintings while you were downtown? Are you riding in Rolls-Royces yet?" I got used to the nagging, stopped listening. I did sell paintings occasionally—to a relative, to somebody who came to see the League exhibitions. That money went to my mother. I never felt guilty I couldn't give her more.

I was twenty-one—1918—when she died. A stroke, the doctor said. A tense woman, always under great tension, that's what brought it on. If you worry too much about the things around you—money, food, furniture, people—you get strokes. You have to roll yourself up into a tight ball, concentrate your energy on what really matters.

I saw her in the coffin, the day before the funeral. Thin lips pressed together, red spot on each cheek. Tense as ever, I thought. Was she spitting out her Yiddish at God?

I was alone now, in the apartment on 128th Street. I used to think it was too small, couldn't move without bumping into Mother. Now it was too big. Ugly furniture. Her smell was everywhere. I wanted to move downtown, near the League. The problem was the stationery store, three blocks from the apartment. It was all I had in the world, it could give me enough to live on, like it gave her. But I had to run it, be there every day. What I wanted to do was sell it. There didn't seem to be any chance of that. What was there to sell? The space was rented—only enough stock on hand for a month or two. Goodwill, people told me. I wondered how much goodwill a stationery store could have. Who cares what store they buy their stationery from? It isn't like the artist's name on a painting.

I could see myself back in prison. The iron bars were newspapers, magazines, pads, and pencils. Then, all of a sudden, I was rescued again.

The Boroff family—Abe and Sadie, their son and daughters—my father's cousins. I never saw much of them before my mother died. They didn't get along with her, they considered her ignorant and crude. She didn't like them any better, she considered them snooty, her mouth was always full of Yiddish curses at them. The Boroffs were the only family my father had in America—my mother cut him off from them.

Now she was dead, the Boroffs came into my life and rescued me.

They arranged the funeral—I was never good at making business arrangements. For a week afterward they put me up in their apartment, on 125th Street, only a few blocks away. I slept on the sofa in their living room—underfoot every minute. It couldn't have been very convenient for them. None of them ever complained in my hearing. When I went back to my own place, one or the other of the daughters came over every night, cooked dinner for me. Mostly Janet, who wasn't the pretty one.

They found somebody to buy the stationery store. An old man

who had worked with Abe Boroff in the New York State civil service. Retired now, with some savings. Looking for an easy one-man business to add a bit to his income, keep himself occupied. A nice sum of money came to me. It would give me another two years—painting, studying—if I was careful how I lived. Frugal. I learned how to do it then. It's come in handy through the years.

After the money was used up, I would have to think about what next, of course. Two years was a long time. It seemed to be then, when I was twenty-one. Nowadays it's two blinks of the eye.

I found a place near the Art Students League. Way west on Fifty-Sixth Street, almost to Tenth Avenue. Really not much more than a big attic room in what used to be a warehouse. Dirty, creaking floorboards, one flight down to the bathroom, drunks from the docks were on the street at night. Crouched, grimacing—Goya. It was mine. I lived there alone. My first taste of freedom.

I saw a lot of the Boroff family. They had me up for dinner once a week, they felt sorry for me, I think, thought I was starving. Because I was so skinny, I suppose. I've always been skinny, even when I'm eating well. Sadie Boroff was a good cook, in the style of the world they lived in. It wasn't French gourmet cooking. It was meat, boiled or roasted, big fat potatoes, chicken broth poured over everything. Not to mention the noodle soup that started off every meal. I didn't care about French gourmet cooking in those days.

The best thing about the Boroffs wasn't the cooking. It was Ruth, the younger of the two girls, the pretty one. Small, dark, nice figure, nice breasts and hips, all on a small scale. I've always preferred small women. Strange really, because it's not the type I like in paintings. My taste goes to Rubens, Renoir, Degas, Bonnard. Big hefty women, folds and folds and folds of flesh, plenty of opportunity for shadows, curves, layers of color. That Italian—what was his name?—peculiar little man, never sober, killed himself with absinthe—Modigliani, that's it. Those matchstick women he specialized in never appealed to me at all.

Ruth was my type in real life. I liked her personality too. Cheerful, talkative, full of jokes and giggling. She liked it that I was an artist. Told me my pictures were wonderful, how sensitive I was, what a deep nature I had, what a beautiful soul. Such nonsense . . . so long ago.

The rest of her family couldn't appreciate me. Friendly and kind, didn't know a thing about art. Terrible pictures on their walls: old prints of Greek ruins, medieval castles—smudged, heavy, ugly drawing. Sold by the dozens in those days to people who wanted to look cultured. And they had a cousin—Celia something, recently divorced—terribly fat girl, made Rubens look like El Greco. Studied to be an actress once, used to give recitations from plays and poems. Very exaggerated gestures. That was the Boroffs' idea of art and culture.

To tell the truth, they didn't even *care* about art. They looked at my paintings and said, "How nice!" It could be the worst thing I'd ever done, it could even be unfinished. Then they changed the subject, back to what really interested them—clothes, money, family gossip. Irving, the son, told jokes, dirty ones, about medical school. Everybody laughed, then they turned to me and explained what was funny. A lot of people talk to artists that way, I've often noticed it. They think we're childish, feebleminded.

I felt like a stranger to all of them, except Ruth. Very odd. Why did I single her out? She wasn't any different from the others really. Laughed at the same jokes, applauded those awful recitations. A part of me knew it even then, while I was telling myself the opposite. The time, for instance, when I took her to see my Degas.

I was thirteen when I first saw my Degas. I had been to the Metropolitan Museum many times before, on that morning I turned into a new room. She was waiting for me on the opposite wall. Ballet girl, white dress, arms lifted, feet in the first position. Eyes lowered—shy and modest maybe. Or maybe just listening to the music, worrying she might miss her cue to start dancing. A little awkward and dumpy, of course—she would never be more than an obscure member of the *corps de ballet*. Degas loved the obscure ones.

She was beautiful. She took my breath away. At thirteen I often had my breath taken away. Rembrandt's man in the helmet did it to me. That enormous Rubens nude—who was she? Persephone, some such mythological character. Nothing had ever hit me as hard as my Degas did. It changed my life. It made me see what kind of painter I wanted to be.

I didn't realize that at the age of thirteen. I realized only that I wanted to keep coming back and looking at her. It was ten years later when I took Ruth to see her.

"Oh yes, I've seen this one before," Ruth said.

She hadn't ever mentioned it to me. That was hard for me to understand. Then I realized *I* hadn't mentioned my Degas to many people either. There was no pleasure in talking about her to people who wouldn't understand, wouldn't love her as much as I did. Maybe Ruth had been feeling the same way.

"Don't you think she's beautiful?" I said.

"Oh yes. Beautiful. I don't think she could be much of a dancer, though. She's got such thick calves. She should take off some weight."

I loved those thick calves. I said something about the curving lines, the shadows around them. "Oh, I certainly see what you mean," Ruth said. "You're not bothered by her ankle? The right one. Why is it twisted up in that funny way?"

"It's the first position. Dancers stand like that in the first position."

"Oh yes, of course. I can't think of anything I love more than the ballet."

"You've seen a ballet?" I looked at her with wonder. I had never seen one myself, it was the dearest wish of my life.

"Oh yes. When my parents took us all to the vaudeville show at the Palace. On my brother Irving's last birthday. One of the acts was a ballet. The girl was a nymph, and the man was a hunter chasing her through the woods. I didn't like *him* very much—he could jump quite high, I'll give him that, but I think it's so *feminine* for a man to wear tights. But *she* was marvelous. Very tall, and what a trim figure! I'd give anything for a figure like that."

She paused. A few years later, thinking back on this conversation, it occurred to me she wanted me to say something in that pause. How her figure was as trim as any ballerina's, something like that. No such idea was in my head. These things always occur to me too late.

She went on talking. "She didn't look at all like this girl here, in this picture. It's a wonderful picture, of course, a real masterpiece, but don't you think it's a shame Degas couldn't have found a more attractive girl to paint, somebody who could do the first position more *gracefully*? It wasn't his fault, I suppose. The really good models must have charged a lot of money, and since he was a struggling artist . . ."

I took her by the arm, led her into the next room. Landscapes mostly. I was a little hot, I could feel it on my cheeks.

I learned an important lesson from that experience. If there's something that means a great deal to you, gives you special pleasure and satisfaction, don't tell other people about it. Especially not people who mean a great deal to you too. Don't take the risk of spoiling two good things for yourself.

After that I saw Ruth as much as ever, loved to be with her as much as ever. She made my heart beat faster, just looking at her. We had lovely times together. When she wanted to go to a museum or an art gallery, though, I always made some excuse. We went somewhere else.

And then, in 1920, early in the year, everything changed for me. . . .

S A U L

. . . The following Saturday I went to work. For this advertising company, Rubin and Rosenblatt; they had an office uptown, on Broadway in the twenties. In those days that was uptown for me. It was an up-and-coming firm at that time; ten years later, when the big money moved into advertising, it got slaughtered.

I was an errand boy, office boy, wastebasket emptier, and pencil sharpener, but also they let me write some copy and go out sometimes to talk to a prospective client, if he wasn't such a big one. I did a pretty good job of this, so they let me do more and more of it— which was what I was after.

I was looking for some promising businesses I could buy into, and I saw a lot of possibilities. Once I came damn close, a company that manufactured toys. Today I could be Saul Glazer the Toymaker. But at the last minute I noticed something fishy about their books, so I pulled out of the deal.

So I kept my eyes open, kept making contacts, and finally I saw what I was looking for. Je Suis Belle, Incorporated. It used to be a very solid firm, one of the best, but the old man died and the son was the playboy type, only interested in throwing away his money on chorus girls and horse races. The big ambition of his family was to unload the firm before he managed to run it into the ground for good. If I paid cash on the line right away, I could pick up the whole shmeer cheap.

It looked perfect, and frankly my tongue was hanging out. But there was one small hitch to it. I didn't have enough money saved by myself yet. So I brought in a partner, Oscar Kaplan, who was also working for the advertising company. He was exactly my age, and he came from a family of immigrants that wasn't too different from mine, only they lived in Chicago. His father was a tailor, ruining his eyesight in the back of a dark little shop, and Oscar's brothers, older than him, were already on the way to doing the same. So Oscar had decided this wasn't for him, and got out at the age of sixteen and came to New York to change his luck.

He was a smart fellow, and an even better salesman than I was. He had a certain flair, a certain chutzpa which was special. The fancy words he came out with! He was a great reader of Shakespeare, no less, and was always throwing him into the conversation. Also he had looks—I mean *looks*. He was the dark type, with shiny hair and long eyelashes like Rudolph Valentino, who became popular in the movies a few years later. He dressed like something from a magazine ad, with always a flower in his buttonhole. God knows how he could afford his clothes, he was as broke as I was.

In other words, we were the perfect combination. Oscar had the sex appeal, also the wild merchandising ideas that you wouldn't think they could work but half the time they did. (All right, Oscar, I can almost hear you snorting at me—three-quarters of the time!) And I was the steady practical type. I kept track of the accounts, made sure the books balanced and the orders got filled on time and Oscar didn't throw away all the profits on some crazy scheme.

It wasn't long before we started doing very nicely. World War One was a big help to us, I couldn't deny it. There was a lot of money around, a good time for new businesses. By 1918, 1919, a couple of kids still wet behind the ears, both of us under twenty-one years—and we were executives, tycoons!

Now, all of a sudden, it was important to me to live up to my new situation in life. Things I never used to give a thought to—like polish, elegance, high-class manners—I now had to give lots of thought to. Where was I going to learn about such things? Who was going to be my teacher? Oscar—who else?

The first lesson was the night of my twenty-first birthday. Oscar took me out for dinner that night to the fanciest steak house in New York, and after we finished we took a stroll down Broadway, the Great White Way. A nicer street to stroll down than it is today. Not so many people, not so much garbage in the gutters, the neon signs weren't so big and glarey. There was even an occasional tree on the corners.

And in those days everybody around you wasn't mad at the world, like today, didn't stick elbows into your ribs to get past you. It was possible, while we strolled, for Oscar to take hold of my arm and talk to me in a leisurely manner, using his wise man-of-the-world voice, like he was a millionaire uncle visiting his poor relation in the sticks.

"You're twenty-one years old, Saulie old pal," Oscar said. "That's the legal age of manhood in these United States of America. You arrived at your *first* manhood at the age of thirteen, when you went through that quaint old ceremony, the bar mitzvah. They taught you Hebrew prayers, which have no doubt come in very handy for you in later life. So now, for your second bar mitzvah, I'll be giving you information and instruction which will be equally if not more useful."

Sometimes it could take Oscar a long time to get to the point. He *did* love the sound of his own voice! So I broke in and asked him what the hell he was talking about.

"I'm talking about education," he said. "Eight years ago you were educated in how to take your place as a Jewish man. Now you have to be educated in how to take your place as a rich man."

"But I'm *not* a rich man."

"You're getting there, you can't avoid it. And when the time comes you have to be prepared. Now just for openers . . ." And Oscar reached into his inside pocket and pulled out a shiny silver case, which he snapped open, revealing a row of black cigars.

I could imagine what was coming, and I knew there was no escape, but I tried some delaying tactics anyway. "*You're* prepared?" I said. "When were *you* rich, I'd like to know?"

"I've been rich all my life," Oscar said. "In every way except for the money. I always knew it was only a matter of time before my bank account caught up with my tastes. All right, the first thing to know about being rich—cigars. Big ones. They should be expensive. More important, they should *look* expensive. Carefully observe this little collection here. Note how the combination of shape, color, setting, atmosphere practically shouts out that these cost money. Light up one of these little bombshells after lunch and dinner, and when you're sitting behind your desk putting on a show for a buyer.

She won't *dare* refuse to give you an order. Of course it helps if you know *how* to light it up."

For the next ten minutes I got my initiation in how a big business executive smokes his expensive cigar: the whole process of snipping off the end, rolling what's left between your fingers, maybe even holding it up to your ear while you're rolling (though God knows what you're supposed to be listening for: Oscar didn't even pretend to know), giving a sniff or two, then lighting up in quick short puffs and letting the smoke out very slowly, and giving a big satisfied sigh. The big satisfied sigh was the hardest part for me that first night, because I thought I was going to be sick right there in front of the old Astor Hotel. But I wasn't, I exercised my self-control, and after a year or two, the satisfied sigh actually got to be genuine.

"Now the second thing you have to know about," Oscar said, "is highballs. Not too many, one or two a day, in a tall glass. That's important—business tycoons don't fool around with drinks from small glasses. I can recommend a nice brand of Scotch—"

"As a matter of fact, I don't much like the taste of whiskey."

"Sorry, but you'll have to grin and bear it. That's one of the sacrifices you make on account of being rich. That's what people like J. P. Morgan and John D. Rockefeller mean when they tell the newspaper reporters about 'the responsibilities of wealth.' Now the third thing is your golf game."

I reminded Oscar that I didn't *have* any golf game, but he brushed this aside easily. "I'm going to get you one. We'll go out to the public course this weekend, and I'll start teaching you. I'm in the process now of negotiating membership into a club—a little tricky when you're as young as me, and you don't come from the highest-class family, but I've got my contacts. It's out in Westchester, this club, not one of the old German ones but not too kikey either. As soon as I'm in, I'll get myself on the admissions committee and take it over, and then I'll have them elect *you*. In the meantime, though, you should be learning the game. Number four—your clothes."

This annoyed me, because one thing I was a little proud of in myself was my taste in clothes. I asked him what was wrong with them, and my annoyance must have showed through, because he immediately put on a soothing voice. "Don't get insulted, there's absolutely nothing personal in this. Objectively and impersonally now—look at that whatever-it-is you're wearing. Is that a suit, or is it an old sack you picked up in the garbage? A man lets the world know who he is by the way he drapes himself. 'The apparel oft proclaims the man.' *Hamlet* by William Shakespeare. A play about a fellow who neglects his clothes, and everybody thinks he's crazy. Anyway, I'll make an appointment for you with my personal tailor."

"Since when do you have your own tailor?"

"As a matter of fact, it's my older brother Harry, he just moved to New York and bought a shop. But the point is, people like us—the leaders, the ones who have been singled out to run this world—should be ashamed to put on a suit that doesn't fit our individual personality. Would you go to Macy's basement and pick up a pair of arms and legs off the rack? Would you let yourself be seen in a ready-to-wear prick? Incidentally, when we've finally got some civilized suits and shirts for you, I'll give you my famous lesson on neckties. Their color, shape, and length. I don't want to hurt your feelings, old pal, but some of the ties I've seen around your neck I wouldn't use them to wipe my ass."

"I get the point," I said, and I have to admit there was now a definite stiffness in my voice. "I'm a mess. So please don't spare me, any other ways I can improve myself?"

"Plenty of others. I haven't even scratched the surface. How much you should tip to waiters and cab drivers. The types of jokes you should tell. The difference in your tone of voice when you're talking to your help, to the buyers, to your fellow card-players at the club, to men in the industry who are bigger than you. The list is endless, but let's work on the obvious disaster areas first, later on we'll get to the fine points."

"You're sure it's worth the trouble? Maybe I'm so far gone there's no hope for me."

"Yes, I can see why you're worried. You are a tough case, no doubt about it. But don't get discouraged, tough cases are what I thrive on. I *like* it when the odds are against me. 'We shall be remembered—we few, we happy few, we band of brothers!' *Henry the Fifth* by William Shakespeare. A play about another fellow that enjoyed a good fight." Oscar looked at his watch. "The night is still young—plenty of time for the most important lesson of all." He stopped walking and started waving at the street. "Taxi."

"Where are we going?" I said. "A lesson in what?"

"Women!"

A cab stopped. Somehow, even on Saturday nights at busy corners, cabs had a way of stopping for Oscar—there was something magical about his waving. We got in, and Oscar gave an uptown address, then leaned back with a contented sigh. "Women," he said. "In our business you have to know how to handle them. Smoothness, finesse, sophistication—at every stage of the relationship, from the restaurant to the boudoir. You have to learn the elegant way, the rich man's way, to do everything from lighting their cigarettes to stroking their boobs."

"For God's sake, Oscar, are you taking me to a whorehouse? You know, I do have some experience along those lines—"

"The type of woman *you've* got experience with—she wouldn't know finesse and sophistication if they came up and bit her. She thinks you're being elegant if you take off your shoes before you jump her. No, I'm definitely *not* taking you to a whorehouse. We're paying a call on a couple of ladies who are specially equipped to instruct you in the finer points of sexual dalliance."

"I assume they get paid for their services?"

"They do—and handsomely. But you're the birthday boy, so it's all on me."

"It isn't the money I'm worried about. I'm just wondering what you'd like me to call them if they're not whores."

"Pedagogues," Oscar said. "And I'm counting on you to address them with proper respect. No lewd looks or coarse phrases, okay? Tell yourself we're going to Paderewski's place for piano lessons."

At this what could I do except laugh? That was Oscar. You could never stay annoyed with him for long. Sooner or later, with the big production number he made out of everything, he'd have you laughing.

And he did polish me up, I have to admit it. In fact, once I started wearing decent neckties and talking correctly to the help, the next step was inevitable. I decided the time had come for me to get married.

I was still only twenty-one, but it never occurred to me or to anybody else I knew that I was too young for such a step. We got married younger in those days than the kids did a generation later. Maybe because we started earning a living younger too—or maybe because we were too ignorant about psychology and sex and so on to realize what we were getting ourselves into. They tell me, incidentally, that early marriages are coming back with this new generation, the one my grandchildren are growing up into. I suppose that's because they're all sleeping together anyway, from about the age of twelve, and getting a divorce is easier than getting a driver's license used to be.

So my reasons for considering marriage were naturally very practical. I was still living at home with Papa and my three kid sisters, and the place was much too small for me. My sister Doris—she was supposed to be the "pretty" one, frankly I could never see it myself—brought home a different boy every night, and I could constantly hear her nagging at them in that high shrill voice of hers that went through me like an electric shock. My sisters Goldie and Dodie, who were on the plain dumpy side, *didn't* bring home any boys, and they were constantly weeping over this in each other's arms.

Another practical reason for me to get married, I was sick and tired of the neighborhood. Papa's jewelry store was doing pretty well, he had moved it uptown to West Forty-Fourth Street, but he positively refused to move his residence uptown too—it took me another five years to talk him into that—so when I looked out the window I saw the same old rotten surroundings, the signs in Hebrew letters, the people hollering from the other windows. What kind of an atmosphere is that for an up-and-coming young businessman?

Oscar was always after me to get myself a bachelor apartment, like he had—and I could certainly afford it. But to tell the truth, the idea of living alone didn't appeal to me. Oscar enjoyed going to restaurants, but I liked home-cooked food that I could eat in peace, without a lot of strangers talking at the next table and waiters hanging over me and interrupting my conversation. Oscar could live in a mess, with stuff all over the floor, unmade beds, laundry piled up—which was very peculiar, considering how elegant and spotless he always was in the outside world—but I wanted everything around me to be neat and clean. Most of all, Oscar liked having his private love nest where he could bring a different girl every night, but I liked my life to be steady and predictable. I wanted a girl I knew all about ahead of time so she wouldn't surprise me. In other words, I was definitely the type that needs a wife.

It was 1920, and I was twenty-two years old, when Oscar introduced me to this girl that he met at the Metropolitan Museum of Art.

Not that Oscar actually went in for paintings and sculptures and that type of thing. What he used to say was, "If you're at loose ends and bored stiff with the old stuff, the best way to find something new is go to the art museum. There are always a few pretty young things there looking at the pictures, and you've got a much better chance to strike up a conversation with one of them than you would anywhere else. She knows you must be respectable and serious-minded, and also have a sensitive soul, or what would you be doing in a museum in the first place?"

So Oscar had struck up a conversation with this pretty girl, and they went out for a cup of coffee afterward, and then they arranged to meet there the next day. This went on for a few weeks, until Oscar started to get the feeling that this girl had ideas about marriage. Oscar had an infallible sixth sense about this sort of thing. He used to say he could smell ideas about marriage through a woman's pores.

"Well, naturally it's time for me to pull out," he told me. "Before I break the poor girl's heart. Or worse still, before she fixes it so that I don't."

"If she's such a lovely girl," I said, "why *not* marry her?" I knew the answer to this question, of course, but I always got a kick out of hearing Oscar say it.

"I'm too young to take on such a responsibility," he said. "I need more ripening. I won't be ready till I'm a mature man—about fifty-seven, say."

So his idea was that the next time he was supposed to meet this girl at the museum, he'd take me along with him, then he'd leave for an urgent appointment, and I could pick up where he had left off. "By the way," he added, "her name is Ruth Boroff."

Thinking back on it now, what amazes me is that shivers didn't go running up and down my spine at that moment. My whole life was about to be turned inside out, and not even one little shiver. My God, I'm shivering right now, fifty years later! Because ten minutes after Oscar introduced me to Ruth Boroff, I could see there were possibilities.

She was one year younger than me, almost twenty-one. Nowadays, the way she tells it, she was only eighteen, but the truth is twenty. For quite a while now Ruth has been automatically knocking a few years off her age whenever the subject comes up. Even when she fills out official documents, like passport applications or insurance forms or her social security, she can't stop herself from lying about her age. She has this idea that one of the privileges of having money—*my* money, that is—is that you don't have to grow old as fast as the poor people do.

In those days she was also the physical type I've always been attracted to. Small, a nice thin figure, dark hair, big eyes, a cute smile and manner. She liked to tease you and make cute jokes at you, but it was a little-girl teasing, no sharp sarcastic remarks. If there's one thing I didn't want in a wife, it was sarcasm. I've known women like that, believe me. I've got this niece, my sister Goldie's girl—I haven't exchanged two words with her for the last fifteen years, on account of this totally uncalled-for sarcastic remark that she made once.

Another thing about Ruth back in those old days—if you happened to tease her back, she didn't realize half the time that you were doing it, and when she finally did catch on she blushed so hard you had to feel sorry for her. What I'm getting at is, she had no sense of humor. Absolutely none. But the peculiar thing is, in those days this was a trait that gave me a big kick. I didn't want a woman with a sense of humor. I wanted a woman who could take things seriously—especially me.

One of the things she had even less sense of humor about than anything else was her family. They weren't so different from my own family, though God forbid she should ever admit it. Her father worked for the state of New York, he did something with an adding machine in the real-estate bureau. They were quiet people, typical immigrants, except their accents weren't as heavy as Papa's. To *my* ear, that is. To somebody who wasn't familiar with such accents, I suppose there wouldn't be anything to choose between them. Ruth likes to brag how her mother was a native-born American, but that's strictly a technicality. Her grandmother was in her last month all the way over on the boat, and it was touch and go if the baby would get dropped before or after they got through immigration. As for Ruth's brother and sister, they didn't have anything special about them. Irving was studying to be a doctor when I first met the family, and he practiced for many years, but he never exactly developed into another Louis Pasteur or Jonas Salk.

Her sister Janet—in fairness you could say she's somebody special. She's certainly done something with her life that most people never do.

The point I'm making, Ruth used to brag about this family of hers as if they were the Roosevelts or the Rockefellers or the Royal Family of England. She never noticed how funny she was being, and to tell the truth, at the beginning I got a kick out of how she didn't notice. I thought it was a charming trait of character, believe it or not.

That very first afternoon I met her, for instance, when I took her for coffee after the museum, she started in with the bragging about her family. We were talking about some movie we both had seen, I told her how unrealistic I thought it was, and she got upset and asked me if I didn't believe a woman could sacrifice money and social position and everything for the man she loves. I answered that I was in business five years, with plenty of opportunities to study human nature, and frankly I didn't notice much sacrificing going on. And that's when she came out with the bragging.

"My mother did just that though," she said. "Her family disapproved terribly of Daddy, they thought he wasn't good enough for her. Because in their opinion he was a foreigner—when she met him, you see, he had just come over from the—" She stopped herself fast. I could tell she was just about to say "the old country," but I suppose that sounded too lower class to her, so she said "from Europe" instead. "Mother was born in this country, you see, right here in New York. She was a Steinbrunner, you know, a very fine family. *Her* parents, my grandparents, they're dead now, came here at a very young age—they came from Germany—well, very close to Germany, practically on the border—"

"Where did your father come from?"

"My mother was a Steinbrunner—did I mention that yet? And *her* mother was a Mayerhoff. Though personally I think people who pay attention to that sort of thing are just snobs. I don't see what a person's family background has to do with anything, as long as he's a nice person."

"I absolutely agree with you about that," I said. How could I keep it out of my mind at that moment that family background wasn't exactly my strongest point?

"Besides," she went right on as if I hadn't spoken—it really didn't matter what you said to Ruth, once she got up a head of steam, "even though Daddy was born in Europe, he came from a *very* fine family, one of the outstanding families in—where he came from. His father was a rabbi."

"My father's father was a rabbi too. Quite a coincidence."

"My second cousin Nathan Steinmetz, he's from Atlanta, Georgia, the southern branch of our family, is studying to be a rabbi right now, as a matter of fact. So the point is, Daddy's side is just as cultured and artistic as Mother's. We're cultured and artistic on *both* sides."

"Myself, I'm pretty ignorant about that sort of thing."

"But you're obviously a very intelligent and sensitive person. I'm sure you could appreciate art and literature and all, only you've never been exposed to it."

"I've been exposed. Only I happen to be immune."

"I don't believe it. I'll go to work on you for a while. I'll take you to the museum with me—I go there every month or so. I could look at the old masters for hours. And I play the piano too, I've been playing for three years, all the classical composers. I took lessons from my mother's sister, my Aunt Etta. Musical talent runs through the Steinbrunners. Did I tell you my mother was a Steinbrunner?"

"I thought you said she was a Mayerhoff."

"No, no, *her* mother was a Mayerhoff. Anyway, I love to play the piano. I just lose myself in the music, I feel like I'm floating up in the air. It's a very spiritual experience."

"Is it anything like getting drunk?"

"Well, I wouldn't know. I've never *been* drunk, though I did have some champagne at my cousin Celia's wedding—" She broke off suddenly and stared at me with her eyes wide, and then gave a puzzled little giggle. "You were making fun of me, weren't you?"

"Now why should I do a thing like that?"

Her giggle got more confident. "I like people with a sense of humor. My brother and sister are always making fun of me, but what I say is, if you can't take a joke—"

"A sense of humor must run through the Steinbrunners," I said.

"Oh it does—we all have it!"

All right, it was like shooting at a sitting duck. But I didn't mean anything cruel by it. It made me feel like I was closer to her. I did it for pleasure. Later on I did it for other reasons.

Anyway, before we said good-bye that afternoon, Ruth invited me for dinner at her home, to meet her family. . . .

M O R R I S

. . . And then, in 1920, early in the year, everything changed for me.

The money from selling the store had almost run out. I wondered what I was going to do. I had a teacher at the Art Students League— old Augustus Kelly, did still lives mostly, very fine draftsman, nobody like him for laying out a bowl of fruit—died of pneumonia in the 1930s. He liked my work, thought it was time for me to go to Europe. He was a personal friend of Marcel Brulard at the Académie Julien—Brulard used to be a pupil of Degas'. Kelly felt sure he could get Brulard to take me on, without any tuition.

How was I going to get the money for the boat passage, living expenses in Paris? The bars of the prison again.

Something always came along to lift those bars. Kelly knew Mrs. Charles S. Newberry—the widow of the railroad tycoon—a great patron of the arts. One of the things she did was to support young artists who wanted to study abroad.

Kelly showed her some of my pictures. She liked them, he told me, wanted to meet me personally. She never agreed to help a young artist till she met him personally, decided if he was the right type. What did that mean? It worried me terribly—my mother's influence. I was sure Mrs. Newberry would lose interest in me as soon as she realized I was Jewish.

She lived in a house on Gramercy Park. Four stories, beautiful red brick, marble hallways, sweeping staircase, Roman busts. The oddest collection of pictures. Beautiful masterpieces—Degas, Corot, Gainsborough—all mixed up with terrible muddy portraits of her ancestors. That house was torn down years ago, apartment building there now.

She had me ushered into the drawing room. Bay windows. Chippendale furniture, very valuable, a little heavy for my taste. A plump little woman with snow-white hair, carefully coiffed, curled, smoothed. She poured tea for me, asked me questions about myself. Soft voice, never showed excitement, annoyance, pleasure: that's how they're brought up. I can't remember much about what was actually said that afternoon. It isn't failing memory. I couldn't remember ten minutes after I left her house. I remember I didn't exactly answer her questions untruthfully, I just left things out. I left my mother's Yiddish out. I said my father had been in the stationery business.

Every minute I was with her I was frightened of spilling tea on her expensive carpet. Here's a funny thing: in the next fifteen years I visited her many times, often had tea in that drawing room. I never got over being afraid of spilling it.

When I left her I was sure I had made a terrible impression. Pains in my stomach, the usual symptoms. I had dinner with the Boroffs that night. They knew something was wrong with me: I couldn't eat seconds of Sadie's pot roast. Afterward I went for a walk with Ruth, told her how badly I had done. She told me she was sure I had done very well. If Mrs. Newberry didn't like me and agree to help me, that proved what a silly old lady she was, no taste or judgment at all. Someday, when I was a world-famous artist, I could laugh right in her face.

That was the night I knew I loved Ruth. If I went to Paris, I wouldn't go alone. I would ask Ruth to marry me and come with me. . . .

A week later I heard from Mrs. Newberry. Indirectly, through old Augustus Kelly.

He greeted me in class with a big smile. Network of wrinkles on his face, every wrinkle turned up now, as if it was smiling on its own. Mrs. Newberry had come through, he told me. She liked me and believed in me, she would pay my passage to France, give me a grant for a year. Not a very large grant, enough for my needs if I lived modestly. No problems there—I was used to living modestly. I might have had trouble living any other way.

I went to Ruth after my last class that afternoon. She was at home, putting polish on her nails. Terribly earnest absorbed look on her face . . . light from the window reflecting off red nail polish . . . Vermeer. She spent a lot of time on her hair and nails—didn't have a job, didn't work very hard helping her mother keep house.

I told her my news. She laughed, cried, threw her arms around my neck, told me how much she envied me, she would give anything in the world to go to Paris. This sounded like the opening I needed.

"You don't have to give everything," I said. "Just marry me."

"What's that, Morrie?"

"Marry me. Be my wife."

I turned my head away. The surprise on her face . . . of course, it was a shock to her. Stupid of me to imagine she could ever think of me in that way.

Then I felt her fingers on my arm. "Oh Morrie!" she was saying. "Oh, that's the most flattering thing anybody ever said to me. . . . You'll give me a little time to think it over, won't you?"

As much time as she wanted—how could she even ask? You can't expect women to make decisions on the spur of the moment—that much I knew about them. They're like artists, indecisive, always wavering back and forth. They see all the different sides of things and worry about them. A man—most men, that is—does the first thing that comes into his head. He won't see more than one side of anything. He calls this being businesslike.

A few days later she asked to come down to my studio. She had never been there before. I had never brought a woman there—too dirty, the smell of paint on top of everything else. Her voice was full of excitement. I knew I'd be spoiling it for her if I didn't let her come.

I opened the door to her, she got her first glimpse of the place. She gave a little gasp. Then she got hold of herself. She smiled—did it very well, I have to give her credit. "Why, this is wonderful," she said. "I don't know what you're always complaining about. It's a real painter's studio. Just being here makes me feel artistic."

Very nice, but what was her answer to my proposal? She had to sit me down next to her on the sofa first—ratty old sofa, stuffing and springs popping out—and take my hands, look into my eyes. Soulful. Used to see looks like that in the movies all the time.

"Oh, Morrie darling," she said. "I *will*, I *will*. . . ."

But it turned out she didn't want anybody to know about it yet. We'd be secretly engaged till June, when I left for Europe. So much more romantic to keep it a secret, she said. Then, just before we sailed, we'd go off quietly to the registry office, make it official, tell people afterward. How amazed they would be—she could imagine their faces. "Do you give me your solemn promise? Not one word?"

Of course I gave her my promise. It was like a fairy tale, I thought. Like the story of some ballet. I was the prince. She hugged me, kissed me, told me the next three months would be simply beautiful.

I watched the smile on her face, sucked it in with my eyes. Creases at the corners of her mouth, reflected by creases at the corners of her eyes. That's the trick about doing a smile. I learned it that day, been using it ever since.

Ruth was right. It was beautiful being secretly engaged. . . .

S A U L

. . . Ruth invited me for dinner at her home, to meet her family.

I can't remember too many details about that dinner. Ordinarily I've got a good memory, but my feelings that night were all mixed up, and after fifty years how am I going to straighten them out?

What I do remember is, I'm not the type that gets nervous about meeting people—I figure I can hold up my end of the conversation in *any* crowd—but on that occasion I was nervous. It didn't help any when I saw the neighborhood they lived in. A Hundred and Twenty-Fifth Street and the West Side, the section that turned into Harlem about ten years later. Today nobody you'll ever know personally would be seen dead up there, but in those days it was one of the neighborhoods where the immigrants moved as soon as they began to make a little money. The Boroffs lived in a building that was fairly new, made of gray stone, around ten stories high. A European palace or a southern mansion it definitely wasn't, but for a kid like me, whose father positively refused to budge out of the Lower East Side, it was pretty impressive.

Maybe the most impressive thing about it, at least in my eyes, was that it didn't have any fire escapes running down the front of it. All my life I've had this peculiar hatred for fire escapes. To me they're like some kind of badge, or like stripes or something, that a building wears to let the world know what a low-class dump it is.

The inside of the Boroffs' apartment impressed me too. I didn't know a damn thing about furniture, and I still don't—and who wants to?—but I could tell their stuff was a lot better than what we had at home. It was newer, more up-to-date—more American, that was the only word for it. Today I realize it was strictly Macy's basement, but in those days I was comparing it to the heavy, faded, old upholstered chairs and couches on the Lower East Side, which had a smell that made me think of goats and mud, even though every piece had been bought in this country—secondhand, from peddlers on the street.

What made me most nervous of all were the signs of culture and education all over the Boroffs' apartment. There were pictures on the walls—real pictures, showing old Greek ruins and castles and cows grazing in the fields and so on—not just family photographs, like at home. There were shelves filled with books, some of them new and shiny, some of them old and thick and looking as if only a rabbi could read them. There was a piano in the living room, the biggest piece of furniture in the place. To prove what a stupid kid I was in those days, I took one look at all this stuff and I began to feel sure I was going to say some ignorant thing at dinner, or make some terrible mistake in my table manners, or otherwise show them what a lower-class slob I was.

As it turned out, though, nothing like that happened. The evening passed by without a single disaster. I didn't even spill anything on my jacket. Ruth's family were a loud bunch, they loved to hear themselves talk, but also they were interested in hearing *me* talk. I got on to one of my favorite subjects, the importance of advertising in putting over a product nowadays—which was something, without bragging or exaggerating, that I knew a little bit about—and they all listened to me with great interest and had a lot of questions to ask. Then I told some jokes—most of them I picked up in the last few months from Oscar—and everybody appreciated them. And just so I wouldn't be a complete bust on the culture front, I told them about Papa and his opera records. And it turned out that Ruth's sister Janet—who was a year older, Ruth said—was crazy about opera too, and even had some records of her own. So all in all it wasn't such a bad evening.

So why was I still feeling mixed up when I went home that night? I won't beat around the bush. What confused me after that dinner, and went on confusing me for weeks, was Ruth's sister, Janet.

I couldn't understand how I felt about her. Because in every respect that I could think of she was exactly *not* the type that appeals to me. In fact, she was the direct opposite. She was tall, almost as tall as me, and I like a woman to be short, I want her to look up at me when she talks to me. And Janet definitely wasn't pretty: her figure was all right, though there was a little too much bosom for my taste, but her nose was too long and her chin was too sharp. Truthfully she looked a little bit like a horse. She had quite a smile, that much I'll admit. Suddenly she would switch it on, and it made her whole face and the surrounding area light up with pleasure, with joy. But even this smile, though I found myself waiting for it, watching her hard and hoping it would come breaking out, made me nervous when it did. It was—how can I explain this?—such a *positive* expression. There was something so *positive* generally about Janet, about her facial expressions, her gestures, her voice. She wasn't loud—as a matter of fact, she had the softest voice of anybody in that family, and she did a lot less interrupting—but you always knew, whatever she said, that she really *meant* it, she was going to follow through on it, she was throwing herself into it all the way. Another way of saying this maybe is that Janet had a mind of her own. You got a feeling that if she didn't agree with you she'd say so in no uncertain terms, and that if she thought you were talking like a damn fool she wouldn't hesitate to laugh at you.

As a matter of fact, once or twice during that dinner, she came out with certain quiet little remarks that I couldn't exactly understand at the time, but later on I began to wonder if they hadn't been jokes at my expense.

So for all these reasons I should have disliked her very much, I should have put her down as a pain in the ass and forgotten about her. But that was the peculiar part of it—I couldn't forget about her, she kept running through my mind. And what was worse, I couldn't dislike her either. In fact, from the first moment I laid eyes on her I liked her, and I got to like her more and more as the evening went on.

After a while, in fact—the way it always is when there's somebody in a room whose good opinion you particularly value—I started looking out of the corner of my eye at her, to see how she was reacting to what I said. Was she showing an interest in my ideas? Was she laughing at my jokes? And before long, even though I wasn't necessarily using her name or staring straight at her, I was really addressing all my remarks to her.

When I left I shook hands all around—a long warm one for Ruth, a short quick one for Janet, and I didn't look her in the eye.

Is it any wonder I felt confused when I got home that night? And went on feeling that way for the next four months? The truth is, I couldn't make up my mind.

Now to most people, maybe, that wouldn't seem like a matter of much importance. But I'm a man who knows his own mind, weighs the pros and cons of a problem and makes a decision. Indecisiveness I positively can't stand. I find it in somebody who's working for me, I get rid of him pretty damned quick. All my life I never liked wishy-washy people.

I took Ruth out a lot in those four months. I took her to the movies and to restaurants, once or twice even to a show on Broadway. Even in those days I liked the musicals and the farce comedies better than the straight dramas. After a hard day's work, with plenty of depressing people that you have to come into contact with, who wants to go to a theater and see *more* depressing people up on the stage? And pay good money for the experience too?

All this time, while I was going out with Ruth, I wouldn't ask Janet to go out with me. *That* hornet's nest I didn't want to stir up.

But that didn't mean I wasn't seeing a lot of Janet anyway. Plenty of the time I spent with Ruth I was also spending with her family. I got to be a regular dinner guest, twice a week, sometimes even more, and I had a standing invitation to drop in on Sunday afternoons, when the Boroffs were always at home and members of their family used to gather. I met her cousin Celia Solomon, the one whose wedding Ruth tasted champagne at. She was a divorced woman then, built like a blimp, used to drive everybody crazy with her poetry recitations. I met her cousin Nat Steinmetz, who was studying to be a rabbi, and already he couldn't open his mouth without sounding like he was giving a sermon. That's one of the big things they teach them at rabbi school. I met Morris Unger, the painter that she told me she once had a crush on, but it was all over with a long time ago. And what I'm getting at, on these various occasions I saw Janet.

And we did a lot of talking together, even though the room was crowded with her family. We went into a corner alone and talked together, we might have been all alone. And if somebody came up to us, I always looked up surprised, because my conversation with Janet made me forget there was anybody else in the room.

What did Janet and I talk about? That's hard to say after all these years. It wasn't the same things as Ruth and me, that's for sure. For one thing we did a lot of laughing, which I didn't do with Ruth—giggling maybe, but not laughing. But also we were serious, which I also wasn't with Ruth. Sincere maybe, but not serious.

I used to tell Ruth about what was happening in my business, for instance. She used to listen to me and give a nod or a gasp from time to time and tell me how wonderful and exciting and complicated it all sounded, and how much she admired me for being able to keep all those things straight in my head. She cared about it for *me*, that's what I'm getting at. She cared about it because *I* cared about it. But I could tell from the start that she didn't care about it one bit for *itself*; there wasn't anything in *it* which interested her or excited her or which she was even willing to bother thinking about and trying to figure out. And pretty soon, if I ran down a little, she'd start talking about her clothes or the movies she went to or her wonderful family, the things that *really* mattered to her. And that was fine with me. I loved to listen to her talk about such things, I loved to see that little-girl enthusiasm come bubbling out of her.

Now with Janet it couldn't have been more different. I talked to *her* about my business too, but what I got back from her weren't nods and gasps but questions: how did this work, what did that mean, why did I make such-and-such a decision rather than such-and-such a decision? And often enough, when I answered the questions, I'd get from her more questions, even suggestions, sometimes even arguments. It was annoying as hell, in a way—this little snot-nose girl should be telling *me* how to run my business!—but also it made me feel good in a way, because she was really paying attention, thinking about what I told her and taking it seriously. Then she'd tell me what *she* was doing: her job with this big firm of stockbrokers, how she wished she could be more than a secretary, she wished she could actually learn the business. She'd explain the ins and outs of the stock market to me, and I loved to listen to her. Not the way I loved to listen to Ruth though. It wasn't the *way* Janet talked that gave me pleasure, it was what she talked *about*. There aren't too many women you can say *that* about.

So I'll try to sum up my feelings during those four months. When I was with Ruth I always felt very nice and comfortable. She made me see that I was somebody a woman could admire, that I'd be on top of things all my life. When I was with Janet I felt upset and irritated half the time, like I was a balloon and she was a pin. Who needs it? Life is too short for such aggravation! But the other half of the time I'd feel what I never felt with Ruth. Excitement. Like when you're on a fast train, the window is open, the wind is whipping against your face. I've always been crazy about trains.

So what was I going to do? I wanted to get married, to spend my whole life with a woman—and here were two women, and I liked them both, and all I had to decide was which one did I want to spend my life with. And incidentally, I had a pretty good idea that either one of them would have said yes to me if I had asked—which was important, because it's been a principle of mine all my life, one of the chief reasons for my business success, that I never get myself involved in a deal unless I'm pretty sure I can pull it off. But here I was, going

along for four months without being able to decide which deal I
wanted to pull off.

I've never been in the habit of letting other people make my
decisions for me. But I got to feeling so desperate that I actually asked
Oscar's advice. Which turned out to be of no use at all.

"Personally I wouldn't touch either of them," he said. "One of
them will whine you to death, the other one will argue you to death.
I'm very fond of both of them, you understand. Whichever one you
marry, you'll get my heartfelt congratulations—as long as it's you,
not me."

I couldn't go on like this forever. Eventually the balance had to tip,
and sure enough it did. . . .

One night, it was the middle of May, when I came to pick Ruth
up for dinner I learned she was in bed with chicken pox. She refused
to let me into her room—afraid I should see her with red spots on her
face. I remember thinking if Janet was the one with the chicken pox,
she wouldn't give a damn how she looked with her spots, she'd
probably be making jokes on the subject.

I had a reservation at a restaurant in Greenwich Village where you
could get lobster, so I asked Janet if she'd mind standing in for Ruth.
She told me yes, and looked pleased about it—and I don't think I'm
flattering myself either.

Lobsters are delicious food, but they're conversation killers. We put
on our paper bibs and got down to the job of sucking, digging, and
prying, and it wasn't till we had the remains of the two corpses in
front of us that we could talk. Then, through salad, coffee, and apple
pie, we talked about everything—politics, women's fashions, the latest
shows. She wasn't shy about disagreeing with my opinions, and tonight, for some reason, I liked it.

We did some walking after dinner—up Fifth Avenue, a clear warm
night. And suddenly these crazy words came out of me: "Tell me
something, Janet—what's it like to live with your sister Ruth?"

She didn't say anything for a second or two, then her voice came very quiet. "She's my sister, she's only a year older. I love her. I've never had any trouble living with her."

"Even though the two of you are so different? You work, you earn your own living, and she stays at home and takes it easy all day long."

"Don't give me credit for working, for heaven's sake. It's my natural temperament. I can't be still, it drives me crazy if I'm not *doing* something. You're the same way yourself, a maniac for work. But Ruth—*her* natural temperament is to sit back and let other people work *for* her. She's been that way since the day she was born. As long as I can remember Mother and I have been picking up her clothes after her and making her school lunches for her and ironing her dresses before she went out on a date."

"So how come you haven't got a first-class resentment against her?"

"What on earth would be the point? Ruth won't ever change. What's more she'll never *have* to. She'll find a nice rich husband someday, and he'll hire people to do things for her."

"That's probably true," I said. "Your sister is a terrific girl. Beautiful, vivacious, intelligent. The things she knows about—art and culture and so on—it's no wonder she's got plenty of men after her. A man could do worse than have a wife who can handle that side of life for him, who knows how to decorate a room and arrange a dinner party—who can give him a little class. And he'd be marrying into a good family too, a fine old German background."

She wasn't saying anything, so my voice trailed off and I turned to look at her. She was shivering. It was a nice spring night, no chill in the air at all: how could she be shivering? Suddenly it seemed to me that she looked terribly small—delicate even. Her face didn't remind me of a horse at all—her nose seemed to have shrunk.

She'll be a handful, I told myself. But how could I live my life without her?

So right then and there, in the middle of Fifth Avenue, I asked

Janet Boroff to marry me. And right now, fifty years afterward, I can feel the way my heart went into my mouth while I waited for her to say something.

"Oh Saul," she finally said, "I don't know what to tell you. I know you're in suspense, and I do want to give you an answer. . . ."

She wouldn't give it right away though—just like a woman.

"We can't talk in the middle of the street," she said. "Couldn't we go someplace where we can have some privacy?"

Personally I didn't see why this was necessary. The people walking down Fifth Avenue around us had their minds on their own business, they weren't interested in listening to our conversation. But Janet felt this way about it, so naturally I was willing. The only problem was, where could we go for this privacy she mentioned? *She* lived with her family, and *I* lived with my family; both our places were full of relatives. In the end, all I could think of was to head uptown and sit in the waiting room at Grand Central Station, which is like a big empty deserted cave at that time of night.

So that's where we went, and sat down at one end of a long bench, as far away as we could get from the bums who were curled up for their usual night's sleep. The lights above us were dim—the railroad company wasn't wasting money on electricity this late at night. Janet's face was in shadows when I asked her my question again.

"Saul—darling," she said, making me shiver a little, because "darling" was something she never called me before. "My feelings for you are . . . You'll be a wonderful husband—any woman who's lucky enough to get you—"

"Any woman? Meaning not you?"

"I didn't say—I'm mixed up, it's such a surprise. What I've thought all these months . . . It's Ruth you've been taking out. Ruth was the one you were interested in. I never let myself think—"

"If it's Ruth I'm interested in, why am I proposing to you? Am I the type that doesn't know my own mind?"

"Of course you're not. I'm not saying . . . What you don't understand—all my life it's Ruth who attracted the boys. She's the pretty one. Any boy who came to the house, naturally he preferred Ruth."

A fine way to do business, I thought. You run down your own product and build up the competition! This running-herself-down habit was her one big fault. Maybe it was also one of the reasons why I wanted to marry her.

"Another thing," she was saying. "You ought to know something about me. There was a boy once—Donald. Donald Shannon. We went to high school together. He was a very sweet boy, very shy and intellectual; he played the violin."

I hated him already. I could picture him in my mind: skinny, with a pasty face and his hair too long, the type that didn't have enough guts to wipe the snot off his nose. "So what happened to him?" I asked.

"Our senior year, he proposed to me. I told my folks. There was a terrible uproar. He wasn't Jewish—he was Catholic—Irish. *His* folks were pretty upset about it too, I guess. He told me, if we couldn't get permission from our families, we'd elope. But . . ."

She stopped talking, and squinting in the dim light I could see the tightness on her face. She went on with the story, but I could've figured it out by myself. The violin player, with all his big talk about elopement, caved in on her in no time flat. I felt sympathy with her, nobody can say I didn't, but let's face it, what kind of a life would she have had with that long-haired pansy?

"You don't see this fellow anymore?" I said. "You don't still think you're in love with him?"

"No, of course not. Sometimes I wonder what I ever saw in him."

"So why bother your head over him? You didn't even have to tell me."

"I wanted you to understand certain other things about me."

"What other things?"

"After all that with Donald—I got over *him*, but I didn't get over what *happened*. If you see what I mean."

I didn't and said so.

"That I could let somebody do such a thing to me, *that's* what I couldn't get over. That I could be so stupid and naïve and—and so *dependent*. On somebody else—on one silly boy! My whole happiness in life, and I let it be ruined by *other people!*"

She was getting excited and angry, and to tell you the truth I didn't like it much. What she said about not wanting to be dependent on other people, that I could understand, I had the same feeling: why else was I in business for myself? What bothered me was that a *woman* should have this feeling. How was a woman supposed to get used to her future in this world if she wasn't willing to be dependent?

"So once I was over the shock and thinking clearly," she was saying, "I made a promise to myself. I promised myself I'd never let it happen to me again. Maybe I'll fall in love with somebody again, but I'll never again give up my freedom and my independence—and my belief that I *matter*. Not just because somebody else wants me, but for *myself*, even if nobody wants me."

I was liking all this less and less. "I don't see what this has to do with us," I put in fast. "*I'm* not going to run out on you like that no-good pan— what's-his-name. You don't have to worry anymore that nobody wants you."

"It *isn't* that I don't trust you, Saul. You're the most dependable person I ever met, and you've got a kind heart too—though you'll never admit it in a million years, you think you're such a ruthless businessman. But I still have to feel a certain way about myself. That's why I've got this job now, with Hillman and Sons. When I graduated high school, I wanted to go to college, but my folks wouldn't let me. They sent my brother Irving, and they had enough money to send me, but my father said it would be a waste. You don't need college to learn how to run a household and bring up a family."

Personally I could see her father's point of view, but this didn't seem to be the time to say it.

"Then I told them I wanted to go to business school, to learn typing and shorthand and some accounting and so on. They told me this would be a waste too. But I went anyway."

"How did you manage that?"

"My aunt, my mother's older sister, died about ten years ago, and she left some money to all her nieces and nephews because she had no children of her own. My share wasn't much, but it was in the bank in my own name. So I used it to pay for that year in business school."

"Your parents had a fit, I'll bet."

"I didn't tell them. When I left the apartment in the morning I told them I was going out for a walk or shopping or visiting friends. They never suspected a thing. It wouldn't have occurred to them, you see, that I could lie to them. Ruth has always been the one who lied to them, but they didn't think I had enough courage. The only hard part of it all was, how I could practice my typing. But this girl who was in the school with me let me keep my typewriter in her apartment."

"After the course ended, did it take you a long time to find this job of yours?"

"It was the first ad I answered—I was very lucky really. After that, of course, I had to tell my folks what I'd been doing. They didn't take it too well. The look on my father's face . . ."

I knew what she was talking about. I could remember that look.

"And it's going to be even harder, I think," she said, "when I tell them I'm moving out, I won't be living with them anymore."

"They'll be happy, believe me. Parents are always glad to see their daughters settled—"

"No, I don't mean *that!*" Her face was so startled and amazed that I wasn't exactly flattered. "I'll be moving out in a week or so, as soon as I can find my own apartment. I don't need anything very big—"

"Wait a second, let me get this straight. You're planning to live all by yourself?"

"I have to. If I'm ever going to be independent. I *love* my parents, I really do, but sooner or later a grown person just can't go on *living* with them."

"That'll cost a lot of money, won't it? You can afford the rent on a secretary's salary?"

"Well . . ." A funny look was suddenly on her face—guilty almost.

"That's really the big thing I wanted to tell you. I just found out about it this morning."

I didn't like the sound of this, though naturally I kept my feeling out of my voice. "Found out about what?"

"Mr. Hillman's been thinking about it for a long time. I've learned a lot about the business and the stock market and so on, and now he wants me to move into the regular part of the firm—actually working with customers, selling, analyzing, having accounts of my own. It's not much to begin with, of course. I'll only be doing what a dozen other junior people are doing, and there's no guarantee I'll ever rise any higher—"

"Hillman has women handling people's accounts?"

"I'll be the first one. Mr. Hillman says that more and more of the clients are women, widows who inherited money from their husbands and they're looking for investments. He thinks maybe some of them would feel better discussing their financial affairs with another woman than with a man. Anyway, he's going to try the experiment." Her face lighted up—that big excited smile which positively made her look pretty. Only this time I wasn't so happy to see it. "It's the chance of a lifetime, Saul!"

The chance of a lifetime! And what about the chance *I* was offering her for her lifetime? "It's a crying shame, in a way," I said. "On the other hand, if you ask my opinion, the idea wouldn't have worked. It didn't stand a chance. A rich widow might want to talk to another woman about her love life or her hairstyle, but when it comes to money—"

"*Didn't* stand a chance?" Janet was staring at me, her eyes wide open. "I don't follow you. The idea hasn't flopped *yet*. I mean, don't write me off before I've even *begun*."

"I wouldn't do that, I've got a lot of admiration for your ability. But since you aren't *going* to begin—"

"Who on earth says I'm not?"

"Well, after we get married, how are you going to be a wife and a lady stockbroker at the same time?"

Now believe me, I understand how this question would sound if somebody came out with it today, 1970. We've got Women's Lib. We've got not only lady stockbrokers but lady lawyers, lady plumbers, lady governors of states. Nowadays every woman thinks she's got a right to hold any damn job she pleases, no matter how lousy she's going to be at it. But that conversation I had with Janet Boroff, in the Grand Central Station waiting room, was in 1920. Her ideas about herself, what she was going to do with her life, were ideas that nobody else was having—nobody *we* knew anyway. I was entitled to get mad at her, back in 1920.

"Or was that all just a lot of phony talk you were giving me before?" I said. "What a wonderful husband I'll make! You're so happy I didn't choose Ruth! You never let yourself think—"

"Saul, *no!* I *love* you!"

"You've got a funny way of showing it. 'I love you, but excuse me, I'm going to be a big shot on the stock exchange so I can't marry you!' "

"I *will* marry you!"

I had to give my head a shake. "So what's all this with the stocks and the widows? Would you make up your mind please, one way or the other?"

"It doesn't *have* to be one way or the other. It can be *both* ways. We can get married, and we can *both* have our business careers."

I looked at her a few seconds, and this time I couldn't stop myself coming out with it. "You're crazy," I said.

"But why can't we? Is there some law against it?"

"How about the law of nature?"

"That's the silliest thing I ever heard in my life."

"Because you weren't listening to *yourself* just now," I said. "What about children? Marriages occasionally produce them—"

"I *want* children," she said. "I think I'll be a good mother."

"How are you going to find the time, if you're such a big shot with the stocks and bonds?"

"A mother doesn't have to spend every *minute* with her children, does she? Even women *without* careers don't do that. Look at all the rich women who hire nurses and governesses, and go out shopping or playing cards or having lunch with their friends. Why is it all right to be away from your children for *that* kind of thing, but it's a crime to be away from them so you can do a useful job that you're good at and love?"

"The two situations aren't the same at all," I said. "If you weren't so stubborn, you'd see there's no comparison between them."

"*You're* the stubborn one! I mean, that's a wonderful logical argument you just gave me, isn't it? You know why you're taking this attitude? Because you're *afraid* to marry me!"

"Afraid! What of?"

"That your wife might turn out to make as much money as you do. You're afraid people might laugh at you or something. That's the one thing in the world that worries you most—making a fool of yourself! Saul darling, if you're going to be happy, sometimes you *have* to make a fool of yourself—"

"This argument is getting ridiculous," I said. "It isn't worth going on with."

We went on with it for a while longer, though, until it was midnight and we both had worn ourselves out. So I took her home.

I wasn't mad at her anymore—that was just a momentary reaction. How could I be mad at having my eyes opened in the nick of time, seeing the truth before it was too late, being saved from making a terrible mistake? At her front door I was glad to shake hands with her and agree we wouldn't stop being friends. After all, she was still the most interesting woman I knew, when it came to having a serious discussion or laughing at jokes.

I went up to the Boroffs' apartment first thing the next morning so I could ask Ruth to marry me. That's what I'd been intending to do all along, I realized. She was the one I met first and got interested in first. It was only some kind of temporary brainstorm that pulled me off the track.

Today she was willing to talk to me, but even so she kept her room dark. I practically couldn't see her face, and she wouldn't let me turn on the light. She said it gave her a headache. When I came out with what I had to say, she hemmed and hawed, acted like it was a big surprise to her. Strictly a lie, but that's all right, you wouldn't want a woman to be too eager when you propose to her. In the end, of course, she said yes. In fact, I made it downtown to my office by ten o'clock.

That was the middle of May. We decided on a wedding late in June. . . .

M O R R I S

. . . Ruth was right, it was beautiful being secretly engaged. Exciting to sit in the living room with her whole family around us, to listen to her talk, watch her face, all the time knowing we shared something that nobody else could guess.

The pleasure was the greatest when we took risks. Unnecessary risks, those were always the best kind. Ruth put herself next to me on the sofa. While her father made a speech about the economic situation—he had some small civil-service job, he talked sometimes as if he were the president of U.S. Steel—she let her hand slither down to mine, until our fingers were touching, clasping. For a long time we sat like that, anybody in the room might have noticed. Once I felt sure her sister Janet noticed. She was intelligent, sharp eyes, talked less and saw more than the other Boroffs. But she never said anything to Ruth or me. Maybe she didn't notice after all.

We took another risk when the Russian ballet came to town. Augustus Kelly had two seats for the weekend matinee. He got sick and was confined to bed, he gave me his tickets. I never could have afforded them myself. They were the most valuable objects I had ever owned. Kept taking them out of my wallet, fingering them, making sure they hadn't disappeared in a puff of smoke since the last time I looked.

I invited Ruth to go with me. Her family didn't approve of shows on Saturdays. They were old-fashioned people in some ways, still believed in the Sabbath. Ruth was twenty years old, lived at home and depended on them. She couldn't go against them openly. She told them she was going to a friend's house, then she met me on the corner.

Four short ballets on the program. I wouldn't think much of them now, I suppose. I've even forgotten the names of the dancers—long and Russian, of course; dancers had to have long Russian names in those days. To me every one of them looked like a great star. To me there had never been so much light, so much color, all in one place— and the bodies turning into light and color—whirling, exploding in my eyes. I was seeing what Degas saw. That was what took my breath away.

In the intermissions—and afterward, when it was all over—I didn't say anything to Ruth. I pretended not to hear her, broke in with a different subject, when she started to make comments. I loved her— with my whole heart and soul—but I knew it would all be spoiled for me if I talked to her about it.

At five-thirty I brought her back to the corner. She went the rest of the way by herself. Would her parents really believe she had been at a friend's house for such a long time? I worried about her, but she never got into any trouble over the incident. Ruth could make her parents believe anything.

One thing about the secrecy I didn't like. To throw people off the track about our engagement, Ruth went out with other men. "I've always been popular," she said, "I've always had so many dates—I can't help it, it's just the way it's been. If I stopped having dates suddenly, it would look suspicious." Then came the soulful look again, and clasping my hands. "They don't mean a thing to me,

Morrie, honestly they don't. You can't feel more terrible while I'm on them than I do!"

There was one fellow, she knew him before I proposed to her. Saul Glazer. Lived down on the East Side somewhere, the kind of neighborhood everybody else had moved out of years ago. A year or so younger than me, six inches taller. Thick lips, nose, eyelids—Soutine maybe—somebody who likes to use thick lines, smear on the paint. He was established in business already, making a lot of money, Ruth said. She met him at the Metropolitan Museum. I had to laugh at that. What was he doing in an art museum? He was the businessman type, he grubbed for money, he didn't look at pictures. He must have gone into the museum to use the toilet.

I had dinner with the Boroffs, also went to their Sunday afternoon get-togethers, several times when Saul Glazer was there. His only conversation was boasting about the business deals he had pulled off. I couldn't imagine why everybody wasn't bored to death. I didn't like the way he talked to me either, making sniggering little jokes I was supposed to be too stupid to understand. Business types like to laugh at artists. They're frightened of what they can't understand—they make jokes to convince themselves they're not frightened.

Ruth egged him on. She laughed at his jokes as if there was really something funny about them. After dinner she went out with him—to the movies usually. That's all he could enjoy—taking her to something like the ballet never would have occurred to him. I talked to her about him once, told her I wished she would stop paying so much attention to him. She laughed and said, "But it's the perfect camouflage. The more I go out with Saul, the more I fool people."

"I think you're fooling *me*," I said.

She laughed again, a little gentler. "You're jealous, aren't you, Morrie? Oh, I'm so flattered." She gave me a pat on the cheek, the way you might do to a child. "You don't have to worry, honestly you don't. Saul isn't my type at all. He doesn't care one bit for cultural things, for paintings and ballets and so on. Do you think I could be interested in a man who has no appreciation of beauty and art and the finer things of life? After I've known *you*?"

I believed her. What choice did I have?

I had a friend, Danny Glick, who was studying to be an actor. At the American Academy of Dramatic Arts, a block or so west of the Art Students League. I met Danny at the Horn and Hardart's Automat on Fifty-Seventh Street. Little square windows with food behind the glass—looking neat and clean, could have been made out of papier-mâché. We both went there on our lunchtime. One day we sat down at the same table, started talking, got along nicely. Pretty soon we were having lunch together three or four times a week. Very odd really. We never got together any other time, any other place—only the Automat at lunch.

I told Danny about my secret engagement. Yes, I had given Ruth my solemn promise. But Danny didn't count. Ruth and he would never meet. I knew them in different worlds.

Every day I gave him the latest news about our engagement, told him the latest incidents. He asked me questions, gave me advice, worried. He was as interested as if it was a serial story in a magazine. One day I told him about Saul Glazer, asked him what he thought.

He put on his angry look—very common look on his face. That thin long face, sharp chin, sharp nose, black eyebrows curving up when he laughed or frowned—like the devil in a movie. I used to wonder, did he practice that expression in front of a mirror? "They're all the same," he said. "They'll do it to you every time."

"Who'll do what?"

"Women!" Out came his sharp laugh—cynical, sardonic—that devil again. "Poor Morrie!"

"But she *hasn't* done anything to me!"

He just shook his head. "Wait, wait. As soon as they get a whiff of money and success—penthouses, mink coats, servants—say good-bye to everything else."

"Ruth isn't that type at all!"

"They're *all* that type. Don't I know it? Didn't I go through the same thing with Loretta Levy?"

Danny was always talking about Loretta Levy, this girl who had thrown him over a few years ago to marry a doctor. In the end, according to him, she couldn't face the sacrifices that would have been required of an actor's wife. She betrayed him. For a long time he was in despair, now he was glad it had happened. The experience had taught him about reality. It had stripped him of all illusions. It had given him emotional depths he could now reach into for his art.

Actually, I couldn't quite understand why Loretta Levy had thrown Danny over, if she was really so mercenary. The fact was, he came from a well-to-do family. His father manufactured men's hats—you saw his hats in stores all over the city. Even if he never made a living as an actor, Danny would always have a good income. He stood to inherit a lot of money someday.

"Loretta Levy and Ruth Boroff aren't the same person," I said. "And if you wouldn't mind, I'd like to change the subject."

Danny shrugged. "If you can't face up to the truth—if you want to blind yourself to reality . . ." He started talking about the audition he had gone to earlier in the week, some drama about Jesus Christ—they were looking for Roman soldiers. It didn't sound as if Danny was really the type. He was short and skinny like me, fragile looking. You couldn't imagine the Roman army drafting him. He was optimistic about his chances. That was a strange thing about Danny—he expected everything else in life to be a disaster, he was always full of hope about becoming a successful actor, playing Shakespeare, Ibsen, Chekhov someday. In spite of the fact that he still hadn't got any professional parts.

We had this particular conversation many times. I wouldn't let his gloomy predictions worry me. I trusted Ruth. I told myself you couldn't love somebody, be engaged to her, if you didn't have complete trust in her.

In the middle of May, Augustus Kelly got a letter from Marcel

Brulard. He was still in the south of Italy. He'd be back in Paris in three weeks. The time had come to arrange my passage to Europe.

This meant seeing Mrs. Newberry again. She invited me for tea so she could give me her first check—she liked to give money to her protégés in person. In return I gave her a medium-sized pastel drawing that I had done of her from memory. She seemed to be pleased by it. It was the first of many, I can't remember how often I did her in the next fifteen years. Including the full-length oil portrait.

I don't want to think about that now. That comes later in my life. One painful memory at a time.

From Mrs. Newberry's house I went straight to the offices of the French Line, made my reservation for a third-class cabin on the *Ile-de-France*, sailing the last day of June. The old *Ile-de-France* that was—superior in every way to the one they replaced it with in the late thirties. Second Empire-style furnishings and decorations—a bit pompous, awfully handsome, much nicer than the art deco fruit salad they came up with later. The third-class cabins were holes-in-the-wall, of course—they weren't decorated in *any* style.

In those days, by the way, you didn't have to make your reservations half a year ahead of time. There were plenty of ships crossing the Atlantic. They were seldom full. They didn't have to be, the shipping lines made a profit anyway. Everything cost less. You got good food, even in third class. The crewmen had no union, they worked for practically nothing—stewards lived on tips. Outrageous really, the way people were treated fifty years ago. It made for elegant ships though.

I reserved a cabin for two. My hand trembled as I signed the paper. I had no idea where I would get the money for Ruth's passage. Unless I took it out of Mrs. Newberry's check, meant not only to pay my fare but take care of my expenses for the year. If I did that, how would I manage those expenses—especially for the two of us? I told myself I'd work it out somehow. Everyone said Paris was very cheap—that *was* the good old days! Maybe I'd sell some pictures. I was told the French went in for art much more than the Americans. Not true at all, of course. People have some odd ideas about the French.

After I left the French Line I took the subway uptown. The Boroffs had a telephone. They'd had it only a year, they were very proud of it—in those days not everybody had one. I didn't feel like calling. I wanted to see Ruth's face when she heard the news.

It was almost six o'clock when I got there. Everything was in a state of confusion. Janet was hurrying out the front door, she had just time to tell me she was going to the drugstore for medicine. Ruth was sick in bed—chicken pox. I remembered having it as a child. Terribly itchy. Sadie Boroff went into Ruth's room to tell her I was there. She came out again a few minutes later. Ruth wasn't feeling well enough to talk to me. I should wait a day or two till she was a little better.

I understood right away. Ruth didn't want me to see her with the red spots on her face—that wasn't hard for me to figure out, knowing Ruth. I couldn't blame her either. A woman always wants to look her best. It's what she ought to want. A woman in bed with the chicken pox—miserable, itchy, spotty—doesn't look her best.

Sadie asked me to stay for dinner. I said I had a previous engagement. No desire to make conversation with the rest of them if Ruth wasn't going to be at the table. I accepted a dinner invitation for three nights later. Sadie was sure Ruth would be up by then.

When I got off the elevator in the lobby—the Boroffs' building had an elevator, small and creaking, any elevator at all meant splendor in those days—I was face-to-face with Saul Glazer. He was waiting to get on, a bouquet of flowers in his hand. Red roses. Sad looking. He bought them a bit too late—going to wilt at any moment. Why is it that the favorite flower of people with no eyes in their head, no artistic bones in their body, is always roses?

I wondered what he was there for. One of his dates with Ruth no doubt. Camouflage.

We gave each other a nod. I didn't tell him about Ruth's chicken pox. Let him find out for himself that his evening was about to collapse.

Three nights later the Boroffs had me up for dinner.

Sadie opened the door for me. Her eyes bulging, her lips quivering. She was excited about something. Reminded me of a small child who's trying to keep a secret, can't bear to hold it in.

Janet came up to her quickly, pulled me away by the arm. Ruth wanted to talk to me in her room, she said. They had special instructions from Ruth—they weren't allowed to say a word—she wanted to tell me herself.

Tell me what? All I felt was puzzled. Nothing worse—no premonitions. I've never been much for premonitions. Anything terrible that ever happened to me in my life, it's always caught me completely by surprise. . . .

So I knocked on Ruth's door. Her voice said, "Come in." Very small, quavery.

Inside the shades were drawn, the light was dim. I could barely make her out as she lay on the bed. Mysterious shape in the darkness—halfway swallowed up by shadows—minor Rembrandt figure, one of the crowd at the Crucifixion.

"Don't come too close to me," she said. "I'm still contagious."

"I've had chicken pox," I said. But I stopped a few feet away from her. It wasn't the contagion that bothered her, I realized. There were still spots on her face.

"Morrie darling," she said. "I'm sorry—I'm so sorry—"

She started crying. I could hear those gulping noises coming out of her. I couldn't see her face too well. I had watched her crying before, I could imagine the redness and the puckering.

"I never wanted it to happen this way," she said. "It's Saul and me—Saul Glazer—oh Morrie, we're engaged!"

"Engaged to do what?"

Yes, I know, I couldn't have said anything more stupid. My mind doesn't work too fast at moments of crisis. It takes me a long time to get used to new ideas.

"To be *married*! In about a month—near the end of June."

I've often wondered about myself since then. My thoughts at that moment should have been terrible—shattered by grief and disappointment. What I was actually thinking though—dim light through the shades, pale fragile figure in the bed, tall manly one standing by the bedside. Bad painting of the Pre-Raphaelite School. Is there something terribly wrong with me? I don't have any real feelings, only ideas for pictures?

I spoke to her very calmly, my voice was perfectly steady. "When did you decide all this?"

"The day before yesterday." Her sobbing got loud for a while, then it got soft again. "I couldn't help it, Morrie. It just came over me—like some force that was bigger than me. I suddenly realized that I *loved* him!"

"You said you loved *me*." I remember bringing this out very matter-of-factly, not getting angry, not reproaching her at all.

"Yes, yes! And I really did—I *do*! I'll always love you, Morrie, I wasn't deceiving you or leading you on—it's just that my feelings for Saul are a different *kind* of love. Well, a person can't control her *feelings*, can she? You just can't control what you *feel*."

It came into my head what I ought to say to her. "You just can't control your appetite for mink coats and penthouses and servants to order around. Money and success are what you've got such uncontrollable feelings for." I didn't say it. I kept my mouth shut. What was the use? Hurting people, making people angry at me—that wouldn't make me feel any better. I've never been able to hit out at people like that.

"You *do* understand, don't you, Morrie?" Using her little-girl voice at me now. The voice she used when she wanted something from somebody, sweet and helpless. I had heard her using it many times before, with her family. It worked especially well with her father. I had always loved it myself.

"Yes, I understand," I said.

"And you forgive me, don't you?"

"There's nothing to forgive. You're a free person, you can do what you want."

"Oh Morrie!" The weeping got louder. I could hear what was underneath—the little sigh of relief. The hard part was over, she could enjoy herself now. My hearing was pretty good in those days.

"You're the kindest human being who ever lived," she said. "I know what I've done to you. You'll never get over this—you'll *say* you have, you'll put up a brave front, nobody will know what you're really going through except me."

Her hands reached out from under the covers. "Come over here, you can come close to me now."

I went up to the bed. She grabbed hold of my hands, smiled up at me. I was close enough to see her face quite clearly, even in the dim light. I could see that smile-between-tears quite clearly. "You'll be a great painter someday, Morrie. I know you will. I'll be so proud to be your friend. Maybe you'll even let me buy one of your paintings—if Saul and I ever have enough money."

She gave a little laugh. I understood its meaning exactly, she might as well have said the words out loud: We'll have enough money to pick up dozens of the damn things!

"Give me one kiss, Morrie. Not good-bye, because we're *not* going to stop seeing each other. Just one kiss to wish each other happiness— even though we'll be walking on different paths."

She was having the time of her life. No little girl ever got more enjoyment out of dressing up in her mother's clothes, playing at being a grown-up. I felt this terrible wave of anger rising up in me. Why should I go along with her childish game? She kicks me in the teeth, she expects me to build up her vanity by telling her how much I admire her for it! Why should I go along with that? I won't do it, I told myself. Not in a million years.

I leaned over, gave her a kiss on the cheek. I actually felt ashamed of myself at that moment, because I was having such unkind thoughts about her.

Then I noticed the red spots on her face. Chicken-pox marks, like little red wounds. I wondered if they would leave permanent scars. I don't think I hoped so—I just wondered.

Out in the living room there was nobody but Janet. I told her I was suddenly feeling sick, would she give my apologies to her parents, I couldn't really stay for dinner. She said she understood, she hoped I'd be feeling better soon. How much *did* she understand? Her face didn't give away a thing. I never could bring myself to ask.

I walked all the way downtown. From 125th Street to my attic room on Fifty-Sixth Street, that's quite a walk. It took me about two hours, darkness came while I was at it. One minute the streets were glowing, yellowish—next minute nothing but black all around me. I was exhausted when I finally got home—just what I wanted to be. I went to bed without eating anything. My stomach wouldn't have taken food even had I forced it into myself.

I couldn't get to sleep. My mind was on Ruth. Every word she had said to me in that dark room was being said all over again in my mind. And all the words she had *ever* said to me, all the times we had spent together in these last two years. Why couldn't I wipe my mind clean, like wiping out a charcoal line if I made a bad start on a drawing?

I had made a terrible start on falling in love. It would be a long time before I tried it again. . . .

S A U L

. . . We decided on a wedding late in June.

Anybody who's ever been married knows the madness that goes on as soon as you bring the outside world into it. Right away began the parties, phone calls, the shopping trips, all the rest of it. Her family and my family got together, and everybody was very polite, and you could cut the hostility with a knife. At home, every chance he got, Papa came out with sarcastic remarks about "the Germans." "I saw pictures on the wall from Greek temples. Are you positive these Germans of yours are really Jewish?" Or else he made offhand references to Ruth's brother Irving. "He's doing nicely at medical school, the mother told me. I'm glad to hear it. Between you and me, he doesn't have half your brains."

My sisters were no better. They knew they couldn't say disparaging things to me about Ruth, so they said them instead about Janet. Goldie and Dodie sighed, and murmured that the "poor girl" was "such a frump." They didn't like her clothes, her makeup, her hairstyle, her manner. And my sister Doris was out-and-out snotty about her. The "pretty" ones, in my experience, aren't usually too generous to the ones who aren't so pretty. I was careful to ignore all this. Janet was a subject I didn't feel like talking about with my sisters or anybody else. It didn't surprise me one bit that foolish people couldn't appreciate her.

Then came the wedding itself, almost an anticlimax. It was in the Boroffs' apartment, and their cousin, Nat Steinmetz, who had just been ordained as a rabbi, came in to perform the ceremony. Too much Hebrew in it for my personal taste. Ruth's parents, with all their so-called culture, still held on to plenty of superstitions from the old country. One of the first things Ruth and I did, a few years later when we moved into our apartment on Park Avenue, was to join Temple Emanu-el, the big Reform temple, where there's practically no Hebrew in the services at all. Not that this makes them any more interesting, but at least you can understand what's going on.

Incidentally, the joke is that fifteen or so years after our wedding Temple Emanu-el hired Nat Steinmetz as their chief rabbi. So I guess *he* wasn't too fond of all that Hebrew either.

Janet was Ruth's maid of honor and walked behind her carrying flowers. In her blue dress she looked very nice—she could never be a knockout, of course, she didn't hold a candle to Ruth when it came to looks—but on that particular occasion, I wouldn't deny it, she was almost pretty. I didn't actually look straight at her or try to catch her attention, when Ruth and she came walking up to the front of the room—because I didn't want to embarrass her or anything—but I looked at her sort of sideways, and I could see how nicely she had got herself up.

I could also see that her eyes were red, with dark circles under them. As I found out later, that was because she was tired. She'd been up for hours the night before, because Ruth had one of those crying fits that women always have before their wedding, and Janet was naturally the one who had to hold her hand and calm her down.

Personally I wasn't a bit nervous. Once I make a decision I don't waste time or energy worrying about it, I carry it out without a lot of unnecessary sweating and shaking.

Oscar stood up with me as my best man. He looked spectacular in his dress suit—there wasn't a woman there who didn't have her eye on him, the blushing bride excepted, of course. My sisters Goldie and Dodie and Ruth's sister and her mother and all the aunts did the usual amount of crying. At the wedding supper afterward, which took place at Goldblatt's Kosher Restaurant, 110th Street—the Boroffs rented the banquet room in back—Papa and Mr. Boroff sat in a corner and traded stories about the old country. And my sister Doris, who was drinking more than she was used to, kept going up to Janet and telling her how beautiful she looked. But with that shrill piercing voice of hers, even Doris's compliments came out sounding like insults.

Other people were drinking a lot too. Ruth's brother Irving, the medical student—my brother-in-law now, what a thought!—was bawling out songs at the top of his voice, grisly ones about cutting up bodies. His fiancée Rose Levinson, eventually his wife—a nice girl, knew how to keep her mouth shut—was blushing all over the place.

I had a little too much to drink myself. Isn't that a man's privilege at his own wedding? Ruth kept coming up to me, putting her hand on my arm, telling me to take it easy. I just made jokes, which started her giggling. As a matter of fact, it felt nice to have a woman worrying about me, even nagging me a little, because I was such a wild fellow.

Ruth's cousin, the blimp—Celia Solomon—gave one of her recitations, of course. Her special wedding number—something about Indians.

> "As unto the bow the cord is,
> So unto the man is woman,
> Though she bends him, she obeys him,
> Though she draws him, yet she follows,
> Useless each without the other!"

After all these years, for some reason, those cockamamie lines still stick in my head. That poet might have known a lot about archery, but about marriage he was strictly an ignoramus.

As usual, though, that Solomon woman got a big round of applause from the family. From her side of it anyway.

The big climax of the party came when Oscar, who loved nothing better than making speeches in front of an audience, stood up and lifted his glass in the air and delivered a toast: "In the words of William Shakespeare, 'So smile the heavens upon this holy act.' That's from *Romeo and Juliet*, a play he once wrote about Ruth and Saul Glazer."

Leave it to Oscar to drag in William Shakespeare and give the occasion a little class.

After that toast everybody started getting very sentimental and crying. I told Ruth to change her clothes so we could get out of there. . . .

A couple of hours later we started on our honeymoon, taking the train to Niagara Falls. That sounds pretty corny nowadays, I admit it, because outside of the movies who goes to Niagara Falls for a honeymoon anymore? But back in 1920 there was nothing corny about it, it was a natural thing for a young couple to do. Personally I couldn't get all that excited about the idea—I saw a waterfall once already, and what was Niagara Falls except more of the same, only bigger?—but Ruth was bubbling over about it, like my granddaughters a few years ago when their parents took them to Disneyland. So *I* was happy to make *her* happy.

That's the way it was with us in those days.

That night in our hotel room—the truth is we had a little trouble at first. Don't most people when they're still not used to each other? It's a question of positions—what fits where, who's comfortable doing what, how to keep from bumping into the wrong things when you're reaching for something else. In some of those R-rated movies they come out with nowadays (a lot different, believe me, from what they let us see when *I* was a kid!) the fellow jumps into bed with the girl, and they go rolling around on each other's shoulders and hips, and the music gets all excited in the background, and she's purring like a kitten and he's neighing like a horse that just won the Kentucky Derby, and when it's all over they're lying next to each other with big blissful grins on their faces, looking like cats who just swallowed some mice.

Well, come on now, everybody knows that's a lot of crap. Sure, it's terrific fun—otherwise why would it keep on being so popular with the human race?—but it's like any game or sport, golf or gin rummy, for instance. Some days you're at the top of your form and other days you keep getting schneidered or hitting into the rough.

So on the night of our honeymoon, after it was over, Ruth and I got up from the bed and went to the window of our hotel room. We looked out at the moonlight, in the direction where the falls ought to be. To tell the truth, I couldn't get a room that actually had a view of them, I wasn't so experienced at finagling with hotel people in those days. And in spite of a few pinches and bruises, nothing serious, and a couple of tricky moments back there when it looked like nothing was going to happen at all except mussed-up sheets, I guess we were both feeling pretty pleased with ourselves and pretty affectionate to each other.

Ruth took me by the arm and held me close to her, and we looked out the window awhile, and then she said, "You love me, don't you, Saul?"

Women are always asking you if you love them. I found that out a long time before I got married. The question isn't supposed to get serious consideration. What you're supposed to do is answer yes, and that's what you'll do if you have any sense. "That's why I'm here," I said.

"I hope you'll tell me so from time to time. People have to tell me things. I don't have any confidence in myself."

Could that be? I wasn't exactly a blind man, and I'd noticed how she wound her father and everybody else around her little finger and was never too shy to ask for what she wanted. I told her that her lack of confidence didn't show on the surface.

"You're the only one I ever confessed this to," she said. "Not even to Janet—I love you so much. I dreamed all my life, since I was a little girl, about marrying a man like you. Strong and handsome, a forceful personality."

This was getting me very uncomfortable. I don't like it much when people flatter me to my face. Especially if it isn't the truth. Handsome I'm not, and never was—my jaw is too square, my lips are too thick. This is something I've never kidded myself about. So the only way I could handle what she said was to make a joke out of it. "That's me, a real movie-star type. Douglas Fairbanks in the flesh."

"Well, that's how I see you," she said, with one of her little-girl giggles. "Now you're fidgeting, you're embarrassed."

"Who's embarrassed? It's chilly in here."

"Don't get embarrassed when I say nice things to you. Please don't. I get such enjoyment out of it. I know I'm just like a little girl sometimes. Well, I am, I can't help it. So you'll have to be careful how you talk to me, Saul darling. You have to be very careful how you talk to children."

Then she had her arms around me again, and we stopped looking out the window and went back to bed. It seemed like the thing to do.

So now I was a married man. And God, or whatever it is up there, must have liked the idea. My luck, which hadn't been so bad up to then, suddenly turned spectacular. Five days into the honeymoon—we had reservations at the hotel for a week—I got a long-distance call from Oscar. A big deal we'd been working on for a long time—an order from Marshall Field, the department store in Chicago, one of the biggest stores outside of New York—looked like it was about to come through. If it did, there was absolutely no doubt that other stores in other big cities, which we were never able to sell so far, would follow Marshall Field's lead. We wouldn't be only a little local operation anymore, we'd be doing business on a national scale. But the Marshall Field buyer was going to be in New York that night, and she was a very temperamental type, like a lot of those tough biddies. She'd be insulted if both partners in the firm weren't on hand to kiss her ass. Honeymoons wouldn't cut any ice with her. Young love wasn't part of her inventory.

So I explained to Ruth that we had to cut the trip short and get right back to the city. Naturally she was a little disappointed at first, but pretty soon she understood what was at stake. She agreed with me completely when I pointed out to her how rotten we'd both feel if I let this opportunity slip out of my hands.

One thing I'll say for Ruth, she wanted me to go up in the world as much as I wanted it myself. In all the years of our marriage, this was the one subject we never disagreed about.

So we packed and checked out and took the train back to New York. The honeymoon was over. . . .

M O R R I S

. . . I had made a terrible start on falling in love. It would be a long time before I tried it again. I was still telling myself that when I woke up the next morning. Oddly enough, I had an appetite for breakfast. And my work at the League went rather well.

I met Danny Glick for lunch at the Automat. Naturally I poured out the whole story to him. I didn't even hold off long enough to take the wax paper off my egg salad sandwich.

His face darkened. Angry. Really angry for once, not just the devil from a movie. "Bitch!" He spat out the word, made me jump a little. Skinny, pale, fragile-looking Danny. "Empty-headed little bitch! All right, if you want to know, I'm *glad* she did it. I never thought that little bitch was good enough for you. Another Loretta Levy! You're better off without her."

I stammered out some words. God help me, I was actually defending Ruth, finding excuses for her. The power of habit.

Danny just rode right over me. The way he whipped himself into a climax of anger—he really ought to play King Lear someday, I thought. Long white beard, fists raised to the storm, purple splotches in the sky. I wondered if he'd be willing to pose for a picture.

"We're artists, Morris," he was saying. "We haven't got time for these silly little flyspecks, with their moronic airs and pretensions. Dogs yapping at the heels of lions! They hold an artist back, keep him from realizing his vision. You might as well make up your mind to it—our destiny is to reach the heights alone!"

He really made me feel a lot better. I took the wax paper off my egg salad sandwich. Found it quite tasty. After lunch I went down Fifth Avenue to the offices of the French Line, told them I'd be using only one passage on the *Ile-de-France*. They were very nice about it, gave me back half of my deposit. People were much nicer about money in those days.

New York is full of nice people, I told myself as I left the French Line. They were streaming by me on Fifth Avenue. Lovely soft light glowing on happy faces . . . elegant suits and dresses . . . pretty magazine-cover world where nothing could turn out badly.

All of a sudden my stomach was hurting. She isn't going to Paris with me, I thought. It's all over. I love her, she's marrying somebody else.

That's how it happened for quite a while afterward. It came over me in waves, leaving me shaken, tears in my eyes. Then it would subside, I'd be quite all right, cheerful even, for a long period of time. Then the wave would sweep over me again, always without any warning. It was almost a year before the last wave subsided. Sometimes I think I *am* capable of real feelings.

I mentioned the power of habit? It was so strong, even during this first month, that I went right on seeing the Boroffs. Yes, it's true, within a week I was having dinner with them. Everything the same as ever—only I didn't address too many remarks to Ruth. What amazed me, *she* addressed remarks to *me*. Made jokes at me, asked me questions about my work, as if nothing had happened. Maybe, for her, nothing had.

So it was back to my once-a-week dinner schedule with her and her family. Somehow Saul Glazer was never there. His nights turned out to be different from my nights. Could it be pure coincidence? Somebody must have arranged it. Janet, of course, who else could it be? Ruth would never have thought of such a thing. Ruth would have *enjoyed* having the two of us for dinner together.

The wedding was three days before I sailed on the *Ile-de-France*. I had no excuse to refuse the invitation. Besides, I asked myself, why *should* I refuse? I enjoyed weddings. The food and drink would be much better than anything I could afford on my own. I was a great lover of good food and drink in those days. Still am, fifty years later. I'm content to live without it. When I can get it, I never turn it down.

The ceremony was in the Boroffs' living room. They had a young rabbi, somebody's cousin, went on forever in Hebrew. Interesting to watch Ruth's face—pretending she was listening intently, spiritually carried away, in direct contact with God—at the same time trying desperately to keep from yawning. A pity caricature was never in my line. Daumier maybe?

Also interesting to watch Saul Glazer. Tall and heavy, running to fat, his chin would be double in ten years. Big nose, thick lips, jaw like a bulldog—a lower-class face, a businessman's face, no sensitivity or delicacy in it at all. But for one moment, as I watched him standing in front of the rabbi, I felt a twinge. A very odd feeling. What was it? I couldn't place it. I'd have to think about it—it would come to me later.

After the ceremony we went to a restaurant for the wedding dinner. Abe and Sadie had hired the banquet room in back. What a lovely meal! Chopped liver, herring, roast beef, potato pancakes, apple strudel—the food I loved best in those days. I still have a taste for it, hidden somewhere deep inside of me.

A pianist and violinist were playing dance tunes, the latest hits. I danced with every female at the party. I had one dance with the bride. We laughed a lot, didn't say much to each other. Just before the dance was over she gave my hand a squeeze, spoke in a low voice. "I'm so grateful to you, Morrie. For taking it like this."

I looked her straight in the eye. "Taking what?"

I made my expression genuinely puzzled. I made my voice that way too. I'm positive, the way her mouth fell open, that she believed me.

The fat girl—Ruth's cousin—gave one of her recitations. Poem about Indians. Couldn't figure out why Indians were appropriate for the occasion. Didn't take in much of it, I'm afraid. Too interested watching her chins quiver. Toulouse-Lautrec—only one I can think of who ever got that effect in paint, illusion of quivering flesh.

Saul Glazer's best man, his partner in business—what was his name? traveling-salesman type—made a toast. He quoted from Shakespeare. Everybody cheered, I cheered too. Kept asking myself, How did that traveling salesman ever find out about Shakespeare? Fellow came to a bad end years later, if I recall.

After that I got drunk. Then I got sick. Then I went home. . . .

Two days later I made my last visit to the Metropolitan Museum. I said good-bye to my Degas. She lowered her eyes modestly.

The next morning I got aboard the *Ile-de-France*. The Boroff family saw me off—except Ruth, she was still on her honeymoon. Danny came too, gave his eyebrows the devilish lift while the poetry woman was saying her piece, something about the ship of state sailing on. Augustus Kelly and a few of my fellow students from the League brought champagne—ended up drinking most of it themselves. Mrs. Newberry sent a basket of fruit.

It was nice of them all to give me so much attention. My eyes got wet as I stood on the deck and waved good-bye.

Underneath, though, I can't say I was sorry to be leaving. I was scared of what lay ahead of me, my stomach was playing all its old tricks. Even so I wouldn't have wanted anything to be different. A misty day in the harbor. The crowd, the dock, the New York skyline, all swallowed up quickly once we were under way. Everything in the world can be swallowed up by mist, turned into something better. Monet taught me that. Whatever it is, mist can make it beautiful.

I remembered the twinge that came to me while I watched Saul Glazer being married to Ruth. I understood it now, what that feeling had been. Pity. I had pitied him. Poor fellow, didn't know what he was getting into.

And mixed in with my pity, was there maybe a little bit of relief? There but for the grace of God . . . ?

It's finally happening to me, I thought. I'm finally getting out of prison. Not just a temporary reprieve. Forever. Doing what so many other artists have done before me. On the other side of the Atlantic Ocean, in Paris, freedom is waiting for me. . . .

S A U L

. . . The honeymoon was over. Real life was beginning. But that wasn't bad. The Marshall Field deal went through smoothly. Like I predicted, it was a turning point for Je Suis Belle, Incorporated. Before we knew it, Oscar and I were getting orders from stores we thought it would take us ten years to crack into. Some of the biggest stores, even out on the West Coast, were falling all over themselves to get hold of Je Suis Belle nightwear.

What was the reason for it? Well, we made a first-class product, that's the most important reason naturally. But also the time was ripe for us. It was the 1920s, and the boom was on. Pleasure and entertainment were what people wanted in America, so they could forget the war and pretend there could never be any others. Speakeasies, jazz music, riding around in Ford cars, wearing those crazy coats at football games—all the things everybody's read about, the Roaring Twenties and so on, it was absolutely true, every bit of it really happened. And along with the boom in everything else, I suppose, there was a boom in men going to bed with women, and Je Suis Belle got the benefits.

So in a year or two Ruth and me were rich, just like Oscar told me I'd be. We could buy things neither of us could ever afford before, or even dream about. I was crazy about some of those things myself, I wouldn't try to deny it, but the biggest kick I got out of it all was from watching the kick Ruth got out of it. She was like a little girl opening the presents on her birthday. She couldn't get enough of them. Every present was better than the one before. Then she'd throw it aside and pounce on the next one. For instance, we got a car, a big black shiny Pierce Arrow, the fanciest car they made that year, with one of those little bronze statues sticking out in front, some Greek god with wings on his feet. Ruth had conniption fits when she saw that car, but then right away she said we had to hire a chauffeur to drive us around in it. I pointed out to her that we both had licenses and knew how to drive, but her answer was, "We can't drive a car like this around *ourselves*! The police would stop us, they'd think we were stealing it!"

So we hired a chauffeur—and a lot of other servants too, especially when we moved into our new apartment. It was a penthouse on Park Avenue and the Eighties, and it had a terrace that was big enough to hold the whole apartment that I grew up in on the Lower East Side. And the building had a doorman and elevator man that wore uniforms, with gold braid and silver buttons. They made the uniforms on the U.S. Marines look poverty-stricken. I hate to remind myself the rent I paid for that place . . . well, it was worth it to see the pleasure on Ruth's face. Anyway, this apartment was full of rooms for servants, so naturally we had to get some: a butler and a cook, a married couple, Swiss, and a maid who was Hungarian. Ruth made them all dress up in fancy uniforms. There was a department at Saks Fifth Avenue in those days that sold nothing but servants' uniforms and advised you what styles were proper.

Also this apartment had a dining room that could hold as many people as some of the restaurants I've been in, with a spectacular crystal chandelier hanging over the table, so naturally we gave dinner parties. Half a dozen a year, and as many as ten, twelve couples showed up on the average. Sometimes I wasn't even sure of their names when they came through the front door. The food, if I say it myself, was terrific: caviar and smoked salmon with the cocktails, a soup, a big roast beef with Yorkshire pudding and three kinds of vegetables, a salad, something fancy for dessert like baked alaska or cherries jubilee. And just to give it genuine class, before the dessert there were always finger bowls. I remember the first time we had Papa for dinner and he saw them. "What's this?" he said. "You're serving the soup *after* the main course? This is how it's done among the Germans?"

Another example of how I wouldn't think twice of throwing away money in those days—the presents I gave Ruth, on birthdays and anniversaries and so on. I would have felt like a piker if I had come through with anything less than a mink coat or a diamond bracelet or something on that order. And she'd clap her hands and hug me when she got it. A little girl, like I said.

Also we did a lot of traveling. And we did it in style. We went to Europe first-class on the ocean liners, and we stayed at the best hotels in London and Paris. (We saw everybody we knew there, it was like the high holidays at Temple Emanu-el). We took a couple of Caribbean cruises and gambled at the casino in Havana, and every winter we went for a couple of weeks down to Miami Beach. We got there in deluxe drawing rooms on the streamlined trains—nobody rode in airplanes in those days, but the trains were like resort hotels or ocean liners, only on wheels. They had bands playing in the club car, and a full bar, and a hostess to bring you cards or Mah-Jongg pieces or stationery, and they had names like the *San Francisco Streak* and the *Florida Zephyr.*

Ruth really loved that *Florida Zephyr.* She loved how respectful the colored porters were. They made her feel like some Southern aristocrat on the old plantation. *Gone With the Wind* wasn't even written yet, but Ruth, just by instinct, already thought she was Scarlett O'Hara.

What she liked best about being rich, though, was that she could now go in for art and culture and all that in a big way. We went to Broadway shows, getting our tickets from a scalper naturally. What's the good of being rich if you have to wait in line like everybody else? Ruth got herself a Saturday afternoon subscription to the symphony, and she made me buy a box at the opera for Monday night. The *good* night, Ruth said, meaning all the high-society types went on Monday—only I didn't see how there could have been any seats left for them, so many people like Ruth were there to stare at them.

Papa never got me to like the opera in my childhood and Ruth certainly didn't succeed where he failed, but on the other hand that box wasn't a bad way to impress important business contacts. The women would stay with Ruth and listen to the screaming from the stage, the men would sit it out with me in the bar.

And if no business people were in town, we'd take Papa to the opera—it was seventh heaven for him. Or we'd take Janet and whoever was her latest boyfriend. There was always some fellow that was interested in her—phonies, blowhards, bums, stockbrokers. I didn't like the looks of any of them!

Ruth also started buying paintings around this time. She'd pick up one or two when we went to Paris. None of the artists was famous—*that* kind of money I didn't have—but she put them in gold frames with lights over them and told her friends they were genuine French.

It was on account of the paintings that I finally saw something about Ruth which maybe I was a damn fool not to see a lot sooner. . . .

One of the painters whose stuff she liked was her cousin Morris Unger. They had a crush on each other when she was a young girl. A skinny little fellow with a long nose, and he wore his hair long, the way artists do. Right after our wedding he went to study at an art school in Paris, France, and he never came back to America. He got himself a place to live there and set up as a full-time professional painter. Whenever we went over—and other people in the family too—we took this Unger out for dinner, and he paid back the favor by showing us the sights, the genuine French nightclubs and cafés and so on. And of course we went up to his studio to look at his latest things.

That studio! Who could imagine a human being deliberately living like that? It was four floors up, no elevator. If the stairs didn't collapse under you you'd die of coughing from the dust. A bed, a few sticks of furniture, a dresser crowded into one little room. The other room was a nice big one with a skylight, but that one he wouldn't live in, he had to use it for his painting. Well, Unger wasn't married—I suppose he figured he could get away with living like a slob.

He wasn't exactly a world-famous artist, but I think he was earning a living from it—especially the way *he* lived. Years later I met an art dealer at a UJA fund-raising dinner, and I asked him what the opinion of Unger was in the art business. He answered me, "Unger is strictly an imitator of Degas and the Impressionists, only he hasn't got their genius. He's completely unimportant, his work won't be worth a thing after he dies, but it's slick and pretty, he'll always find rich people who are willing to buy it." Which was pretty much the way I had already figured it myself—not on artistic grounds, of course, but because if Unger had been any good, I knew I could never pick up his stuff at such low prices.

The incident I'm thinking of, which opened my eyes to certain things, happened on our first trip to Paris, two or three years after we got married. One day Ruth went up to Unger's studio without me, and she saw a picture there which, she said, she absolutely fell in love with. How do you fall in love with a picture? A human being maybe—but a hunk of canvas with paint smeared on it?

Be that as it may, she made me go up there with her to see it for myself. It was a full-length picture of this woman in a red dress, with a fan in her hand and another one sticking up on top of her head. You could tell from the way she was swaying around that she was doing a dance, and from her long black eyelashes that she was Spanish. So I wasn't exactly bowled over with amazement to find out that Unger called this picture *Spanish Dancer*. He went to his bedroom to have a cup of coffee, so that Ruth and I could stay by ourselves in the studio to talk the matter over.

"You like this thing, do you?" I said.

She put on that "inspirational" smile that people put on when they're appreciating a work of art. "Oh, I think it's beautiful. The color, the lines! Don't you think it would look perfect over the dining-room mantelpiece, where we've got the mirror now? It would blend in so nicely with the chandelier."

"How much does he want for it?"

"Well, ordinarily it would be quite expensive, but we're family, so Morrie says we can have it for two thousand."

"Dollars or francs?"

"Oh dollars, of course. Morris doesn't know anything about currency exchange or things like that—"

"He seems to know a lot about chutzpa, though. Two thousand

dollars! For that kind of money I could get a lot bigger name!"

"I'm in *love* with this picture, darling. You're not going to quibble over a few dollars here and there, are you?"

"Two thousand is a few dollars here and there? And look at her, will you. She's supposed to be a dancer, did you happen to notice that her feet are crooked?"

"Well, yes, I asked Morrie about that, and he says he did it deliberately. It's part of the effect."

"I'm supposed to buy a dancer with crooked feet? I'll tell you right now, I wouldn't be interested unless he straightens them out."

"But he *can't* do that! I wouldn't embarrass him and make myself look foolish by asking such a thing. You don't know anything about art, Saul dear, so it's hard for you to understand."

That was when it hit me, the truth about her. Not all at once, but a definite jar, hard enough so it was like a fog clearing up before my eyes. "*You* understand?" I said.

"Well, yes, now that I'm familiar with the picture—"

"So tell me why."

I could hear the panic in her voice at this. "What do you mean?"

"Explain it to me please. *Why* do the feet have to be crooked, *why* is that part of the effect? Give me an art appreciation lesson, I'm waiting."

"I'll call Morrie!"

She took a step to the door, but I stopped her with my hand on her arm. "Never mind Morrie, I want to hear it from *you*. From the big connoisseur!" She gaped and gulped for a while, and couldn't say a damn thing that made sense, and finally I exploded. "You don't know one damn thing about art, do you? You don't know any more about it than I do! All this time, you've been lording it over me—"

Her face was getting all puckered up, and a kind of wail was coming into her voice—it was new to me then, though it got to be very familiar before long. "You've never talked to me like this before! I didn't know you could be so brutal! Is it because you're too stingy to spend the money? You're looking for an excuse—"

That really made me mad. You can accuse me of a lot of things, but stingy was never one of them, and if anybody should have known that it was her. "I'll gladly spend the money! All you have to do is tell me why the feet are crooked!"

Her voice got louder and higher, which didn't seem possible. "How can you talk to me like this? I won't listen! I don't hear a thing!" And then she did something that positively flabbergasted me— if I hadn't seen it with my own eyes, I wouldn't have believed it. She put her hands over her ears, and jumped up and down on the floor, in quick little jumps, and tears came out of her, and her face was red and wrinkled, like the face on a baby that's just been born and hasn't stopped squawking yet. After the first shock I tried to stop her. I put my hand on her shoulder, I told her to listen to me, but it wasn't a damn bit of good—her squawls got louder, her feet went on stamping, her hands stayed over her ears. Any minute, Unger was going to come running in, I thought, and he'd be sure I was beating her or something. (Actually he was sipping his coffee peacefully in the other room: what I didn't know was that already, before the age of thirty, he had a touch of the deafness that was going to become complete later on in his life.)

So the upshot was, I turned away from her, cursing. For God's sake, the woman was crazy! How do you deal with crazy people? You try to be logical, but how can you do it with somebody who won't be logical back at you. "All right, I'll buy it," I said. "I'll buy the goddamned picture. Only shut up already, enough with the hysterics!"

It was amazing how quick they went away as soon as she heard that. She took her hands down from her ears, stopped stamping, and gave me her sweet little-girl smile. The only trace of what she'd just been doing was some redness in her eyes. "Thank you, Saul dear," she said. "I'm sure you'll grow to love it as much as I do. Let's go get Morris."

Two thousand dollars! For a couple of broken feet! That was the big thing going through my head for the rest of the day. But after a while it occurred to me that maybe it was worth the money, on account of the lesson I learned. Because now I saw the truth, and I wasn't likely to forget it. The whole world, I saw, is full of people talking about art and culture, looking down their noses at ordinary businessmen like me, making us feel like morons. And what do they all turn out to be? Phonies! Strictly a bunch of four-flushers! All right, Ruth was one of them. I wasn't happy to find this out about my own wife, but there are things you just have to live with.

And I'll say one thing for myself—from that time on I never let her pull any more of her culture baloney on me. At the opera she'd start sighing and wetting her pants over some singer, I'd ask her point-blank what was so great about him. "*I* think he's lousy," I'd say. "So prove to me I'm wrong." And all she could do to wriggle out of this was burst into tears. And when she finally finished decorating our Park Avenue duplex, a year after we moved in—and I paid a fortune to this fairy that did apartments for all the gentile society people— Ruth said it was in the style of French Regency. Quick as a flash I asked her what *was* French Regency. She answered some foolishness about shepherds and milkmaids, and I laughed in her face. I knew damn well that our apartment didn't look any different from any-body else's, if they happened to have the same money. French Re-gency, Yiddish Regency—it was just a lot of phoniness.

In any case, I was damned if I was going to let it spoil my life. I didn't have to. There were plenty of things happening during these years that made up to me for all my troubles. At least, they could have, if they had worked out right. . . .

M O R R I S

. . . In Paris, freedom was waiting for me.

That first week I didn't feel very free though. I stayed in a hotel on the Left Bank where some of Mrs. Newberry's past protégés had stayed. Very small and dirty. I didn't mind that. What I minded was the foreignness of everything. Peculiar smells everywhere: French cooking, French perfume, French garbage in the alleys. Foreign sounds all around me too: French words shouted back and forth, French music blaring from the radios, automobile horns honking. In French.

A spider crawled across the ceiling of my hotel room. I knew he was a French spider.

The truth is, I was frightened. Everything frightened me. Night came, the shadows fell over the strange streets. I was convinced I could never go anywhere at night—French gangsters would hit me over the head, French urchins would jeer at me. Daytime wasn't much better. I had studied French, I could read the signs, I was beginning to understand what people said to me. Still, it was a month before I dared go down in the Métro and take a train somewhere.

Why did I stay in Paris after that first week? Why stay in a city that was turning me into a nervous wreck? Why not run back to New York where I could feel safe? The answer is, I loved Paris. Fell in love with it at first sight.

It isn't easy to explain. Everything I feared and hated came to me through my ears and my nose. Everything that came to me through my eyes I loved. The light—soft, shimmering, pink, breaking everything up, then putting it together again so it was gentler, happier. Paris faces, so different from New York faces—deeper lines in them, sharper contours, more extremes to them. Eyebrows lifted higher, frowns drooped lower, smiles spread wider, eyes flashed more furiously. And the shrugging, the endless shrugging, each shrug just a shade different from all the others. You could spend a lifetime, with your pencil, trying to catch each shrug. And I loved the buildings too—lacework balconies, crazy-quilt rooftops—not boxcars, like New York buildings. And the long boulevards, stretching as far as you could see—the narrow twisted streets that even the little French cars could hardly squeeze through. Hand-lettered signs swinging in front of stores, doorways with stone gargoyles—and flowers, everywhere flowers, the parks an absolute circus of them. You can't grow flowers in New York parks—people pick them or trample them.

Yes, I was terrified. But I knew I wouldn't leave Paris. I fit there. It was my home.

Not much of a home, though, if I went on living in a hotel. Plenty of apartments to rent in those days, amazingly cheap. The French liked Americans, they really did. World War One hadn't been over very long, lots of Americans coming to Paris, spending money.

I found my place on the Left Bank, near Saint Germain des Prés. Four flights up, quite a walk, especially with the lights going out just before you reached each landing—you had to stumble in the dark before you found the switch. And the kitchen was dreadful: ancient gas stove, a menace—icebox dating back to Napoleon. But that skylight! That southern exposure—no time of day when the light wouldn't be perfect! I grabbed it—signed a year's lease, paid two months in advance, filled it up with secondhand furniture. Been living there ever since. You couldn't make me go anywhere else.

My concierge was Madame Voisin—big fat woman with a loud voice and a mustache. There was a Monsieur Voisin—a little washed-out rag of a man. Skinny little husbands, big fat wives; a common combination in France. He went off early every morning to work as a streetcar conductor, we tenants never saw much of him. Our lives were run by Madame. She lives in my mind still: hamlike hands on hips, shouting obscenities at some tradesman or tenant trying to put something over on her. Can't imagine why I never painted her.

She liked me. I paid the rent on time, that was the first qualification for making her like you. Also she had a motherly feeling toward me—though God knows she had plenty of children of her own. They were always underfoot, I never *could* get an exact count. I was an artist. All artists are like children, Madame thought. So Madame looked out for me. Made sure the gas heating worked in my apartment. Checked my cupboard and icebox regularly, saw to it I didn't run out of food. Wouldn't let me past her concierge's window in the morning without looking me over, deciding if I was dressed warmly enough. Kept visitors from disturbing me while I was working.

From the day I moved in I found it easy to work in that apartment. The skylight, the four flights of stairs, the obscure neighborhood—they set me apart, alone in a world of my own, just me and my canvas in front of me. I threw myself into my work. Got up early, started in as soon as it was light, kept at it till the light faded. Hardly even stopped to gulp down a sandwich, a slice of cheese, a glass of wine.

Three times a week I went to Marcel Brulard's classes at the Académie Julien. To tell the truth, Brulard was a disappointment. Elegantly dressed little man, tiny pointed mustache. Took about ten seconds to look at what each person in the class was doing. A nod, a shake of his head, a *"Bon!"* or *"Pas bon!,"* then on to the next easel. The trouble was, he'd become such a famous sought-after teacher that he didn't have time to teach anymore. Too busy buying clothes, entertaining women, calling his stockbroker.

I kept going to the Académie for four or five months, then I stopped. It took too much time away from my work. By then I knew where good models could be found, at reasonable rates.

By the end of my first six months in Paris I had finished a great many paintings and drawings. Nudes, a few street scenes and still lives, mostly dancers. Spanish dancers were the craze at the cabarets, ballet dancers among the elite. The Russian ballet was on just then, the Opéra had its ballet night once a week—I went to both, as often as I could. Tickets were amazingly cheap.

Was my work good at this time? I thought it was. I really did. You can never be absolutely sure, can you? God can be sure—not you, not the artist himself. You have to push ahead hoping for the best.

I wanted to sell my work. Everyone told me I had to find an art gallery to handle it—I could never find buyers unless an art gallery was willing to exhibit me. I took my paintings around to art galleries. Paris is full of them, there were even more in those days. Two or three times a week I propped up oils, watercolors, mounted draw-ings on the chairs and sofas in some art gallery's back room—plush expensive chairs and sofas, or battered run-down chairs and sofas. Frozen-faced, narrow-eyed, hard-jawed businessmen, well dressed or shabbily dressed, the same men really. They peered at my work, moving up close, moving far back, making a hole with their fingers and squinting through it. For all the world as if they knew what they were doing.

They all turned me down. None of those galleries would handle me. Some of them told me I was old-fashioned. I was painting in the old Degas style, the public didn't want ballet girls nowadays, couldn't I try some dishes of square fruit? Some of the others told me my work wasn't graceful and pretty enough. What the public wanted were beautiful svelte sylphs, not clodhoppers. Someone told me I was a poor draftsman, put too much emphasis on color at the expense of line. Someone else told me my draftsmanship was superb, what a pity I used such muddy uninteresting colors.

I was finding out what I had suspected for a while: nobody knows anything about art. Above all, the people who are in the business of selling it.

I can't say it wasn't discouraging. You do your work for its own sake, of course—the pleasure it gives you, that's the most important thing. Still, you want people to see it. You like to think there's somebody else who gets pleasure from it too.

The most discouraging thing about being in Paris—I could see how many painters there were in the world. Right there in that neighbor-hood, living within a few blocks of me. I saw them at the café down the street, got in the habit of going there after dinner at night for a cup of coffee or a beer. I fell into conversation with some of them. Soon we were a group. Half a dozen of us, we had a regular table that the waiters saved for us. We did a lot of talking at the table. About art, of course. Everyone full of ideas and theories—a great deal of arguing went on.

Most of my fellow artists were French, doing square fruit like the cubists or limp watches like the surrealists. Otherwise in the same position as me. About my age, painting steadily, taking their work around to galleries—nobody doing much better than I was. Occasionally somebody would sell a picture. Even if the price was very low, which it usually was, our group would celebrate with a bottle of champagne. At the lucky seller's expense, of course.

I kept in touch with Mrs. Newberry. Careful not to let my discouragement creep into my letters to her. I sent her some examples of my work, a few drawings and pastels. She liked them. She bought them for her personal collection, paid me over and above what she was already giving me. I couldn't possibly tell her how much this meant to me. Knowing there was *somebody* who believed in me.

At the end of the first year she renewed her grant. And again at the end of the second year. By this time leaving Paris didn't even occur to me. I had a gallery now, Lantin's on the rue de Rennes. Not the best, not the worst. Lantin didn't sell much of my work yet. He seemed satisfied though, told me the sales would come later.

One more thing about my life in Paris, I shouldn't pass this over. Women. For the first year or so there weren't any, not to speak of. There were prostitutes—I went to the boulevard des Italiens. They came out in great numbers as it got dark. You wandered up and down till you saw one who caught your fancy. She took you off to one of the little hotels on the side streets. Oh, those miserable women. Poor complexions, terrible posture—never saw a prostitute who didn't have pimples, whose shoulders didn't sag.

I met other girls too. Nice girls who worked as secretaries, students, assistants in galleries. Pretty in the French manner: turned-up noses, pert little chins and breasts—brisk no-nonsense girls, like newly sharpened pencils. I never encouraged them. I held them off deliberately. How could I take on anything permanent until I saw some permanence in my career? Besides, those girls were too sharp, intellectual, full of themselves. They made me nervous.

Finally I met Louise.

She was a model, a good one—always understood exactly what I wanted her to do. Large girl, big hips and breasts. The kind I like to paint, not the kind that attracted me personally. I had always gone in for the small-breasted ones. Louise was twenty-four. Just my age.

I found her personality appealing. Good-natured, easygoing, laughed a great deal. Not at me though, like my laughing relatives. She wasn't very well educated—no fool either. She had an eye. When she told me a picture was going well or badly, she usually turned out to be right.

We got into the habit of having coffee together, talking a bit, once our sittings were over. She told me about her husband. He used to teach mathematics at a children's school. Educated men were a weakness of hers, she said. He lost his job a few years ago, took to drink, never worked at all anymore. They had a little girl of two or three— Mathilde. Louise supported them all from her earnings as a model. Admirable woman really.

She didn't talk only about herself. She was interested in me too. She asked me questions—people seldom did that. I found myself answering her, telling her about my life, my family, my mother. How I'd always wanted to be a painter, though people looked down on me for it.

She told me I should never let people make me feel bad about myself. Creating beauty for the world to enjoy—what could be more important? She said this quietly—no gushing, like Ruth. She really meant it. There was no way I could doubt that.

These talks of ours, after the sittings, began to mean more and more to me. A day finally came when we did more than talking. That day wasn't for a while yet. I'll get to it later. . . .

Near the end of my third year in Paris a letter came. Blue stationery, expensive, return address engraved on the back in red letters. I didn't recognize the name at first glance. Who was Mrs. Saul Glazer? A moment later, of course, I realized it was Ruth.

My hands were trembling as I opened the envelope. I couldn't imagine why. It was annoying. It was almost three years since I had set eyes on the woman. For most of that time I hadn't given her a thought. News about her had come in bits and pieces from her mother, who wrote to me regularly, felt it was her family duty. She let me know that Saul Glazer was doing very well. Ruth had her mink coat and her chauffeur, and had just moved into her Park Avenue penthouse.

Danny Glick had mentioned her in one of his letters too. Mostly his letters were full of news about himself—his acting career still couldn't seem to get off the ground, though he had high hopes for radio, which was just beginning to hire actors—but in this one letter he mentioned Ruth. "Picked up a tidbit about the yapping little lapdog the other day—the one who used to sniff at your heels, remember? You know my mother, with her charities and her boards and her committees? Well, she told me she just put a certain Mrs. Saul Glazer on one of those committees. 'To bring in young blood,' that's how Mother explained it. Translation into English from Motherese: there's money to be squeezed out of her." I could imagine Danny's grin, with the eyebrows shooting up.

I turned to Ruth's letter. "Darling Morrie" it began. But nothing in it to suggest we had ever been more to each other than friendly second cousins. She just wanted me to know that Saul and she would be taking a trip to Europe this summer, would be staying in Paris for a week. "We'll be at the Ritz," she wrote. "We know, of course, the Crillon is fancier, but we didn't want to overdo it." She finished up by hoping we could all get together.

A stranger reading that letter would have thought she was an old world traveler, she knew Paris inside out, all the bellboys at the Ritz would recognize her instantly. Actually it was her first European trip. I knew why she had got in touch with me. She needed somebody to show her around, lead her to the right shops and restaurants, talk French for her to taxi drivers and waiters. I wondered if I would bother to see her. I was in the middle of a difficult picture. Why should I interrupt my work for a couple of tourists who meant nothing to me?

I went to the Ritz Hotel the afternoon Ruth and Saul arrived. Three years in Paris, I had passed it many times. This was the first time I had ever been in the lobby. Lovely red carpeting, cut-glass chandeliers, boutiques with expensive merchandise. The people looked even more expensive than the merchandise. Ruth and Saul had a suite. God knows why they needed that much space. It made them look small. While she threw her arms around me and he gave me his nod, I thought what very small people they were.

They asked me to suggest a restaurant they could take me to that night. I said to myself, "Why not?" and suggested Maxim's. At the height of its popularity then, the most expensive restaurant in Paris. Another place I had passed many times, never went inside. I ordered the famous *caneton au cidre*. So did Ruth. I could see the surprise on her face when it turned out to be duck. Saul ordered a steak, complained because it wasn't well done enough. Ruth kept plucking at his sleeve, whispering loudly, "For heaven's *sake*, Saul!"

I didn't like Saul Glazer, never have. Even so I found myself admiring him just then. How many people would have the nerve to go into the fanciest restaurant in Paris and order a steak well done?

Before we separated that night, Ruth told me she would love to visit me at my studio, see the pictures I was painting. And tell her friends back home, I thought, that a genuine artist in Paris, France, had invited her up to the quaint little dump where he lived. Then another thought popped into my head. Maybe I could get her to buy a picture. I've never been very good at that part of being an artist, the salesmanship part. It isn't that I don't care about money. I care about it. I just have trouble persuading people to give it to me. Even an idiot, though, could see the opportunity Ruth was dropping in my lap.

She got to my apartment next morning at eleven. Saul wasn't with her—he was inspecting negligee shops, comparing prices and workmanship with his own product. It had slipped my mind that he was in the negligee business. I always have trouble remembering what businesses people are in. Ruth wore a blue dress, cloche hat, latest Paris model, expensive, ugly. "Oh those stairs!" she said, when I opened the door to her. She was huffing and puffing. "I don't see how you manage them. Why don't you move into a building with an elevator?"

Her exhaustion wasn't keeping her from giving sharp little glances around the room. I remembered the look on her face the first time she saw my attic back in New York. It still came as a shock to her that people could live the way I did. "This is *wonderful*, Morrie!" she said. "A real Paris studio! I feel creative just standing here!"

I've never quite understood that really, the idea people have that what you do, the quality of your work, depends on where you do it. A painter needs light, of course—awfully hard to paint in an underground cave—otherwise what does it matter if you're in a big room or a small one, a clean one or a dirty one? Once you get involved with what's on the canvas, *that* becomes your room. People just can't seem to understand that.

I offered Ruth a cup of coffee. While it was heating up she wandered around looking at my pictures. In front of each one she went through the same little ritual: scrunching up her face, nodding, frowning, putting on expressions to suggest how hard she was concentrating, how deeply she was feeling. The usual expressions you see all the time in art museums.

Everything she saw she ended up admiring. "Oh Morrie, this is beautiful!" Found myself wishing she'd tell me one of them was ugly, just to break the monotony. She asked me which picture was my most recent. I showed her my full-length oil of the Spanish dancer. She admired it even more than the others. People like Ruth always prefer the latest model—cars, clothes, why not paintings?

The coffee was ready. She took a seat on the sofa. I was close to her in the old armchair. In my little bedroom wherever two people seat themselves they have to be close to each other. "You're doing so well, Morrie," she said, leaning toward me. Eyes wide and bright. Still a pretty girl, marriage hadn't spoiled her looks one bit. Still the prettiest girl I knew. "Your work is getting better and better, I just love it!" she said. The most absurd spurt of pleasure went through me. As if her opinion actually meant something. "I'm so glad for you," she said. "I realize now that we made the right decision."

"What decision?"

"About marriage. When we agreed you weren't ready to get married. Three years ago, I mean. We decided a wife would just be a burden to you in your future career, and how true that turned out to be!"

It was hard for me to believe my ears. The satisfied little smile on her face—not a sign she didn't believe what she was saying. I almost started believing it myself.

"I've thought about you so much during these years." She leaned forward a little further. I began to be alarmed she'd spill her coffee on my trousers. "Saul's the most wonderful husband in the world, he gives me everything I could possibly want—I don't just mean material things, I mean kindness and understanding. But there was something *we* had between us, Morrie—those wonderful long talks about art and beauty and so on. . . ."

I couldn't remember them exactly. As usual, she didn't need any response from me, she went sailing right on. "If Saul has one limitation, he doesn't know much about art and beauty and so on. He's a very sensitive person basically. He could develop his artistic taste if he'd ever give it a chance—but he *won't*, he doesn't think it's important. It's a whole side of my nature he just can't share with me."

Her voice was softer. She was reaching out, taking hold of my hands. "You're the only person I've ever known who *could* share it with me!"

She stopped talking, still holding tight to my hands. I had the feeling I used to get with her back in New York—that she had given

me a cue, now there was a line I was supposed to say. This time I
knew what line she was waiting for. I was older now, more experienced with women. There was a moment—I have to admit it, one
terrible moment—when I was tempted, when I felt how nice it would
be to give her what she expected.

Only a moment. Then a suspicion came to me. What would she
do if I actually took her up on this suggestion she was making? She
would be panic-stricken, wouldn't she? A child who plays a game of
cowboys and Indians doesn't want to be shot by an arrow. None of
this is real to her, I thought. She's not a cruel person. She's even rather
kind, in a way. She isn't a serious person.

It's difficult to explain how much these words, coming suddenly
into my head like that, did for me. They cured me. Of what? Hadn't
I cured myself of *that* a long time ago? Somehow, knowing she wasn't
a serious person made it impossible for me to have a relapse.

I heard myself saying an amazing thing, something I never would
have expected to come out of my mouth. "If you want to cultivate
the artistic side of your nature," I said, "you ought to own some
paintings. You were just admiring my Spanish dancer. Why don't
you buy it?"

She looked confused at this. It obviously caught her by surprise. "Is
it for sale?" she said.

"To you it would be."

Where did *that* come from? Such trickiness. Such salesmanship. I
was shocked at myself. Pleased with myself too. I was even able to
push it further: "That love of art we share—what better way to go on
sharing it with me than to have one of my pictures in your home?
Whenever you feel like escaping from the routine of your ordinary
life, you can look at it, and we'll be together in a way."

That was the right thing to say. I saw the satisfied little smile
trembling at her lips. She was thinking, How convenient, how safe.
She could have an admirer around without the nuisance of actually
having him around. I'm not ordinarily very perceptive about other

people's motives. At that moment it was as if I could hear her thinking.

"Oh Morrie, that's a *wonderful* idea," she said. "It's such a beautiful picture, I'm in love with it already! It would go perfectly in our new dining room, the carpet has exactly that shade of red in it. How much would a picture like that cost?"

I must have been inspired that morning. Once again I amazed myself, heard myself rising to new heights. "Not too much," I said. "Since you and Saul are family, I wouldn't charge you my usual price. I'll let you have it for two thousand dollars."

That made her blink. As a matter of fact, it made *me* blink too. Now that I had said it, I couldn't imagine how I could be such a madman. Still, I *had* said it, there was no way I could back down.

She recovered herself, gave her little laugh. "Well, that *isn't* much, is it? I'll talk to Saul about it. He'll want to see the picture himself, of course. He doesn't know anything about art, but—"

"But he knows what he likes," I said. "Oh yes, I understand."

I told her to bring him around the next morning. I wasn't a bit anxious. I was going to make this sale, I knew it. Saul would be against it. The last thing on earth he wanted to look at every day was one of my pictures. She would make him buy it anyway, wouldn't give him any peace until he did. That was your fate—I saw it clearly now—if you lived close to her and didn't give her anything she asked for.

She brought him to my apartment the next morning. I sat in the bedroom drinking a cup of coffee, while they sat in the studio and argued over my Spanish dancer. Eventually she burst into tears. She used to do that a lot with me, I remembered.

He gave me his check before they left that morning. I took it straight to the bank. What a champagne party my friends and I had at the café that night!

I said a little prayer when I went to bed. I thanked God—the one I didn't believe in—for watching over me three years ago, saving me from making the mistake that would have ruined my life. Then I fell asleep, feeling sure that the sale of my Spanish dancer would change my luck. . . .

S A U L

. . . There were plenty of things happening during these years that made up to me for all my troubles. At least, they could have, if they had worked out right.

I'm referring, of course, to my son Jeffrey, who was born in 1924, and as it turned out he was our only kid. There were complications and Ruth couldn't have any more. We gave him a nice-sounding American name, nothing old-fashioned or foreign about it. Not like my name, for instance. Well, how could you expect Mama and Papa to know any better? He was a good-looking baby, chubby, a tight grip, a lot bigger than I was at that age. The first time I set eyes on him, I said to Ruth he'll grow up into a football player. I had to laugh at her hysterics.

I won't deny it, I was crazy about that kid. If he had turned out to be a girl, I still would have been crazy about him—her—but let's face it, a man wants a son. You build up a business, you want a boy who can take it over after you're dead.

So Jeffrey getting born could have made the craziness around me minor and unimportant, but pretty soon I saw it wasn't going to. The craziness was still in the family. It didn't go away. If I didn't watch my step, it could mess up my son's life like it was messing up mine.

That was how I felt in certain moods. In other moods I wondered what the hell I was worrying about. Wasn't my kid getting everything a kid *could* get—what else was money for? Compare him to my sisters' kids. Goldie and Dodie, inseparable like always, had married a pair of brothers, both of which turned out to be deadbeats. So now Goldie and Dodie each had a little girl, and what could they do for them, what advantages could they give them?

Believe me, it was different with Jeffrey. His clothes came from the most exclusive children's shops. He put in his stomach only the healthiest food from the most expensive butcher and grocer in the neighborhood. When he was sick, and even when he wasn't, the biggest pediatrician in New York looked him over. We fixed up a room for him in a separate section of the apartment, so he wouldn't be disturbed by the noise from the adults, and we also fixed up a playroom, with stuffed animals and electric trains and a miniature circus and a basketball game, everything you could think of that would appeal to a real boy. And on the wallpaper we put pirates and baseball players and Tom Sawyer. I liked the looks of *his* room better than my own.

Also we spared no expense hiring people to take care of him. From the age of one year we had a combination nurse and governess, a woman with special training. She was a German and we called her Fraulein. She had a name, but nobody ever called her anything but Fraulein. She was big and beefy, in her late fifties, and she had references from some of the best families in New York. They all said what a good job she did keeping their kids healthy and teaching them manners and whipping them into shape.

Nowadays, of course, young parents don't go in much for nurses and governesses, even if they can afford them. But in those days, if you had the money, you wouldn't think of *not* hiring a Fraulein—or it could also be a Mademoiselle or a Nanny—and she saved you the trouble of putting the diapers on the kid, or feeding him from his bottle, or cleaning him up in the tub.

All right, I can hear my dear sister-in-law Janet saying it. "Who saved you what trouble? You never would have done any of those things even if you had been dead broke." Well, you're damn right I wouldn't. That's the woman's job. In those days we knew the difference between a father and a mother.

So why was I worried about the way Jeffrey was being brought up? The answer, in a nutshell, was Ruth. I knew when I married her that she was impractical and illogical, and spoiled too. That was part of what made her attractive to me, a successful man *should* have a wife who enjoys spending money and being waited on. But who could have predicted, in a million years, how positively *crazy* she would behave when it came to her son, her baby, her only child? I think back on those first years of his life, and almost the only events I can clearly remember are the fights Ruth and I had over him.

They happened at least once a week, but one in particular is still in my mind, because it was definitely the biggest. In fact, just thinking about it now, after forty-three years, is making me hot under the collar. I have to push myself through it though.

He was three years old. One night before dinner when I was stretched out on the couch reading the evening paper—which was how I liked to relax and unwind myself after a hard day at the office—Ruth came stamping into the living room and told me she had something important to discuss with me. In the first year or two of our marriage I used to ask her if she couldn't wait till later, but by this time, 1927, I knew that waiting was one thing Ruth could never do, even if her life depended on it. So I put down the paper, and she started in.

"Fraulein is very upset," she said. "When I went into the nursery this morning she was practically in tears. You know how much she cares about Jeffie."

A hundred times I had told her to stop calling him Jeffie. If that name stuck to him, the kids would make his life miserable when he went to school. But when could you ever get Ruth to stop doing something just because it was a crazy thing to do? So I let it pass and said, "If that woman was practically in tears, it's the biggest miracle since the Red Sea opened up. She looks to me like she cries about as easy as Max Schmeling."

"*You're* the one who's upsetting her. She says you've been doing things to Jeffie." And then Ruth came out with it, the damnedest rigmarole you ever heard. First of all, how I went up to see him when I got home from the office, and lifted him over my head and swung him around in the air, and how I put him on my shoulders and ran across the room with him.

"That's not so good for my back maybe," I said, "but the kid loves it."

"Fraulein says it's the worst thing for his digestive tract. It makes his water slosh around inside of him. You know he drinks a full glass of water three times a day, after every meal—to make the digestive juices flow."

"A full glass of water three times a day! My God, how could a three-year-old kid get it all down?"

"Oh Fraulein makes sure of that. She stands right next to him at the bathroom sink, until he's swallowed every drop. But the point is, when you jiggle him around like that you throw the balance off."

"All right, what's the next charge, your honor?" I said.

"At breakfast last Sunday you fed pieces of bacon to him off your plate."

"I do it every Sunday, he's crazy about bacon."

"He's *too* crazy about it, he'll stuff himself with it if you let him. Fraulein's worked out his diet very carefully, and he just can't be allowed to go over his weekly fat allowance. And another thing you're doing, dear—you've got into a terrible habit, whenever we have a date at night you go into Jeffie's room before we leave and you look down at him on the bed."

"What's wrong with that? He's used to my face. It doesn't scare him."

"But it wakes him up, dear. Seven o'clock is his bedtime. Fraulein won't allow him up even one minute after. If you take him off his schedule, you'll completely upset his nervous system. He's a sensitive highly strung child as it is, and you're making it worse—".

That was all I needed to hear. I kept my voice very quiet to begin with because it was my intention, before I was through, to get very loud. "Is that it? Any more complaints from the Kaiser? Then I'll give you my answer. I'll take up the points one by one."

I ticked them off on my fingers, making my voice a little fuller and more positive with each finger. "First—if I want to lift the boy up and swing him around and give him piggyback rides, I'll do it, and I don't care how much it sloshes the water. It's *my* water, *I'm* paying for it, so whenever I'm in the mood I'll slosh it. Second—if bacon is what gives him pleasure on Sunday morning, bacon is what he'll get from me. He isn't going to be some kind of picky eater when he grows up. He'll be an eater like his father, and that means he'll put a lot worse than bacon in his stomach before he's finished, so he might as well start getting used to it right now. And third—any time, day or night, that I want to look at my son, I'll go into his room and look at him, and the whole German army isn't going to stop me. And don't worry about his nervous system, because no son of mine *has* one—and if he has, he better get it knocked out of him early. It'll be a big liability to him later on in business. And fourth—what's fourth? Oh yes. Stop calling him Jeffie, for God's sake! He's a *boy*—he isn't some little doll in a little girl's dollhouse! Do you follow my meaning? Good. The discussion is closed."

But it wasn't, of course. With Ruth no discussion is *ever* closed, not until it closes her way. She started in with her screaming, that voice that goes through me like a stomach pain. "What are you trying to do? You're trying to ruin your son's health for the rest of his life!"

"I'm trying to keep you from turning him into some kind of pansy! I'm trying to make sure he grows up into a *man*!"

"Whatever you're trying to do, if you don't stop pretty soon Fraulein won't *let* you have breakfast with him on Sunday mornings anymore—and she won't let you come in to see him either!"

"What's that you said? Am I hearing right? Some female wrestler who talks like a dialect comedian in a burlesque show won't let *me* see my own son in my own home? I'll fire her! I'll kick her right out on her ass!"

"You won't do anything of the sort!" Ruth's voice was going up to the hysteria level. Pretty soon we'd have the tears and the jumping up and down. "My God, do you know how hard it was for me to get her? She had offers lined up, society people were after her, some of the biggest families! Do you know how lucky we are, how all my friends that have children are envying me? What do you think people will *say* if we lose her?"

"Let's find out!" I was on my feet, heading in the direction of the door. "I'll call her in here and fire her right now. Fraulein! Hey, Fraulein!"

Here it came, just the way I knew it would. "Stop it, stop it! My God, you're killing me! You hate me, you enjoy seeing me humiliated, you're deliberately trying to kill me!" Weeping, waving, wailing, jumping up and down—the whole bag of tricks. I had to shut my eyes. I'd seen the show too many times before.

And I knew what I was going to do, naturally. Sooner or later, so why not get it over with? "All right, all right, I won't fire her! Do you hear me, I won't fire her!"

The noise calmed down a little. She looked out at me from the hysterics with one suspicious eye.

"I'm only trying to establish the principle of the thing," I said, suddenly feeling very tired. My unwinding time before dinner was knocked to hell and gone. "Have you got enough logic to understand the principle of the thing? I admit she's an expert, she's had more experience with kids than I have. But even so, if a father can't see his own son—"

"Of course you can see him, dear. It's only that you have to be careful, you have to remember there are certain rules."

"And if a father can't lift up his own son—" Her one unhysterical eye began to roll and get wet, so I went on talking very fast, before the show could start up again. "That's only a detail. I'm not making an issue out of details. As long as you understand the general principle, the overall policy."

And that was the end of it for that night.

Maybe I didn't put up enough of a fight? Maybe so, but what the hell more was I supposed to do? I was a busy man, I had a business to take care of, I was earning the money to keep this family going. It was my job to work out the overall policies, it was *her* job to worry about the details. Besides, it wasn't as if I stopped fighting completely. I just got worn out from time to time and had to take a breather. But I was always in again, slugging away, for the next thing that came up.

Time went on, and even after that German left, when Jeffrey got to be school age, a million things came up, crazy things that Ruth wouldn't stop doing.

Here's an itemized list, by no means complete: The girly-girly clothes she dressed him in. The screaming and yelling every time he fell down and scraped his knee. The whole shmeer about taking him for haircuts to her ladies' beauty parlor instead of a man's barber. The way she made all the servants call him "Master Jeffrey" instead of by his real name. And the walks I took him on in the park, the only time in the kid's life that I got to be alone with him—but if we were ten minutes late she'd have the chauffeur out looking for us!

I went on fighting, believe me. On every point I fought with her until I was too worn out to come up with another sarcastic crack. But how is a man supposed to defend himself against crying and screaming and not listening? And if a man makes absolutely no headway against the mess in his family, how is he supposed to keep himself from going crazy?

I can think of one answer only. He tries to find a way of pulling out of the mess.

What way? . . .

The first way that came to my mind was exactly what would occur to most men in my situation. I said to myself, I'll find another woman and have an affair. I'll take a mistress. Why not? I always did have a way with women, didn't I? You wouldn't last very long in the negligee business if you didn't.

The only trouble was, while it's all very nice to tell yourself you're going to take a mistress, from the practical point of view where do you find her? Do you go to an employment agency? Do you look in the Yellow Pages?

Oscar could have told me right away, of course. I could imagine him telling me. "Saulie old pal, this city is full of women who are positively panting to go to bed with you. Allow me to draw up a list. I'll rate them according to quality—like bonds."

Fortunately I wasn't crazy enough to go to Oscar.

The basic problem, what was making it so hard for me, seemed to be that after eight years of marriage I couldn't remember what type of woman appealed to me. I considered the models that worked for my company. Twice a year, during the buying season, we hired these models to show off the new line in our style show, and some of them were spectacularly beautiful girls. I used to kid them and tell them slightly dirty jokes. They all got a kick out of me. But to tell the truth, I was thirty years old, and they were in their early twenties, if not younger, and with girls like that I never really felt I had very much in common. There wasn't even a single one of them who was Jewish.

So I considered the out-of-town buyers. They were close to my age, most of them, some of them a little older, and they shared with me an interest in the industry. And some of them weren't unattractive either, they made enough money to keep themselves looking nice. On the other hand, I had a certain type of relationship with those women. Twice a year they came to town, I buttered them up and took them out to shows and nightclubs and gave them free liquor, and they told me how bighearted and generous I was, and what a wonderful host—and all the time *I* knew and *they* knew that I was trying to sell them a product and they were trying to get it from me as cheap as possible. With such knowledge between a man and a woman, how romantic are either of you going to feel?

So then I asked myself if Ruth and me had among our friends and acquaintances any women, divorced or still unmarried, who maybe I could get something started with. I went through every one of them in my mind. I even sat down one day and made a list of names. There were half a dozen eligible women on the list—but the trouble with them, how many of them were that much different from Ruth?

Well, I'm not exactly a dope. I knew what was in the back of my mind while I was drawing up these lists and making these calculations. I knew that what I was looking for was right under my nose the whole time. So stop futzing around, I finally told myself. Get on the phone and ask her out to lunch.

I started to buzz my secretary to look up her office number, then I decided I'd better ring her up all by myself. So I did it, and she accepted, and I took her to the fanciest restaurant in New York, with a genuine French menu. Stingy, was I?

The headwaiter had a face that was carved out of marble, and he looked twice as classy as most of the customers. He put us in a booth in the corner, and we spent a long time trying to decipher the menu. Finally we had our orders in, and it was time for me to get down to brass tacks. So why didn't I? I had a hunch. It told me that in this case a little more finesse and diplomacy might be appropriate. Instead of jumping right on top of those tacks with both feet, it might be better to creep up on them gradually.

So while all these fancy dishes were put in front of us—the French chopped liver, the potatoes made out of strings, the tiny chickens that looked like they were cooked a few minutes after they got hatched— we talked about things that didn't matter.

We talked about the stock market. This was 1928, and the boom was really booming. Everybody was putting every bit of their stray cash in stocks—except me, but I'll get to that later—and Janet told me she was worried about it. It meant a lot of business for Hillman and Sons, and she got a big bonus that year, but she had a feeling the bubble was eventually going to burst. She was advising her rich widows to put some of their assets in government bonds and real estate, items that didn't bring in too much income but looked safer to her in the long run. Hillman, her boss, wasn't too happy that she was giving this advice. Investors who curled up snugly in nice safe harbors didn't bring in nearly as much commission as speculators who jumped like monkeys from one bonanza to another.

"He had me on the carpet about it last week," Janet said. "But I told him I had a feeling the firm would be grateful for it someday. Meanwhile, we're making so much money off the speculators, can't we afford to do a little less well off the widows?"

One thing I always said about Janet, you couldn't beat her for common sense.

The conversation turned to my son Jeffrey. Janet was crazy about the kid. She dropped by to see him whenever she had the chance, and she was always bringing him toys and games, and getting down on the floor to show him how to play with them. I noticed too that she was even willing, from time to time, to stand up to Ruth for the kid's interests. A few years before, for instance, they had a screaming fight on the subject of that German nurse Fraulein. Janet told Ruth she ought to get rid of that tyrant who was taking all the joy out of the kid's childhood, and Ruth told Janet that a woman who didn't have any children of her own and couldn't get any man to marry her ought to keep her mouth shut about subjects she couldn't possibly understand. Ruth won the fight in the end, of course. Nobody ever wins a fight with Ruth, on the same principle that nobody's head ever makes a dent in a stone wall.

So now Janet asked a lot of questions about how Jeffrey was getting along, and I answered that he was doing fine, all things considered. And this naturally led to me complaining about Ruth.

It wasn't the first time I had complained to Janet about Ruth. We didn't get many opportunities to be by ourselves, but sometimes—if we found ourselves, say, in a corner of the room at a big cocktail

party, with Ruth in the opposite corner—I'd manage to come out
with a complaint or two. Well, who else was I supposed to come out
with them to? A man can't keep his feelings bottled up forever.

She listened to me with a look of sympathy on her face, and then
she said, "I know she's got her foibles. She always did, you knew all
about them when you married her. But look at the good points she's
got. You say she wastes her time on shopping and silly luncheons and
so on, but look at all the time she gives to doing really nice things for
people. She keeps track of everybody's birthdays and anniversaries
and so on, and she always sends a card or a present. Anybody who's
in the hospital, she sends them flowers or candy. She does do a lot of
shopping, I admit that, but for every item she buys for herself she
picks up another two or three to give to somebody else. Relatives and
friends, and even her friend's relatives. Not to mention that she's
constantly writing letters to raise funds for her charities and organi-
zations—she must write as many letters every week as *I* do for the
business. When a person spends that much time going out of her way
for others—"

"She gets paid back," I said. "She lets them know for the rest of
their lives how bighearted she's been."

"All right, that's Ruth, that's just her nature. At least she *is* bighearted, and there aren't too many people you can say that about."

"She's still your spoiled sister that you're picking up after," I said.
And maybe my admiration showed in my face, because suddenly
Janet gave a blush.

It was one of those blushes that turned her into a young girl again.
And me into a young fellow, with feelings inside of me that I had to
let out. End of finesse and diplomacy, I thought. It was time to say
what I wanted to say. "I've been feeling something lately—"

And just then I heard a noise from across the restaurant. I looked
around and saw this woman laughing, at a table against the opposite
wall. It was one of Ruth's friends. I couldn't remember her name, she
belonged to this group, the Literary Ladies, they called themselves,

who got together one afternoon a week and pretended to talk about some current book, only what they really talked about was the current gossip. This woman didn't see me yet, and probably wouldn't since I wasn't in her line of fire—but I can't deny it, her being there made it hard for me to go on with what I'd been saying.

"This damn city!" I said. "Like some small town—you can't go anywhere without running into people you know!"

"Suppose we skip dessert," Janet said. "You could come up to my apartment, I'll give you some coffee."

Her apartment, which she had just moved into a month or two before, was in a reconditioned brownstone house on a side street on the East Side. Her two rooms, plus bathroom and small kitchen, took up the whole third floor. High ceilings, big bay windows, thick walls. Nobody else in the house could hear a thing through those walls.

I nodded. My mouth was too dry for me to talk.

I paid the check. We walked out of the restaurant. I walked slightly at a slant, my head turned away from the wall where Ruth's friend was sitting. We got out to the sidewalk, and the doorman started hailing a cab for us.

There was a sick feeling in my stomach, a dizziness in my head. What was happening to me anyway?

I was coming to my senses, that's what was happening. I was coming out of that crazy dream—second childhood, for God's sake!—and starting to think like a grown man again.

The cab pulled up to the curb in front of us. I looked at my watch and let out a groan. "Oh my God, what a dope I am. I completely forgot! A buyer's coming in this afternoon—from California. It's the only time she's got to see me—"

"You couldn't even have your coffee?"

"I'm sorry, Janet. I'll be late as it is. Believe me, you don't know how sorry!"

She thanked me for the lunch and gave me a kiss on the cheek, and then I put her in that cab and slipped the driver a couple of bucks. I got another cab for myself. I was feeling slightly nauseous all the way back to my office.

I won't pretend that I got much work done that afternoon. I had too much thinking to do. It took me a couple of hours to get everything sorted out. But I did it, believe me—I always do—and it was finally clear to me what had happened. Janet and I had been tempted, there was no getting around that. But how much danger had there ever been of us giving in? The fact is, we still had the same natural common sense and willpower that saved us from making this same exact mistake eight years earlier. We were leading pretty good lives, both of us—the lives we *wanted* to be leading—so who needed complications?

Take marriage, for instance. What Janet wanted from marriage, she couldn't get from me—because my ideas would have interfered with her success in the stockbroking field. And what I wanted from marriage—I had to face up to this—I couldn't get from Janet. What's more, I already *was* getting it from Ruth. She could be a pain in the ass, but she kept my home running smoothly, she got the meals on the table and mostly it was what I liked to eat, she kept track of social engagements and parties and so on, she sent out thank-you notes, she made sure I wasn't bothered by a lot of details that would take my mind off important matters. As for her whining and her bragging and her crap about art and culture—wasn't I pretty experienced by now at shutting my ears and thinking about something else?

As for anything else between Janet and me—short of marriage, that is—we weren't the type. Writing false names in hotel registers, avoiding each other's eyes at dinner parties, ducking our heads if we saw somebody we knew at a restuarant—that kind of life wouldn't appeal to either one of us.

I called her late that afternoon to apologize for running out on her so suddenly. She couldn't have been nicer and more understanding. We decided we'd get together for lunch again, maybe once a month, but we agreed—though we didn't say this to each other in so many words, it was strictly between the lines—that from now on it would be only friendship.

As a matter of fact, we went on having those lunches more or less regularly for years. Sometimes I'd see a look in her eye—that temptation was coming over her again. Thank God I've always been able to be strong for both of us.

Which brings me to something I don't much feel like remembering. I mean, the end of 1929. . . .

M O R R I S

. . . I fell asleep, feeling sure that the sale of my Spanish dancer would change my luck. And it really did.

A week later Lantin, at the gallery, told me he had sold one of my pastels, nude getting out of the bathtub, to a stranger who came in off the street. An American. My things have always sold better to Americans. A few days after that Mrs. Newberry wrote me about a friend of hers—Mrs. H. Walter Carlton, husband in banking, very rich people—coming to Paris in two weeks, wanted to look at my work. Big woman, built like a house, as the expression goes—bust was the front porch, jaw was the second-story balcony. Bought two small pictures: ballerina at the rehearsal bar, ballerina waiting in the wings. Both of them had a lot of pink in them. Pink was her favorite color. After that Mrs. Carlton was a steady customer—every year I put aside a couple of pink items for her.

A month later Augustus Kelly sent me a cablegram. A New York gallery, Kleinsinger's on Fifty-Seventh Street, wanted to handle me. Word was around that Mrs. Newberry and her friends bought my work. Old Anton Kleinsinger was betting other buyers would follow their lead. Big man with a black beard, Rumanian or Hungarian or something, nobody ever knew for sure. Wanted me to come to New

York, bring along oils, watercolors, pastels, anything else I had on hand.

I hadn't even thought of going to New York. The passage was too expensive, not to mention the cost of living once I got there. Paris suited me—in the autumn especially. Pink light turns gold and brown, same color as the leaves on the chestnut trees. Women start sprouting the new fall fashions—lots of trailing lace this year. But Kleinsinger's request made me reconsider. I booked third-class for October. Just past the tourist season, the rates went down.

It turned out to be the first of the trips to America I made every year—by ship whenever possible. I've never liked airplanes. Too cramped, nothing to look at through the window but clouds. From the artistic point of view clouds are overrated.

That first trip was a big success. I sold seven pictures in New York, big ones too. In art it's like everything else—people want you if they think other people want you. As soon as they think other people don't, they stop wanting you. Found *that* part out a little later.

One of the people who wanted me was Luis Hernandez. The movie actor, well-known silent-movie villain, the one who stroked his mustache and kidnapped the girl. He wasn't a Spaniard actually. His real name was Louis Hertzberg, a Jewish boy from Brooklyn. Pudgy little fellow, round face, black pencil-line mustache—half the actors in Hollywood wore them in those days. He collected paintings. Not just for show. He really liked them, had things to say about them.

I met him at Kleinsinger's gallery. He bought a full-length ballerina in white, with a melancholy expression. I did a whole series of melancholy ballerinas around that time. He was leaving for Hollywood by train in two days, insisted I come with him. He'd put me up at his place, introduce me to prospective buyers. Lots of people out there were suddenly making money, didn't know what to do with it, collecting paintings looked classy to them. Well, Louie was a hard man to turn down. Rubbing his little hands together, grabbing you by the shoulder, talking a mile a minute. People like that have always been able to do anything with me.

So I took my first train ride across the country. Louie was bored, wanted to play cards all day long. I wanted to look out the window. Fascinated by wheat fields and deserts. Two kinds of orange. Sun beating down, closer to the earth than it ever was in Paris or New York. And those long hard spiky shadows—beautiful, sinister. Also they made me thirsty. Then came Southern California—palm trees, green lawns, bright blue skies. Didn't look like anything you'd ever see in reality. Found out a dozen years later what it *did* look like—when I saw my first Technicolor movie.

Louie's place in Hollywood was like a bigger shinier version of Nôtre Dame Cathedral. He threw a big party for me the night after we arrived, I sold ten paintings in a week. Made a lot of good contacts too, people who kept buying from me whenever I showed up in Hollywood with a new batch. Very odd people really. Always wearing sunglasses. Everyone calls everyone else "darling." Lots of money for paintings though.

I got back to Paris in November, wrote to Mrs. Newberry right away, telling her I wouldn't be needing her grant anymore. I could stand on my own feet now. She had made it possible for me. Now I hoped she could do the same for someone else like me.

Those other artists at the café told me I was crazy. They thought I should go on taking the money from the rich American woman—rich Americans were fair game. Sadie Boroff didn't approve either. She wrote me it was foolish to burn my bridges, count my chickens before they were hatched. I wasn't worried. I was still under thirty. I was full of confidence, the way you are when you're young. The world was starting to treat me well. I couldn't believe it would ever treat me badly again.

One day, a few weeks later, a letter came—official-looking envelope, gold seal. From the French government, Ministry of Fine Arts, director of the Luxembourg Museum. That's the museum that shows only living artists. After you die they take you off exhibition, store you away in the cellar or transfer you to the Louvre with the old masters. The director was pleased to inform me the French government was buying one of my works. Just a small one, a charcoal drawing—old musician playing the cello in the orchestra pit while a ballerina dances—you see only her legs, his cello takes up the foreground.

Did this stroke of luck make me practically an old master? Not really, of course. Chances were a lot better I'd wind up in the cellar than in the Louvre. I remember walking around for a week in a kind of trance. I passed people on the street, I said to myself, "Wouldn't they stop to look if they knew they'd just come close to the latest old master?" When you're young, vanity comes easy. . . .

It gets knocked out of you easy too. A month later I was invited to a dinner party, the director of the Luxembourg Museum invited me. I'm going to be a lion, I thought.

It was in his house, big three-story mansion overlooking the river. He couldn't live like that on his government salary—his wife's money did it for him. Lots of people there. I was seated far down the table, never said a word to my host and hostess all night. The guest of honor was Matisse—Henri Matisse, fellow who used to paint all those Algerian girls—very big reputation just then. Little man with lots of whiskers—big talker, never let anybody else get a word in edgewise. Much too far away for me to hear what he was saying.

After dinner—pretty good food, I admit, at least as good as Maxim's—I mingled with the crowd, trying to edge closer to Matisse. Suddenly I heard a voice, man's voice, high-pitched carrying kind of voice. ". . . Imitating Degas, in this day and age—unbelievable how some people will spend their lives—no, no, absolutely of no importance whatever . . ."

I looked in that direction, couldn't see who was talking. Matisse was over there. I wondered if the voice had been his. I didn't believe it. People said he was a nice fellow, in spite of the ego.

I left there early. Went straight home, didn't stop at the café,
though I knew my friends would be there. I didn't feel like telling
them I had left the party early. There had been a lot of jokes when I
made my sale to the Luxembourg Museum. They didn't think much
of the Luxembourg Museum.

Louise came to sit the next morning. I was doing another Spanish
dancer—a blue one, companion piece to the red one I had sold to Saul
and Ruth Glazer. Couldn't make any progress that morning. Threw
down my brush. Louise changed clothes, made coffee, sprawled on
the sofa while we drank it. Skirt pulled up slightly, round calves just
barely visible—dimpled softness, like the sofa cushions, only a lighter
color. Milk against *vin rosé.*

She asked me what was wrong. I told her what had happened at
the party. Very odd really. I would have died before I told that to
anybody else.

"But why should you think he was talking about *you?*" she asked.

"People *have* accused me of imitating Degas. Because I do ballet
girls. That's all most people can see in a picture, the subject matter—
not the style, the manner—"

"You don't imitate anybody," she said. "How often you've explained it to me. Real artists learn from the great masters, build on
them. Matisse knows that too, he's always saying the same thing."

"You've worked for Matisse?"

"I know a girl who's one of his regulars. He admires all kinds of
painting, she says, even if it's different from his own. So you see, he
couldn't have been the one you overheard."

She was so positive, her manner wouldn't allow for any contradic-
tion. I began to feel better. Though I couldn't admit it just yet. I've
always had to hold on to my doubts awhile, nurse them along, stroke
them, before I feel I have a right to let them go. I brought in my
friends at the café, told her how some of them occasionally called me
"Degas"—a friendly nickname, a joke.

She gave a laugh, sharp and contemptuous. Only a Frenchwoman is capable of such a laugh. Even a softhearted Frenchwoman like Louise. "Have any of your friends sold pictures to the Luxembourg Museum?"

"I don't think so."

"How many of them have regular customers at all? You don't have to tell me. Don't I see artists all the time in my line of work? Don't I know how few of them can sell things, paint pictures that give pleasure to people?"

"Is that so? It's really so unusual?"

"I'm telling you, you're head and shoulders above the rest of them. Why do you think they're jealous of you?"

"Oh no, I'm sure they're not—"

"You never see anything bad in anybody. You think everyone is just like you. My poor naïve Maurice."

That was the first time she called me her poor Maurice. It became her regular name for me in the years that followed. I still remember the tingling that went through me whenever she used it. I feel it now, I think, that tingling.

She got up from the sofa all of a sudden. She came to my chair, her hand was on my arm. "You're a very nice man," she said. Her voice got softer. Always I'd thought of her as rather loud and hearty. Now her voice was remarkably soft. "Believe me, I know. When you live with a dirty son of a bitch, you become an expert on what's nice and what isn't." She leaned down and gave me a kiss. First on the cheek. Then on the lips. Soft and gentle—infinitely pleasurable. I'm being seduced, I said to myself. So this is what it's like.

We went to bed together. It was very nice. It was nicer than it had ever been for me before. People think artists are all great lovers. People judge us by a few exceptions. Picasso, for instance—in and out of bed with practically everyone—such an unattractive little man too, it's really a mystery. I've never been like that myself. I've always been shy. I have my feelings, I can be aroused. Louise was the first person who ever went out of her way to try.

I decided that big-breasted women *were* my type after all.

"You're so beautiful, Louise," I said. "I think I love—"

She wouldn't let me finish. She laughed and kissed me on the cheek. "You don't have to say that. I know who you are and who I am. We'll just enjoy ourselves, all right?"

We talked it over very seriously then. I realized she was right. What was between us couldn't be called love. It was affection, companionship—but anything like marriage was out of the question. We came from different worlds—French and American, Catholic and Jew, practical businesslike woman and impractical artistic man, mother dedicated to her child and confirmed bachelor dedicated to his work. Art came ahead of everything for me, her child came ahead of everything for her.

Another reason. Both of us had been in love in the past, with other people. Look what came of it. Neither of us wanted to suffer like that again.

We got pleasure from each other's company. We couldn't have got any *more* pleasure. Why let things go any further?

Easy enough to keep this from happening. We set up a regular routine for ourselves. We saw each other twice a week, in the daytime. We saw each other every Saturday night—the little girl went to Versailles on weekends to stay with Louise's mother. The husband was no problem for us. He hardly cared what his wife did, more often than not he was out all night drinking. It was our rule, for our daytime meetings, that work came first. A good long sitting on my latest picture. Only afterward would we be entitled to relaxation. By following this rule we reminded ourselves about our relationship—it was pleasant and genuine, but it was strictly limited.

The years passed. Happy years—the thought came to me often, no time of my life had ever been so happy. The pleasure we took in each other wasn't only in bed either. We went places together. I took her to restaurants. She enjoyed good food, ate heartily, cracked jokes with the waiters. I've never been the type who can crack jokes with waiters. There was one place in particular, near the Sorbonne. Cheap prices, no cloths on the tables, old waiters who grumbled a lot. We liked it. We felt comfortable there.

She always wore bright colors when she went out with me. Polka dots, flower patterns, reds and greens. Splashes of light, even when we were sitting in dark corners.

Another thing she enjoyed was the movies. Never cared for them much myself. I took pleasure in her pleasure. How involved she became—personally involved—in the stories, the lives of the characters. She laughed and wept, got furious at the villains, full of sympathy for the poor naïve heroines who fell into their clutches. I told her I knew Luis Hernandez personally. She was astounded to hear he was really a very nice man, had never kidnapped a girl—no, not one!—in his life.

In all those years there was one thing I couldn't get her to like—the ballet. I took her once or twice. She tried to be polite, she couldn't hide how much it bored her. "Pretty costumes, nice music," she said, "but when I go to a show I like to have a good story. And I want to know what the characters have to say for themselves."

If there was any pain during those years of happiness, it came from guessing what other people were thinking about us. Seeing us from the outside, not understanding what we were really like. Another artist and his model, having a sordid little affair—how typical of Paris! I mentioned Louise's name to my friends at the café, they gave little winks and nudges. For them a woman could be only a wife or a whore, there were no other possibilities.

How I hated them for that! Why couldn't they see it was different between Louise and me? Couldn't they see how I felt when I was away from her for long—on my trips to America, for instance? The terrible empty ache inside of me—how I missed her, how I counted the days till I could be with her again! Was that how a man feels about a whore? But none of those people at the café, nobody I knew, would have believed me. I wasn't foolish enough to tell them my feelings.

I wrote those feelings to Danny Glick sometimes—beginning to do nicely now, getting parts on radio shows, though nothing on the stage yet, which was his great ambition. I explained to him how devoted Louise and I were to each other, how much we admired and respected each other, yet with no impulse to get married, because we didn't feel love for each other in the conventional sense. He never answered those parts of my letters, never mentioned her in his. That was all right. I just wanted my feelings to be on record.

One day Louise told me she was pregnant. The end of a sitting. She was half undressed, late afternoon haze on her shoulders. Suddenly they blurred before my eyes. A certain thought had flashed into my mind.

. She saw it on my face—she never had any trouble reading my face. She smiled, patted my hand, and said, "No, it's not what you imagine. It's my husband's baby. I've kept track of the dates, I can tell for sure."

I had the oddest feeling when she said this. At first a twinge of dismay. I had been assuming somehow that she and her husband no longer got together in that way. Then I told myself I had no right to make any such assumption. She was a grown woman, neither of us had any special obligations to the other, what we had together wasn't *that* sort of thing. I should be relieved about the baby, I told myself. What a catastrophe if it had been mine! Her shoulders were in focus again.

I worked badly that week. Still suffering from the first shock, before she relieved my mind. I kept imagining what the baby would be like if it *were* mine. I'd want it to look like her, of course—and with her common sense and good humor. Maybe just a bit of my talent and seriousness. . . .

She went right on working up to the very last month. I don't know about the rest of her clients—I for one was happy to go on using her. I started doing studies of pregnant women. The swell of the belly, a beautiful shape really. I considered doing a Virgin in the

Manger, type of thing I'd never tried before. Probably just as well I never did it.

The baby was born in March. She stopped working for about a month, I didn't see her at all. I was very restless. I spent more time than usual at the café. When I painted, it was still lives. I didn't feel like doing people.

Then she started working again. The first time she reappeared in my studio—I'd been getting ready for her all day, I had a bottle of champagne, the place had never been cleaner and tidier. I saw her in the doorway, I threw my arms around her. I could feel tears coming into my eyes. I hope she didn't notice.

She showed me pictures of the baby. All babies look pretty much alike—wrinkled, red-faced, crying or burping, not much individual personality. It's one of the subjects that only bachelors are ever honest about. I didn't express this view to Louise, of course—no desire to rouse the tigress in her. I told her he was beautiful, just what she wanted to hear. She had named him Michel. After Michelangelo, she said.

It wasn't long before our life together went back to what it had always been. A great load off my mind. I hadn't realized how worried I had been. What would I have done if she had decided not to come back to me?

Habit, of course, not love. It's amazing how attached you can become to a habit.

And now I come to 1929—when everything got bad for me again. . . .

S A U L

. . . Which brings me to something I don't much feel like remembering. I mean, the end of 1929.

Everybody knows what happened then—the breadlines, the people selling apples on the street. To give my honest opinion, which I mostly kept to myself at the time, people brought it on themselves. They were dumb, they were greedy. They thought they could be millionaires without doing any work. If I was one of the smart ones and stayed out of the market, it's because I knew that nobody gives you something for nothing in this world.

My own partner Oscar Kaplan—such a smart man in so many ways—didn't understand this simple basic fact of life. He was a heavy investor, and he was always trying his hardest to talk me into investing too.

"It's absolutely crazy," he said. "Do you know how much money you've got tied up in insurance? Good money that could be working for you, bringing in dividends, growing bigger every day. In a few years it could be doubled, tripled, quad—"

I interrupted him. "And how is this miracle going to happen?"

"Don't you read the newspapers? We're in the middle of a stock-market boom, the biggest one in the history of the country. People are making millions overnight. *Dopes* are doing it, so why not a man with brains like you? 'There is a tide in the affairs of men, which, taken at the flood, leads on to fortune.' "

"William Shakespeare?"

"Who else? *Julius Caesar*—a play about some ancient Romans who didn't let any opportunities slip by."

"What if I buy stocks and they go down?" I said.

Oscar gave that cocky laugh of his. It always reminded me of a boy showing off, climbing a tree or riding a bicycle with no hands—in all these years that laugh hadn't changed one bit. "What if the Brooklyn Bridge collapses tomorrow? What if the New York Athletic Club suddenly starts taking in Jews? They won't go down. Look around, see what's happening!"

He had his say, so then I had mine. I told him what I always did when I went into a gambling casino. I set aside a certain amount of money that I could afford to lose. If I lost it, I wasn't hurt. If I won, that was a nice extra bonus. I didn't pull out of the bank all the savings I had for my old age and take them into a gambling casino.

Naturally he laughed at this. "I didn't know you were such a philosopher," he said. "But what if the roulette wheel was fixed in your favor, what if you were gambling on a sure thing?"

People like Oscar never learn. In this world there are no sure things. I found that out when I was still a kid, and he should have found it out too. I told him if he wanted to throw away his money that was *his* business, but I wasn't putting all *my* eggs in the stock market.

Oscar shook his head and sighed, the way you do when you're dealing with some kind of idiot. "You want to know something about yourself, Saul? You're so cautious and old-fashioned you're as good as dead. You've got about as much life in you as a dinosaur."

"The dinosaurs lasted for millions of years, didn't they?" I said. Occasionally, if the wind was right, I *could* get a little bit of my own back at Oscar.

But never for long. He always had a topper. "They did," he said. "And you know what finally killed them? They *bored* themselves to death!"

Poor Oscar, he was typical of a lot of other people in those days. They weren't as smart as me maybe, but I still had sympathy with them when the crash came.

My own secretary, for instance—Alice McCloskey—she was in her forties, an old maid, she lived with her mother. She borrowed from a loan company to make up her margin, and now they were threatening to take her furniture. All right, what the hell, I was a sucker. I gave her a check for what she owed. She was a damn good secretary, and they aren't so easy to find.

Another example—Ruth's brother Irving, the doctor. He had to give up the idea of moving his office from the West Side to the East Side, where he could charge higher fees but also the rents were higher. I gave him a loan, and in all fairness he paid back every penny in the next five years.

Another example—my sisters Goldie and Dodie. *Both* their husbands—I used to call them the Klutz Brothers—came to me and told me their businesses were going down the drain. And believe me, those businesses weren't so far *out* of the drain even before the crash. So I bailed them out, knowing they'd be putting the bite on me again in a couple of years.

And then in the summer my sister Doris, who never got married (in spite of being the "pretty" one) and was living with Papa, came to me crying. Papa had just broken it to her that he lost the jewelry store. People weren't buying jewelry anymore. The bank foreclosed because for three months he hadn't paid the mortgage. Three months—and not one word to me! And the worst of it was, he wanted Doris to look for another apartment for them, smaller, in a cheaper neighborhood, maybe downtown on the Lower East Side. After all the trouble I went to, getting him to move *up* from there!

I dropped what I was doing and went crosstown to talk to him. I found him, naturally, in that old chair of his, listening in the dim light to one of his opera records. He had to wait till it was over before he'd look up at me. "So how are you?" he said. "It's the middle of the day, you're not in your office?"

"I could ask you the same question," I said. "You're not in your store?"

"I was going to ring you up and tell you," he said, acting like he wasn't coming out with anything unusual. "I'm a man of leisure now. I'm retired. I got rid of the store."

"How do you get rid of a store?"

"I sold it to somebody, what else?"

"To the bank maybe? For the mortgage you owed them?"

I could see the flash come into his eyes, and the corners of his mouth turned down, the way they always did when he got angry. It was one of my oldest childhood memories. "I told that Doris to keep her mouth shut!"

"She's got some common sense, so she didn't listen. Don't I have a right to know what's going on? I'm your son, your oldest. Some people think I've got a good business head—"

"And I *don't* have a good business head! Thank you very much, it's nice a man's own flesh and blood should remind him he's a failure."

Handling Papa was like handling a stick of dynamite, you had to be careful every second. As quick as I could, I told him I didn't think he was any failure, he got caught in an economic situation through no fault of his own, like millions of other people. The question now was, what was he going to do with himself while he waited for conditions to improve so he could open another store?

He gave one of his sarcastic grunts at that, but I ignored it and hurried on. The question also was, where was he going to live while he waited? And since Doris and he were pretty comfortable here on the West Side, did it make any sense for them to move? Apartments like this didn't grow on trees—why should they sacrifice it?

"Because I don't have the money to pay for it," he said.

"So I'll loan you the money. And maybe a few dollars more for monthly expenses. You can pay me back as soon as you're established again."

The flash was coming back into his eyes. "Wait a second, did I hear right? *You're* offering a loan to *me*? Knowing my opinion of fathers that take money from sons? Fathers should *give* money to sons!"

"Who says so? If you're the one who's in trouble—"

"What trouble?" His voice was louder, he was working himself up into a first-class fit. Well, maybe it would do him good, get some of the feelings of failure out of his system. "Am I some old kocker, can't lift a finger from the rheumatism, he sits in a corner and the spit dribbles out of his mouth, he lives off his children?"

"Look, you can't afford those crazy old-country ideas—"

"Now I'm crazy, is it?" He was on his feet, with an arm up in the air. "I never hit you yet! All the years you were growing up I never raised my fist to you—like some goyisher father that gets drunk! But I swear it—"

And to tell the truth, for a minute there I actually thought he was going to slam that arm down on my head. I even jumped back a step or two.

But then his arm was lowering, he was sinking back into his chair. "All right, all right, it's over," he said. "I'm sorry. You're a good boy. You've always had a kind heart. But this discussion is over, this matter will never be mentioned between us again. I'm turning on Rosa Ponselle."

So there was no point doing any more talking. This high screechy woman's voice came out of the phonograph, and that was my signal to make an exit. But later that day I called up my sister Doris and told her she and Papa didn't have to move, because from now on I'd be sending her a monthly check to cover the rent and expenses.

How did I expect to hide this from Papa? Sooner or later wouldn't he demand from Doris an explanation how they could afford to stay in the old apartment? The answer is, you had to know Papa. I wouldn't have to explain anything to him, I wouldn't have to tell him any lies. He would keep his word and never mention this matter to me again. With Papa what wasn't mentioned wasn't happening. . . .

So 1930 went on, and at the end of it came the biggest thing about the stock-market crash that I wish I didn't have to remember.

It was New Year's Eve, and Ruth and I were giving a party. Japanese lanterns strung up all over the apartment. A five piece band—Sandy Samuels and His Foxy Trotters—they rented themselves out to everybody that year. Couples were dancing in the living room and on the terrace, everybody else was drinking my champagne. Even Ruth's cousin the rabbi, Nat Steinmetz—he had a congregation in Philadelphia, an up-and-coming man in the rabbi business—was doing a lot of dancing and drinking. I didn't want to think what my bill from the bootlegger was going to be.

Oscar Kaplan was there, and just before midnight he came weaving up to me, threw his arm over my shoulder, gave me a cloud of alcohol right in my face. "Happy New Year, Saulie old pal! Welcome, nineteen hundred and thirty-one—farewell, nineteen hundred and thirty. Frankly you weren't the best year of my life, but I won't make an issue out of it, don't believe in fighting with feeble old men." He gave a hiccup, then I caught him before he could fall flat on his face.

I suggested to him that maybe he had had enough to drink already, and I should get his coat and find him a cab. But he shook his head hard and said, "No, no, the night is young and it's a great party. You and Ruthie certainly know how to throw a party. Don't send me out into the cold and dark. Plenty of cold and dark later on. Let me stay here in your nice warm cozy nest, with a nice warm cozy highball, and celebrate my good luck."

"What good luck is that?"

"Didn't you hear? Been waiting for the news for months, today it finally came. Old pal, I've achieved happiness—perfect happiness!"

A terrible suspicion came into my mind. I couldn't actually believe it, but I had to ask anyway. "You're getting married?"

He roared with laughter. "I said happiness, not feeblemindedness, for God's sake!"

"Then what are you talking about already?"

"Very simple. Where does unhappiness come from? The mad pursuit of possessions, material pleasure, worldly prestige—right? Expensive cars, nightclubs, two dozen tailor-made suits, all-night poker games, tall blondes, tipping the headwaiters—in fact, everything I've been madly pursuing my whole life. Well, it gives me great satisfaction to announce that the pursuit is over now."

"What is it, a New Year's resolution? You've decided to reform your life? I'll believe it when I see it."

"I understand your scornful laughter. Don't think I've got the strength of character, do you? You're absolutely right. But the Lord wants to save a man's soul, He's going to save it one way or another—by hook or by crook, you could say. He does seem to be going to extremes in my case, I admit. A stock-market crash and a depression just to make me pure and virtuous."

"What are you getting at?" I said, though to tell the truth I had a pretty good idea already. And I couldn't claim I hadn't expected it either. In this world you make your bed, you have to lie in it.

"I'm broke, old pal," Oscar said, without even a quiver in his voice, like he was making another one of his jokes. "Dead broke. Flat as the proverbial pancake. Couple of little items, thought they might survive the avalanche, seemed to be holding their own—my broker called me today, told me they just went down the drain with all the rest. So here you see before you a man free of worldly hopes, ambitions, and resources—a happy man!"

"You couldn't save anything at all?"

"Not a penny. Not a scrap. What isn't sold already, it's hocked up to the elbows. Matter of a few months it'll all have to go. Latest car, Hispano-Suiza roadster—twenty-three of the twenty-four suits, got to keep one of them to wear out on the street, matter of simple decency, right?—memberships in the dear old clubs, they take a dim view of members who can't come up with the dues—ringside tables at the local bistros, untipped headwaiters seldom produce ringside tables—and the blondes, of course. Swore they loved me for myself, swore they'd be faithful to me forever—till *I* got tired of *them*, naturally. But that kind of devotion doesn't come cheap, requires constant upkeep. You don't get something for nothing in this world—as a certain wise philosopher of my acquaintance has often told me."

I blushed a little at this—that's right, actually blushed. There are times when it's a pleasure to say "I told you so!" to somebody, but this wasn't one of the times. So I spoke up fast, making the usual remark that people make when their friends are in trouble. "If there's anything I can do—"

"Plenty you can do. Pretty soon they'll be kicking me out of my place, my lovely bachelor suite with elegant terrace, top floor of the Savoy-Plaza Hotel. It may annoy them a bit when I stop paying the rent. So you can join me for my kicking-out party. Champagne cocktails on the street, corner of Fifth Avenue and Fifty-Ninth. Special entertainment planned—watching the cops haul away the furniture."

"Listen, if you need some money to tide you over—"

" 'There is a tide in the affairs of men . . .' But that tide is running pretty low just now, Saulie boy. 'Taken at the trickle,' you might say. Drops in the bucket won't start it up again. Instead of money, why don't you give me something useful."

"Such as?"

"Tell me, in your inimitably blunt way, that I'm a horse's ass. Tell me I was conceited, greedy, and reckless. Tell me that even a backward child wouldn't have expected God to shower lovely money on his head forever."

"I don't want to tell you that."

"But I'm looking forward to it. When a man is as far down as he can go, when he's got positively *nothing* in his life, the one pleasure left to him is a good swift kick in the tochis."

How do you answer somebody when he talks to you like that? You try to be optimistic and encouraging. Whatever you may be feeling privately. So I told Oscar, with as much enthusiasm as I could whip up in myself, that he wasn't down that far, he had plenty of things going for him. He still owned half the business, and from what I heard from the buyers we were going to have a terrific season, in spite of economic conditions. Also it was a lucky thing he had to move out of that penthouse. It was always too big for him, a regular theater lobby. And it would be good for his digestion if he ate home once in a while, instead of those rich foods in restaurants. And frankly Ruth and I would be relieved when he stopped riding around in those fancy foreign cars. It was a miracle he didn't break his neck in one of them before now. As for him giving up the blondes, that was the best news yet. Maybe he'd meet a nice girl for a change, and settle down to a normal family life, the way a man was supposed to do.

He just listened to me, with a little dreamy smile on his face, while I came out with all this, and then he gave me a pat on the shoulder. "I always *said* you were a philosopher, Saulie. What you're advising, if I understand you correctly, I should cultivate a sense of proportion. I should realize that a headwaiter snubbing me isn't the end of the world."

"You should realize you haven't lost anything you really need."

" 'Oh reason not the need. Our basest beggars are in the poorest thing superfluous.' *King Lear* by William Shakespeare. About this fellow who gets caught in a storm and doesn't know enough to come in out of the rain. Saulie old pal, maybe it *is* time for me to go home. Where did you say my coat was? Got to enjoy that theater lobby while I still can."

I took him by the elbow and steadied him a little on the way to the coat closet in the foyer. While I helped him on with his over-coat—a thick black one with a fur collar, it must've set him back a pretty penny—I told him to sleep late tomorrow morning, and he'd certainly feel better about things.

"I'm positive of that," he said. "And in the clear light of day maybe I'll be able to figure it out."

"Figure what out?"

"When did we start together in the business?" Suddenly his voice was a lot softer than it had been up to now. His words were clear, he sounded as if he had sobered up. "Fourteen, fifteen years ago? All these years, knocking ourselves out, working for something, reaching for something. Have we been damn fools all along? Was it the wrong thing all along? Was there something else that got away from us—something that really matters?"

I don't know why it was—the sound of his voice was making me shiver a little. "What something? What really matters?"

His expression was confused. And he was looking very tired. "What is it . . . ? I don't know. . . ." He gave his head a shake, and then he headed to the front door. I opened it for him, rang the elevator bell, waited with him till I could put him in the elevator and tell the operator to call a cab for him. But we didn't say another word to each other.

Then I had to get back to the party, because Ruth's fat cousin Celia—I can't remember what her last name was then, she had just got herself a second husband—was about to do one of her recitations. Her New Year's Eve special—"Curfew Shall Not Ring Tonight," I think she called it.

I didn't let it get in the way of my thoughts. Something that really matters—the wrong thing all along. Oscar's words were in my head when the last guest finally left at four in the morning. Ruth staggered off to bed, but I sat in the living room smoking a cigar, with the ruins of the party around me. Way below, through the open window, I could hear the sounds of horns blowing, people shouting—but very soft and faint, like sounds from another world. That damn Oscar, I told myself finally. Why did he always have to make a production number out of everything?

Then I went to bed too.

A few hours later, ten o'clock maybe, the phone woke me up. It was between our beds, but I let it ring till Ruth answered it. In a haze I heard her mumbling, and then she was hanging up the phone, and then her voice was cutting into my haze. Sharp and high—I never heard her sound exactly like that before. I couldn't do any more sleeping.

"It's the Savoy-Plaza Hotel," she said. "They didn't have anyone else to notify. There are no close relatives, he gave us as his references."

All right, to make a long story short, here's what happened. He slept that night, got out of bed in the morning, took a shower, put on one of his new suits—and if I know my Oscar, he spent a lot of time picking out just the right tie. Then he jumped off the terrace of his penthouse. He died right away.

I heard Ruth telling me about it—her voice was clear in my ears—

but also I felt like I was in a dream. The words were coming from far away.

"Saul, are you crying?" I heard her ask.

That did it. That made me mad. "I don't cry! I'm not the type!" ...

M O R R I S

... And now I come to 1929—when everything got bad for me again.

After all, what do I know about money? Nothing at all, I'm the first to admit it I've got relatives who are successful businessmen. They've always looked down on me for being impractical and un-businesslike. They wink behind my back, make little jokes to my face. I've never let myself feel offended. Everybody has to think they're superior to somebody else.

I'm trying to explain, I suppose, why the stock-market crash seemed so far away from me when it first happened. Why I was so surprised to discover that it actually had something to do with me personally.

I wasn't in New York when it came. I had just got back from my annual American trip. Paris has a stock market too, that's true. Who would I know who had any connection with it? The crash wasn't really called to my attention till a year later—October 1930—when I took my next trip to America. I noticed the ship wasn't carrying as many passengers as usual. I asked one of the stewards about this. "It's the stock market! It's ruining me!" he said. I was surprised to hear he had money in the market. "No, no, it's my tips," he said. "They're down fifty percent from last year. The rich people all feel like poor people."

In New York I saw more signs of what was happening. Nobody jumping out of a window or selling apples on a street corner—no signs as obvious as that. It was the faces I noticed first of all: cheeks drawn and pinched, staring eyes, mouths twitching at the corners. Souls going down to hell—one of those Last Judgment pictures out of the Renaissance. Was there a stock-market crash during the Renaissance? Then I noticed the way people were talking Businessmen. They always *have* complained about business conditions, of course—no matter how much money they're making, it's never enough. Now the complaining wasn't as loud and self-satisfied as it used to be. I could hear real worry in their voices. I had experience with people who were really worried about money. You move in artistic circles, you don't need a stock-market crash to get such experience.

People always invited me for dinner when I was in New York. Relatives, friends, regular customers—not many nights when I had to eat alone at my hotel. To tell the truth, this was one of the main reasons why I could afford the trip. This year there weren't as many dinner invitations. Fewer courses for the dinners I did go to. Lower quality of food and drink. One fellow—Sam Rubin, the paper-box business—got rid of his butler since I saw him a year before. Lost him in the stock market, I suppose. Another fellow was very embarrassed, his wife was still wearing her old mink coat.

Mrs. Newberry wasn't much affected—butler, cook, housemaids still in full force. She had the kind of investments that don't crash with the market—gilt-edged bonds, property, that sort of thing—old money with deep roots. Other people in her set weren't in such good shape. Mrs. H. Walter Carlton had me up for dinner—delicious meal, lots of rich people, expensive plates and silver. Afterward she took me aside, told me she wouldn't be buying her usual pink picture this year. Banking was shaky, her husband said they had to tighten their belts. Quite a job, I thought, considering the waistline on the two of them.

Things looked up a bit the next night. Saul and Ruth Glazer had me up for dinner. Ruth's parents too—Sadie and Abe, looking awfully old all of a sudden. They weren't living up at 125th Street anymore, Ruth had moved them into an apartment-hotel on West

End Avenue in the Eighties. They kept saying how happy they were there even though they didn't know anybody in the neighborhood. Also at this dinner was Saul's partner, that Kaplan fellow—still cracking jokes, pretending to quote from Shakespeare. There was a woman with him, a big blonde, dyed hair, tremendous breasts—magnificent actually, Renoir's mouth would have been watering. She did a lot of giggling.

The Glazer apartment, penthouse on Park Avenue, beautiful place. Whenever I went there, I tried to figure out how much money they'd put into it. Ruth mentioned various figures—she was never one to make a secret of what she paid for things. But her figures were different every time she brought up the subject. I don't think she was lying or bragging. I think she didn't actually *know* how much it had cost—made out the checks, never bothered to add it all up, wasn't there always more where that came from? The way her place was done wasn't exactly to my taste. Lots of beautiful things, finest examples of everything—only there was too much of it. Too many different items, too many different styles, none of it went together. More like an auction room than a place where somebody lived.

My Spanish dancer was over the mantelpiece in the dining room. You couldn't get away from her, you looked up from your food, there she was. Not too bad, I thought, considering she was seven years old. Wouldn't do her quite that way anymore, of course. To tell the truth, I didn't look at her very closely. Didn't want people to see me doing it, they might think I was egotistical.

Turned out to be an encouraging evening, actually. All through dinner Saul talked about how good his business was. The crash hadn't hurt his company at all. People seemed to be fighting to buy negligees. "Which proves," he said, "that the economy is fundamentally sound. Maybe this crash will turn out to be a good thing, in the long run. It'll drive the crazy gamblers back into the woodwork, where they belong."

"If you're referring to this crazy gambler," said his partner, the

Kaplan fellow, "the woodwork is a nice comfortable place for me to rest in. Pretty soon I'll come out again, doing better than ever."

Saul laughed at this and said, "The wood must be pretty moldy in there. Too bad you didn't fix it up ahead of time—plug the leaks, fill up the holes, get rid of the dry rot. In other words, put your money in insurance, the way *I* did."

Kaplan laughed right back at him. "A year from now, Saulie old pal, I'm going to remind you of that remark. When this temporary slump is over, and the market's on the upswing again, you'll feel pretty silly with your piddling insurance."

A scowl flashed over Saul's face. He didn't much like being referred to as "silly." Only a second, then he was grinning again.

It's always interesting when the businessmen snipe at each other.

After dinner, back in the living room, I sat down next to Ruth, spoke to her in a low voice—what I'd been planning to say to her. "I've got a new picture with me. Young girl selling flowers on the street—the river and a barge behind her—new subject for me. Perfect for your bedroom, I think. That Horowitz woman is interested—belongs to your literary discussion group, doesn't she?—but I told her she'd have to wait."

It never failed. Ruth came to my hotel the next morning, she saw the picture, she loved it, I made the sale.

That afternoon things looked discouraging again. Old Anton Kleinsinger at the gallery—streaks of gray in that black beard, wrinkles, tired eyes behind the foliage. "Business is lousy," he said. "People are broke, the first thing they give up is art. Who needs it? Can you eat it? Between feeding the soul and feeding the stomach who has any trouble making the choice?" I told him that a businessman I'd met at dinner last night believed the country was about to go into an upswing. Old Anton gave one of his sour laughs and said, "Send that fellow in to see me. I'll sell him this whole place at a good price. Escaped lunatics with money in their pockets aren't so easy to find nowadays."

What all this meant for me was, the part of my income that came from Kleinsinger's gallery would be cut in half this year. Next year maybe worse.

Danny Glick and I had dinner together that night. In the Fifty-Seventh Street Automat, for old times' sake. We met early. He had a radio show to do that night, had to be at the studio by eight o'clock. This was his biggest break yet—a weekly comedy about a typical teen-age American boy in a small town. Danny explained it to me: "Every week he gets into a different kind of trouble—girls, school, money, all those typical teen-age troubles, you know? It takes him half an hour to get out of it again." Danny wasn't the teen-age boy, he was one of his teen-age friends. He was as old as I was, thirty-three his last birthday. They hired him for the part because he could put on a high squeaky voice and sound young.

"This job came along in the nick of time," he said. "No more nice monthly check from my old man."

"You've had a fight with your father?"

"I wish it was that. My father's gone broke. Believe it or not, that fabulous hat business, I was brought up thinking it would keep me in caviar for the rest of my life. Smash, nothing left! He's got some savings, thank God, he didn't put everything in the market. He and my mother have moved to the West Side, much smaller apartment. He's looking for work, going like a beggar to his old competitors. It's no fun to watch, believe me. He built himself up from nothing, a self-made man, started off without a penny. What's killing him is the idea he could end up no better off than when he started. I can see it eating into him. His face gets a little grayer every day."

"What about your own type of work? Any chance *you* could be out of a job?"

"For an actor that's *always* a chance. The producers could decide next month that Dickie Dawson's little chum Pidgy is going to die of pneumonia or move to Alaska or go to jail for pimping. As a matter of fact, though, I'm in one of the *better* professions these days. Radio is booming. Companies are pouring money into radio advertising, because so many people listen to the damn thing. Cheapest form of entertainment available, millions of people staying home every night to giggle idiotically over the kind of crap I make my living out of. It's a sobering thought, isn't it?"

His face lit up for a moment, the old gleam of devilish pleasure that he got from thinking the worst about the world. The gleam faded, he sighed. "You know what the old man said to me the other day? 'It's a lucky thing you were smart enough to get into a good business on the ground floor.' All these years he's been telling me actors are no better than bums. I'm telling you, Morrie, it damn near broke my heart. God, what I'd give for him to start calling me a bum again!"

I wasn't really feeling as sorry for Danny's father as I should have felt. I was thinking about myself. Trying to imagine how I would live if my yearly income was cut in half.

A week later I took the train out to California. The first person I called was Louie Hertzberg. He invited me out to his place for lunch. Smoked salmon, the very best quality. He said he had it flown in from Scotland. He looked tired, he had lost a lot of hair since our last meeting. After lunch he broke it to me that he wasn't planning to buy any pictures from me this year.

"The market really slaughtered me," he said. "Plus I've got a special problem of my own. These damned talking pictures—they're not making any other kind anymore, it's playing hell with my career."

"But you're as good an actor as you ever were."

"Wrong voice, that's my problem. The public looks at me, what do they see? Luis Hernandez, that oily dago son of a bitch with his hair slicked down. The dirty degenerate greaser you love to hate. I open my mouth, what comes out? Pure essence of Brooklyn! Who's going to be scared of a Latin villain with a Brooklyn accent?"

"What are you going to do?"

"I'm working with this elocution teacher, this earl or duke from England, only he's retired from that line of work nowadays. He's trying to squeeze out the Brooklyn and put in more Latin. Between us, I don't think there's a chance, but the studio's making me do it, there's a year to run on my contract. I've got a better angle though. Trying to talk them into giving me a different kind of part. I'll *be* the Latin from Brooklyn, get it? Play it for laughs—put on a phony Spanish accent, then my real accent shows through, the audience howls. Plenty of characters I could do that way—comedy gangsters, stuffed-shirt society types, phony European royalty. Anyway, you see the spot I'm in, Morrie? Next year things'll be looking up, I'll take *two* of your pictures. This year I have to cut down on luxury items."

Did he feel that a mansion as big as a cathedral and smoked salmon flown in from Scotland were necessity items? Well, I suppose they were—that's how those people live out there.

My stay in Hollywood usually lasted two weeks. This time I left in a week. Not enough customers to make it worthwhile. The palm trees and the lawns were greener than ever—less real than ever. My ship wouldn't sail for ten days. Better to wait for it in New York where I had my family, guaranteed free dinners.

The day before I sailed I went to the Metropolitan Museum, couldn't leave without one last look at my Degas.

I sat there for a long time. I thought, How much longer will the world be able to afford such beautiful luxury items? Was everything good falling to pieces, would it all be over with soon, no more ballet, paintings, love, happiness for anybody?

What I wanted more than anything else was to see Louise again.

I was back in Paris at the beginning of November. Autumn at its very best. Chestnut trees red and yellow. Sun sparkling on the water. Girls in the new fall styles. You'd think the world didn't have a care in the world. Louise and I had dinner together my first night home— the little place we liked, near the Sorbonne—no tablecloths, cheap house wine, angry old waiters. Excellent tripe. It's usually the cheapest item on the menu. I was glad I had a taste for it.

I told her about my trip. I didn't hide my anxiety about money. I talked about it all the way back to my place, even when we climbed into bed. She hushed me with a kiss. "It's boring to talk about money at a time like this," she said. "Can all the money in the world do *this* for you?"

Very soon I had to admit it, there were things that money couldn't buy.

What happiness to be home again, to know that America with its depression was only a bad dream. . . .

S A U L

. . . I don't cry. I'm not the type. I went to Oscar's funeral, I said my good-byes to him, then I did what he would have done in my position. I got my people together, distributed Oscar's duties among them, and turned my attention to getting our company through the rest of the 1930s.

Here's a crazy fact about the 1930s, the depression. Business was lousy, unemployment was high, that nut in the White House came up every week with wild schemes that made the situation worse. But if you happened to be one of the lucky ones, or the smart ones, who was making money, you had no right to complain. Rents were down, wages were low, you could pick up butlers and cooks dirt cheap, taxes weren't the legalized burglary they are today, plumbers and painters and so on came on time and didn't knock off until the job was done, and a good steak dinner with all the trimmings could run you less than two dollars. There's nothing like it, being rich when everybody else is poor.

My business was one of the few that was booming. It was like the movie business—the poorer people got, the more they went to the movies, and the more they felt like buying negligees. In both cases it was a way to forget their troubles for a while. So Je Suis Belle, Incorporated—with Saul Glazer sole owner and president—did a bigger volume than ever. Ruth and me, and a lot of other people we knew, were living higher than ever.

So how come everything was less fun than it used to be?

There are some obvious explanations for that:

First of all, things always look better to you afterward than they do when you're actually going through them.

Also, the thirties *were* a rotten time for most people, you could see the signs of it around you. How could you close your eyes to those signs? How could you tell yourself every minute that none of it was going to spoil your pleasure? A man isn't a block of wood!

Also, the news from Europe was filtering through—that Hitler madman—and this you couldn't ignore either.

But along with these obvious explanations, which applied to everybody, there was a special one for me. I mean Ruth, who else? She was impossible enough in the twenties, God knows. I couldn't count how many embarrassing moments she gave me. I'm blushing to this day. But in the thirties Ruth was even more impossible than she had been in the twenties. The life we were leading, the money we had, finally went to her head and made her a little crazy. I don't mean crazy she had to go to the asylum, I mean crazy it was a pain in the ass for anybody who had to live with her.

I've got so many memories of this in my head, it isn't possible for me to run out of them:

Her habit, for instance, of telling everybody at the drop of a hat what a wonderful cultured family she came from—by the 1930s this was so exaggerated a six-year-old child wouldn't believe her. One night we went to this champagne reception for donors to the New York Philharmonic, and I left Ruth alone for two minutes to get drinks. A fatal mistake! When I got back she had her hand on the arm of the conductor—this world-famous Italian conductor!—and she was saying to him, "Oh yes, we've always been very musical in my family. My Aunt Etta, my mother's older sister, studied to be a concert pianist, but she gave up her career to get married. Etta Steinbrunner—that was my mother's maiden name, she was a Steinbrunner, and *her* mother was—"

I pushed in fast, practically shoving the champagne in her face. Anything to shut her up and let the poor guy loose.

Another example of how being rich was sending Ruth off the deep end—the problem she had with chauffeurs. Every year, depression or no depression, two or three of them quit on us. Frankly it's a wonder they stayed a week, the way Ruth talked to them. From the minute she got into the car till the minute she got out again, she kept up the nagging, complaining, criticizing, backseat driving. "Why are we stopping, Charles? Get into the *first* lane, Charles, can't you see there's plenty of room in the *first* lane? I just can't understand it, Charles, whenever there's a little bit of traffic you always manage to put the car in the lane that isn't moving!"

Sometimes, if I was with her, I'd tell her under my breath to leave the fellow alone, he was doing the best he could. But this only made matters worse, because she always answered me as loud and clear as before. "Well, *that's* true, I suppose! If he had any brains, he wouldn't be a chauffeur in the first place, would he?" Ruth had this peculiar idea that the people who worked for her didn't have ears. There was nothing she wouldn't say in the car, or at dinner while the butler was serving, or even while she was getting a massage.

Which reminds me of another lovely habit she had. When a conversation didn't interest her, even if it *did* interest everybody else in the room, she wouldn't think twice about breaking in. "To change the subject," she'd say—as if that was a perfect excuse for making everybody shut up and listen to her.

Plenty of times I got mad at her for this. One night, for instance, when we had Clyde Sheffield for dinner—he owned a very important department-store chain out west and he had a very ritzy wife, gentiles—Ruth pulled that crap, and I almost lost my temper. "To change the subject," she said, while Clyde Sheffield was talking, "did you see the ad in this morning's paper, about the new coats at Bonwit's? It's a limited supply—"

"Excuse me, Ruth," I said, "we were discussing the labor situation. Now what were you saying, Clyde—about the goddamned unions?"

"We're not talking about that anymore, Saul," Ruth said. "We've changed the subject to the coats at Bonwit's."

Clyde Sheffield wasn't the type that gives up easy. That wasn't how he got to be where he was. "They've been trying for a year now to move into my stores," he said. "But this organizer, this wop, doesn't stand a chance—"

"The woman who runs the coat department," Ruth was talking straight at Sheffield's wife now, "knows me *very* well, I do so much business there, so if there's anything you'd like to look at—"

"—Why should my people shell out good money from their paychecks to a bunch of crooks when they've already got A-one working conditions—"

"I absolutely agree with you, Clyde," I said. "I've got a similar problem in my factory, and I'm handling it exactly the same way—"

"Saul dear, I was speaking," Ruth said, in her sweet voice—which is even more infuriating than when she gets mad or excited.

I went right on at Clyde Sheffield, pretending I didn't hear her. "Only in my industry it's getting tougher all the time to hold the line—"

Ruth dropped the sweetness and shrieked like a baby. "Let *me* speak, Saul! Let *me* speak!" The war cry of Ruth Glazer!

It was an embarrassing exhibition, I admit it, But at least it was *she* that made a fool of herself in front of strangers, not me. So to that small extent I was ahead of the game.

But the list of examples wouldn't be complete if I didn't mention her illnesses. Her pains in the back, her rashes, her heart palpitations, her stomach flutters, her headaches, earaches, toeaches—every year a different illness, and a different doctor to cure it. The conversations we used to have on the subject would have struck me funny, if they didn't end up costing me so much money.

She'd say things to me like, "And the reason I have these horrible pains in my feet, according to Dr. Schlesinger, is my polyps. He's got this new treatment he developed, he goes right into your sinuses but he doesn't *cut* out your polyps, he *shrivels* them. Eventually you *blow* them out in your handkerchief."

"He goes into your nose, and that makes your feet feel better?"

"That's right. It's because of the nerve ends. There's a whole network of nerve ends which travel from your head all the way down to your toes—well, Dr. Schlesinger explained it all to me, but it's very complicated, I won't go into it now."

"I don't blame you. How can you expect a layman like me to understand such things? One little question though—what happened to that doctor last year who said all your troubles came from one leg being shorter than the other leg? So for three months he stretched you on this machine in his office?"

"*He* was dealing with my spinal condition. Which he cured— temporarily—it could come back any day, if I'm not careful about how fast I walk."

Sometimes I would give a grunt and go back to reading the paper or something. But other times I couldn't keep it to myself, what I really thought. "You want my personal opinion? You're as healthy as a horse. You never had a day's sickness in your life. The only pains around here are the ones you give me in the ass."

That was usually enough to start the hysterics up in her—it was as good as pushing a button. "No pains? No pains? Oh my God, if you knew what I'm going through day and night! But that's typical of you. You don't care how much I'm suffering, you don't have an ounce of feeling in your bones!"

No feeling in my bones? I couldn't count how many times she said this to me. I wish it was true. I would have been a happier man in my life.

And another example of Ruth's craziness. This I'm a little embarrassed about, even after all these years, but it's a part of the picture. She was jealous of other women. It came over her in waves. She'd go along for months without mentioning the subject, and all of a sudden she'd start accusing me of things, of hanky-panky with the models or the buyers or even our friends' wives. Well, she wouldn't exactly accuse me, she'd *ask* me—with a little laugh, like she meant it to be a joke. But if I answered with another joke, "Sure, I've got a regular harem down at the office!," her lips would start trembling, I could see the tears getting ready to come. So right away I'd have to swear I was only fooling, there was no other woman in my life, she was the only one I loved. And there *wasn't* any other woman! From the day we got married I never laid my finger on anybody else—except maybe for an occasional pat on the fanny, just to be friendly at a party, and that was usually with Ruth standing right next to me. So there I was, defending myself like a criminal in court, and I didn't even have the satisfaction of being *guilty* of anything.

But the funniest part of Ruth's jealousy, whoever else she suspected she never had one moment's suspicion of Janet. We were still having our regular lunches together—all through the 1930s we had them. I always told Ruth ahead of time, because I didn't want any of her literary-discussion ladies seeing us together and putting ideas in her head. The explanation I gave her was that Janet had a lot of inside dope on the business world, on account of being close to the stock exchange, so it was valuable for me to listen to her from time to time. As a matter of fact, that was no lie. Janet was riding high at Hillman and Sons, because of how well her widows, acting on her advice, had got through the crash. Really big customers were asking for her to handle their accounts. I *was* interested in her opinions about the business world.

When I told Ruth about those lunches, she always gave a sad little sigh. "Poor Janet—it must be awful for her, never getting invited anywhere except to discuss business. She just can't seem to get a man interested in her in *that* sort of way."

So I've got a lot of memories of Ruth's craziness during those years. And here's the craziest memory of all, the worst thing of all that Ruth was doing. She was doing it, of course, to my son Jeffrey.

In the 1920s, the first six years of his life, there wasn't much I could accomplish in turning him into a normal healthy boy. A kid that young, what can you talk to him about, what thoughts has he got in his head, how much companionship can a father give him? But now, in the 1930s, he wasn't a baby anymore. He could understand things. He could develop interests that we could share together.

If I'm laughing, it's because that's quite some joke. All the things I was looking forward to doing with him—we did them all right, but what was the good? He wasn't the kid I'd been expecting to do them with.

I took him to baseball games, for instance. All through them he looked at his watch, he was hating every minute. I tried to teach him golf. Six months later he was still sending the ball in every direction but at the hole. I taught him how to play gin rummy. He got schneidered nine times out of ten, and didn't even get mad at himself for it. We took long walks down Fifth Avenue, while I told him about my younger days, how Oscar and I started the business—and couldn't I see he was making practically a superhuman effort to keep himself from yawning in my face?

I also had a scheme for taking him down to my office and out to the factory, so I could show him off to my people and impress him with the business he'd be taking over someday. What a disaster *that* turned out to be!

He was eleven years old. We rode out to the factory together, to Newark, New Jersey, and I introduced him to everybody, and of course he was very polite. That was Jeffrey—not too much enthusiasm, no smiling with pleasure, but plenty of good manners. Then I gave him the grand tour. I showed him the whole place, the rooms with the big machines, the sewing rooms, the stock rooms, the loading area, the packaging rooms—the whole shmeer, it took almost an hour. Afterward we went back to my office, and I gave him a Coca-Cola from the machine, and I sat him down across my desk and asked him what he thought of it all.

"It's pretty big," he said.

Not exactly jumping up and down from hysterical joy! He was a tall kid, skinny, dark—big dark eyes, like his mother—and he wore glasses, since the age of six, and it was a big event, you'd break out the champagne and celebrate, if he gave a laugh or even a grin.

"One of the biggest in the industry," I said. "And strictly modern and up-to-date. That row of sewing machines in the last room—I had them put in only last year."

"They *were* pretty new looking," he said.

"And what did you think of that contraption that fastens on the zippers? It was just invented. We're the first outfit in the industry that's got one. Pretty clever, isn't it?"

"I couldn't figure out how most of those machines worked."

"So do you think *I* can? I've got people, mechanics and engineers, I pay them for that. What *I* have to figure out is how to make those machines work for *me*—how to keep the profits coming in. That's what you'll be doing someday too."

I never claimed to be any genius, but I've got eyes in my head, I could see the way he was squirming and trying to find someplace to look at except my face. It was his usual reaction when I made any reference, even indirect, to him going into the business someday. He had no confidence in himself, that was the problem. His mother had filled him up with her foolishness, made him think he couldn't be a practical businessman like his old man.

So I tried to give him confidence. I made my voice full of it. "Everything you saw this morning," I said, "you'll be taking it all over eventually. And the office in New York, the showrooms, the people that are working for me—the whole outfit will someday be yours, you know that?"

"Yes, I guess so," he said.

"You won't start off running things, naturally," I said. "You'll go to college first. *I* never did, and I don't think it stood in my way, but it's different nowadays, a young fellow ought to go to college. After you get out you'll come in with me, and I'll teach you the business from the bottom up. You'll work in the designing department for a while, and in the shipping room, and here in the factory—not on the machines, in the management end. And you'll come out on the road with me and when I entertain the buyers here in town. So don't you worry. Before I'm through with you, you'll know as much about Je Suis Belle as I do, you'll do a better job here than I've ever done. So how does that sound to you, boy?"

If *that* didn't give him confidence, what the hell ever could? But he still didn't look at me when he answered. "It sounds fine, Dad."

"Sure it does. Only maybe you could pump up a little more enthusiasm."

"It sounds great. I just—"

"You just what?"

"Maybe I won't be so good at it. Maybe I won't be able to sell things. And keep the profits coming in."

"Who says you won't? You're my son!"

Then he did something I never expected. Tears came into his eyes, and he said, "I *do* want to be like you, Dad! I know that's how I ought to be!"

How the hell was I supposed to react to *that*? It made me feel good—the boy never said such a thing to me before—but it also made me feel lousy, because how was he ever going to grow up and be a success in life if he burst into tears whenever anybody looked at him sideways?

"It's time to go home," I said, and I hurried him out to the car, before any of my people could see what he was doing.

There was no mystery, of course, as to *why* the kid was in such rotten shape. The dead giveaway were the things that *did* interest him—books, paintings, operas—even ballets yet! A son of mine! In other words, everything his mother pretended she was crazy about. She had pumped him full of her phoniness when he was too young to defend himself, and it was still in his system. What's more, what hope did I have of pumping it out? She spent more time with him than I could, because I had to be out making money. And even when I was home, *she* was there too, always between us, always sticking in her needle.

Take what she did to him that winter night just before his fifteenth birthday. It was a Friday, and I saw in the paper there was a big hockey game at Madison Square Garden, the playoffs between Canada and the U.S. I suggested I should call a scalper and get a couple of tickets, so Jeffrey and I could make a night of it.

"But I was going to finish my book tonight," he said.

"A book you can finish any night. A game like this comes along hardly ever."

"I've never seen any hockey. I wouldn't know what was going on."

"It's easy. They hit the puck with their sticks for a while, and as soon as they're warmed up they start hitting each other."

That was when Ruth, who was sitting in a chair with one of her women's magazines, decided to put in her two cents. "It sounds horribly violent," she said.

"Sure it's violent. It isn't a sport for weak stomachs. It's a man's sport. So how about it, boy? Should I call up the scalper? I'll get two tickets." Then I gave him a wink. "Unless your mother would like to come with us."

Ruth made a face and said no thank you. Which was what I wanted to hear her say, naturally.

"I don't really think I ought to," Jeffrey said. "I've got this book report due at school."

"This is Friday. It can't be due till Monday. I'm in favor of hard work and being responsible, but a young fellow needs a little relaxation too."

"I know that. But I'm going to the symphony with Mother tomorrow, so that doesn't give me much time—"

And then Ruth was in it again. She couldn't stay out of it—I should have known. "I think you should thank your father, Jeffie, and say yes."

He turned to her, this look of pain on his face. But she didn't let him say a word, she went sailing on. "Your father works hard all day, darling, and he gets to see so much less of you than he'd like to. Now he does plenty of things to please *you*, so I think you should do something for once to please *him*."

I could have killed her, right there on the spot. I'm looking forward to a nice evening by ourselves with my son, watching a game together like a couple of men—the last thing I wanted was that he should agree to it because *she* told him to. It would spoil the whole damn thing if I had to owe it to *her*. "Wait a second," I said, "if he wouldn't *enjoy* a night out with me, I wouldn't force him already!"

But you could always count on Ruth. She wouldn't let things happen in a nice easy natural way. "I don't want to hear any more about it," she said, when the kid opened his mouth. "I'm ashamed of you, Jeffie, being so selfish and inconsiderate. Get the tickets, Saul. He'll go with you, and he'll have a good time, I promise you."

What could the kid do after that? He nodded and said, "I'd love to go, Dad—I really would."

I never saw a lousier hockey game in my life. I felt like some kind of torturer, someone out of a horror movie with a black hood over his head, and I was stretching Jeffrey out on the table.

It's no pleasure, believe me, to see your own son growing up exactly the opposite from the way you wanted him to. So I finally washed my hands of it. I stopped inviting him to games. I stopped making him take golf lessons. The walks on Fifth Avenue stopped too. His childhood was lost to me. He was his mother's boy, and I knew I couldn't do a thing about it.

I tried to cheer myself up by noticing *other* people's kids. My sister Goldie, with that little snot-nose Estelle, she couldn't open her mouth without making some fresh remark, positively no respect for her elders! My sister Dodie, with her peculiar Selma, who seemed to be living up on the planet Mars most of the time, you talked to her and she didn't answer you, she was a million miles away. If you saw a kid like that nowadays, you'd say it was some kind of drugs, but in those days we didn't have such things, peculiar kids had to be their *own* drugs. So the point is, I noticed my sisters' kids, and some others I knew, and I told myself I could be a lot worse off than I was.

And I came up with still another silver lining. He wouldn't be a boy forever, I told myself. He'd grow up, get out of college, come into the business. He'd see me at the office, in the factory, on the road, when I was at my best, on my own territory. And maybe he'd finally start to appreciate me, we'd start being like a father and son ought to be.

In the meantime—what in the meantime? A lot of years had to go by before my son was a man. How was I going to get through them?

What I didn't know was that a war would come along to get me through them, to take my mind off my personal troubles.

Those war years—I suppose I have to think about them, but I want to do it in a hurry. . . .

M O R R I S

. . . What happiness to be home again? To know that America with its depression was only a bad dream? I found out the truth soon enough. It wasn't long before I was having that dream myself. If a certain miracle hadn't happened, God knows where I'd be today.

I'm getting ahead of myself. The miracle wasn't for five years yet. Here's how I lived during those years.

Food: Tripe, porridge, bread, cheap wine to wash it down. Best buy in France were those long sticks of bread. A piece of meat once a week, a slab of fish twice a week. You had to be very ingenious with sauces and gravies to disguise the taste and looks of the stuff. The greatest of all treats was an eclair brought home from the corner *pâtisserie*, removed from its sticky white paper, eaten immediately so the custard wouldn't spoil. For years afterward I was putting eclair shapes in my pictures. Restaurants? Not if I had to pay my own check.

Clothes: Luckily I've never been much interested in them. I used a simple system—kept everything until it wore out, until I couldn't possibly use it again, then threw it away and didn't replace it until I absolutely had to. After a few years I was pretty much down to one of everything. Plus one extra suit—clean, pressed, no holes in it—a bit too shiny, but that couldn't be helped. Never put it on unless it was a special occasion.

This was when I got into the habit of wearing my overcoat thrown over my shoulders like a cape. It saved buttons, eliminated wear and tear on the sleeves. I knew what my relatives were saying when they saw me with my cape on. "Free spirit—Bohemian—typical artist!"

Heat: The old Paris buildings have meters in every room, you get charged by the month according to how much you use. Amazing how much it can mount up to in the course of a winter. I didn't realize that till the winter of 1931, the first winter I kept it turned off most of the time. Also didn't realize how cold Paris could get. Deceptive, because there isn't much snow. You think it must be worse in New York. I'm here to assure the world, Paris cold can rattle your bones as bitterly as New York cold any day.

That winter I painted with my gloves on. One critic praised me for my new style. Soft thick lines, blurred colors. "At last Unger has freed himself from the tyranny of the sharp clear edge." There's really nothing an art critic won't say. No conscience, those people.

Painting supplies: The hardest part of my life in Paris during those five years. Tubes of paint, brushes, canvases, frames, sketching pads, crayons and pencils and charcoal . . . Sometimes I'd think what it all cost, my stomach would do somersaults. I often wondered if I could steal what I needed. Shoplifting maybe. Or breaking into art-supply stores at night. I never actually went that far, thank God. I don't think I would have been any good at it.

What I did wasn't too big a step away from stealing. I found stores that would sell me supplies on credit. They were going through the depression too, they were afraid to turn away customers. I didn't pay my bills, not for months sometimes. I went to other stores, ran up new bills. Sometimes I made an unexpected sale. Then I went back to those stores, paid what I owed, tried to persuade them to let me start all over again.

I could have avoided some of those hardships, I admit it. By giving up the one big extravagance in my life. The ballet—yes, I kept going to it. I *would* rather have starved than give it up. Orchestra seats too. What's the point if you can't see anything?

Here's an odd thing about those hardships: the physical ones weren't the worst. I could stand them, mostly. What bothered me much more was the humiliation. Constantly afraid, night and day, of somebody finding out how poor I was.

The lengths I went to, hiding my situation from people—useless lengths, no doubt. Everybody probably guessed my secret anyway. My friends and fellow artists at the café, for instance—very important I shouldn't stop going there at night, otherwise they might think I was short of money. I *was* short of money, couldn't even indulge myself in my usual late-night sandwich and beer. A small cup of coffee was the most my resources would stretch to. I solved the problem by telling a lie. I told them I was having indigestion, the doctor had ordered me to stop overeating.

They may even have believed me. To those people at the café, though I'd been living in Paris for over ten years, I was still the stranger, foreigner, rich American. If they could believe *anybody* was overeating during the depression, they could believe it about *me*.

Well, that's how I lived for the next five years, until the miracle happened. Why didn't I starve to death first? Or die of exposure, something equally dreadful, before those years were up?

Some people were still buying pictures from me. Mrs. Newberry bought her usual two a year. I sold a few more to loyal old patrons, sometimes they could scrape up enough cash. A beautiful gesture—none of them could really afford it. I couldn't afford to turn the gesture down.

I lived off tourists too, when I could. Friends and relations from America—businessmen and their wives, the ones who were doing nicely out of the depression. They came to Paris on and off during those years—traveled first-class on the luxury liners, made a quick tour of seventeen different countries, stayed at the best hotels, met nobody except other tourists like themselves. None of them were ever in Paris longer than a week. They whipped through the Eiffel Tower, Nôtre Dame, the Folies Bergére, the fancy clothing stores. Then they hurried on to the next country on their list.

They always got in touch with me when they came. It wasn't affection for me personally, I didn't deceive myself about that. To Frenchmen I was an American—to my American relatives I was a Frenchman, the closest they could come to one. I talked the language, I was an artist, I wore my overcoat like a cape, sometimes I even wore a beret—much easier and cheaper to keep clean than any other kind of hat. It gave them a thrill, being shown around the city by me, sitting at the table while I ordered the meal in French, climbing the four flights to my studio. Wouldn't have been nearly as thrilling for them if my building had had an elevator.

I was happy to give them this thrill. They always asked me to recommend restaurants. I always recommended the very best, places I could never even smell from a distance on my income. At some of those places I had arrangements with the management. If I brought in a party of three or more, big spenders, ordering the fanciest dishes and the most expensive wine, I could come back a few days later, get a meal on the house. Not with the most expensive wine, of course.

Did my American relatives realize the truth, that the meals they gave me were the only decent meals I'd be likely to have for months? I tried not to ask myself that question. I couldn't let myself think anyone was feeling sorry for me, giving me charity, treating me like a poor relation. If I *had* thought that, those delicious meals in lovely restaurants would have come to an end. That would have been a terrible shame.

In 1933, in the summer, Saul and Ruth came to Paris. They took me to the Tour d'Argent for dinner. A table by the window, Joan of Arc's statue a white shimmering reflection in the river, pressed duck served in two installments—each one a totally different taste and texture. I ate a bit too fast, not very politely. Knowing the Glazers would be in town, I had done less eating than usual in the last few days.

The next morning Saul arrived at my studio. Quite a surprise, he never came there without Ruth. "I just dropped by," he said. He looked nervous, sat on the edge of the chair. "I told Ruth I was meeting with some department-store people this morning. Trying to get Je Suis Belle into some of the Paris outlets. To tell the truth, I had those meetings yesterday. I thought you wouldn't want her to know I came here."

I couldn't imagine why he would have such a thought.

"Don't worry," he said, "she won't be dropping by here this morning too. She's having her hair done, that'll keep her till lunch." He fidgeted, then stuck out his chin. "All right, I'll come to the point. Answer me something honestly. Do you need any money?"

This question threw me completely off-balance. I managed to stammer out something about not imagining where he ever got such an idea.

"I've got eyes in my head, that's where," he said. "I'm no big intellectual, I don't go in for art and culture like you and my cultured wife. But I'm not exactly a dope either. I was watching you in that restaurant last night, the way you wolfed down that stuff, like you didn't have a square meal in a week."

"I've always been a fast eater. It's got nothing to do with being hungry. I know it's a bad habit, I keep trying to break myself—"

"And look at you, for God's sake. You're skin and bones. Those clothes are hanging on you, it's like a scarecrow."

"I just can't put on weight. It's the way I'm built, my metabolism. Ruth's mother used to comment on it—no matter how much food I took in, I went on being skinny."

"And how old are those clothes of yours? How long has it been since you bought a new suit?"

"I keep these old things around for when I work. It would be ridiculous to paint in any of my new things. Didn't you notice, I was wearing one of my good suits at dinner last night?"

"I could see my face in the seat of your pants. Will you please stop the crap already. It's no disgrace being broke in times like these. Half the people I know are broke—the other half are worried they *will* be. Look, you're Ruth's cousin, her folks have always been fond of you, our acquaintance goes back a long way. You're family—who can you count on in this world except your own family? So what I'd like to do for you—"

"All right, all right," I broke in on him, "I appreciate your concern, I really do. You're very kind—I never actually knew it before—but I'm in no position to take a loan, since I couldn't pay it back—"

"Who's talking loans? What I'm offering you is a job."

He couldn't have said anything more startling. All I could do was blink.

"In my company," he said. "Je Suis Belle, Incorporated. I've been on the lookout for somebody now that we're expanding our designing department—somebody who could also do posters and office displays for when the buyers come in. An artistic type—you fill the bill perfectly. You'd work under my chief designer, naturally, but you'd have plenty of opportunities to contribute your own ideas. I'll pay you a pretty good salary to start with, later on it could go up."

He mentioned the salary. Yes, it was certainly pretty good. I felt a little weak, I sat down on the sofa. "I've never really thought of myself as—I'm no businessman, I'm an artist."

"That's exactly why I want to hire you, because you're an artist. Only for once you'll make a little money out of it."

"I couldn't give up my painting—"

"Who says you'd have to? You could paint to your heart's content on the side. On weekends. So how about it? Say yes, and I'll arrange for your passage back to New York right away. We'll call it a bonus for coming into the firm."

It seemed to me at the time that my thinking on this matter went on for hours. Actually it was only a minute or two. First I thought about buying myself some new suits, going to a restaurant where I could pay my own check, seeing a look of respect on people's faces when I told them what I did for a living. Then I thought about my Degas in the Metropolitan Museum. Her beautiful eyes, modestly lowered—those delicate shadows that molded her hips . . .

"I'm sorry," I said. "It's very flattering, I'm really grateful, but it's just not for me, it isn't what I want to do."

"How many people do what they want to do in this world? You could starve to death doing what you want to do."

"Maybe so—I still have to live my own life."

"His own life! Look at it!" He waved his arm around at the room. "*This* is a life? God damn it, Morrie, it's time you grew up already. I'm offering you a good job, you can't turn it down!"

"I can, and I do!" I was amazed at myself, how loud and angry I sounded. "I don't have to take orders from you! Leave me alone please—let me go back to work."

He was glaring at me. "All right," he said finally, "who can knock his head against a stone wall? The idea just came to me—strictly an impulse. This'll teach me to have impulses. All right, I'm getting out, sorry I took up your valuable time."

He was turning on his heel, marching to the door. I went running after him. "Saul," I said. "I'll never forget—believe me—"

I broke off, feeling like a fool. He gave a grunt and left. I heard him stamping down the stairs. In my mind's eye I saw those new suits crumbling away, the headwaiter at that restaurant kicking me out because I had no money, the look of respect fading from people's faces.

For weeks after the Glazers left Paris I had trouble sleeping. As soon as I turned out the lights, a voice would start screeching in my ear: "You don't have to work for money? You'll eat paint? Bum! Bum!" And my mother's beady little eyes seemed to glow at me out of the darkness. My Degas was no match for her at all. I'll write to Saul in the morning, I told myself. I'll apologize for my rudeness, ask if the job is still open.

In the morning, though, I always saw things clearly again. I saw that I'd be destroying myself if I wrote that letter. Still, I wished something *good* would happen to me for a change. . . .

The miracle started happening in 1935, though I didn't recognize it for what it was at first.

I hadn't made my annual trip to America since 1930. I didn't have the money for the fare. Then Mrs. Newberry wrote to me, wanted me to come in October. Important matter to discuss, she cabled me the money.

She had me for tea. In five years, what a change—yellow wrinkles, yellow eyes, thin yellow veins running down her matchstick arms. Sick yellow, like vomit. She said she was giving her art collection to the Metropolitan Museum. Two rooms, the Sarah H. Newberry Rooms. A portrait of her facing the door—full-length, oils, formal, dignified. She had chosen me to paint it, over all her other protégés.

I could live for a year on the fee. I would have painted her portrait for nothing. Yes, I would have. Still, I won't lie about it, I could use the money.

I had to get started right away, get in all the sittings in these next two weeks. We discussed the pose she had in mind, what she ought to wear, what setting she ought to be in, the color scheme, the mood. I left her house an hour later. If only Louise were with me, so I could share this news with her! It was hours before I asked myself the obvious question: why had she decided so suddenly to give her collection to the museum, why was she in such a hurry?

I couldn't think who to ask. Old Augustus Kelly was dead. I remembered Mrs. H. Walter Carlton. Embarrassing to call her—she had been avoiding me since she stopped buying pink pictures from me. She must still be in touch with Mrs. Newberry, I thought. In any case, she was the type who picked up any rumors that were going around.

She told me what the rumor was. Mrs. Newberry had cancer. Too far advanced for operation or treatment. It moved slowly in somebody of her age, the doctors gave her six months to a year.

I painted the portrait. A sitting every day. No longer than an hour. Even that was too long for her, I thought. I asked her the first day if she wanted to cut it short. She told me that was nonsense, no reason why she couldn't finish out the hour. She wore a formal evening gown, dark blue, a touch of red—her diamond necklace, like a splash of stars—no other jewelry. The expression I gave her was serious, kindly . . . I couldn't help making it a little sad too. I filled out her face a bit, as I painted. It was the woman I wanted up there, not the disease.

When it was finished, she looked at it, gave a nod, said, "It's very good." That was all. Those old families never gushed. She sat at her desk, wrote out my check on the spot. At the door she shook my hand. Fifteen years we had known each other, she was dying, we probably wouldn't ever be seeing each other again. In her world, though, you didn't show your feelings.

She lasted five months and one week. I heard about her death in March, in Paris. I did something I hadn't done in many years. I went to synagogue that Friday night—I had to look in the phone book to find out where a synagogue was—and joined in on the prayer for the dead. I hadn't said those words since my mother's death, twenty years before. Mrs. Newberry had been Episcopalian, of course—I hoped she wouldn't be offended.

I saw Louise the next day, our regular Saturday together. She sat for me after lunch, then I told her about Mrs. Newberry's death. Now, for the first time, I understood what it would mean for me personally. She had been my oldest, steadiest patron. To the end she had bought more of my work than anybody else, provided me with much of my income. With her gone there was no way I could keep going as an artist.

I spent the next hour discussing with Louise what I should do. I talked, that is, and she listened. What sort of job was I fit for now that I had to give up painting? Who was likely to hire me, a man of forty? Would Saul Glazer still have me? Were there fields that an ex-painter was qualified to go into—advertising maybe, teaching, interior decorating? Would I become one of those men in dirty overalls, painting the sides of houses?

An odd noise came out of Louise. If I hadn't known how worried and sympathetic she was, I might have thought it was a laugh.

A little later she told me she had some good news. "Michel won his scholarship to the *lycée*," she said. "The letter came this morning, he was in the top five percent in the examination."

Michel, her little boy, was nine years old. In France they start competing very early for the educational benefits the government has to offer. The grown man's whole future career could depend on how the nine-year-old boy performs on one examination. Michel was supposed to be very bright. Actually I had never met him.

I told Louise how pleased I was at the news.

"Do you see what it means for us?" she said. "The money I've been saving for ten years, so Michel could go on with school even if he didn't get the scholarship—I can use that money for something else now, I can invest it."

"Not in the stock market, I hope."

She looked into my face, her expression was very serious. "I can invest it in you. You'll pay me back as soon as your pictures start selling again. This slump won't last forever, all the newspapers say—"

She had done this before during these last five years. She had so little money herself. Her children cost her more and more as they grew older, her good-for-nothing husband wasn't bringing in a penny. How could I take anything from her? If I wouldn't be a poor relation, I certainly wouldn't be a kept man. I told her what I had told her the other times—the answer was no, I wouldn't discuss the matter.

"You're being foolish," she said. "If we were married and had children, you'd take my money, wouldn't you? To keep our family going?"

"We're not married," I said. "There's no family to keep going."

She gave me a look at this, an odd frightened kind of look. "My poor Maurice—how much do I have to say—" She broke off very sharply, looked away from me.

I felt a heaviness, a terrible weight, inside of me. I couldn't trust myself to speak for a while. I finally did. "Say what?"

"Nothing." Her voice was flat. "Aren't you hungry? I'll cook the dinner tonight."

After lunch the next day, Sunday, I took her to the Métro station as usual—she had to be home before her children returned from Versailles. I didn't go back home. I walked the streets, paying no attention to where I was going. A storm was coming soon—dark purple blotches, like bruises, rolling across the sky. Crazy thoughts went through my head. I told myself I had to push them out again. Where could they lead? What could I do with them?

That was the low point of the depression for me. Things couldn't get worse after that.

All this time, though, the miracle had been happening.

I found out about it a few days later, when the letter came from

Mrs. Newberry's lawyers. I was mentioned in her will. She had left me an annuity, it would be paid to me every quarter for as long as I lived. About twice as much as I had been getting from her when she was buying my pictures.

That old lady—she had done it again. When I was a boy in my twenties she rescued me from prison. Now she was reaching out from the grave, rescuing me for the second time.

The year was 1936. What could possibly go wrong with my life from now on? I could see nothing ahead of me but perfect happiness.

I wasn't counting on a war, of course.

That war—I hate to remember it, I'm going to push through it as quickly as possible. . .

S A U L

. . . Those war years—I suppose I have to think about them, but I want to do it in a hurry.

There are people, I'm told, who remember the war with pleasure— with nostalgia yet! Believe me, I'm not one of them. For me it was nothing but a nightmare. First of all, there was that madman Hitler, taking over all the countries in Europe, dropping bombs on people. You could see him in the newsreels, rubbing his hands together when- ever another country bit the dust. My God, it sent shivers up my back! In 1940, as a matter of fact, I did something I never thought I could bring myself to do—I voted for Franklin D. Roosevelt.

Second of all, there was the condition of my business. Je Suis Belle, Incorporated, was making nightwear for the Women's Army Corps, in addition to our regular line, and the money was rolling in. But also I was working longer hours than ever, shorthanded, half my men in the army, secretarial help impossible to get if you didn't pay a fortune, rationing, a million government forms to fill out, shortages of elastic and silk.

Worse than that, it was during the war that the goddamned shlock houses started springing up like weeds in every part of the garment trade. Any crook or shnook could start one on a shoestring. In a few years he'd be riding around in a Cadillac, smoking a big cigar, acting like he had money all his life. My objection to these chiselers wasn't that they were cutting into my profits. I was handling all the orders I could, and they were getting strictly the leftovers. But what were they doing to the standards of the industry? What were those cheap chiselers doing to the quality of the product? Even then I could see the handwriting on the wall—shlock moves in, quality moves out!

Here's another thing about the war years that didn't exactly make me jump for joy. Jeffrey had his eighteenth birthday and got drafted into the army—no deferments for college students in those days. Naturally I was anxious, who wouldn't be? But plenty of people I knew, including some of my own cousins and in-laws, had sons that age in the army or navy. A couple we were friendly with, their boy got killed in North Africa. So whatever I had inside of me, obviously I had to keep it to myself.

But not Ruth. Oh no, you could take bets on it, *she* wasn't keeping any feelings to herself. Her little angel was in danger, she never even noticed if anybody else was going through the same thing. My God, even when we went to pay a condolence call on these friends of ours right after they got the news, Ruth talked all the time about how worried she was over Jeffrey. And at that time he hadn't even been sent overseas!

And the way Ruth nagged at me, I should pull strings to keep her baby safe. I should put pressure on big shots, use influence that John D. Rockefeller himself didn't have. And when I told her I couldn't do it, she talked to me like I was a murderer, I wanted to kill my own son. Didn't it ever come into her head that maybe *I* was feeling something too?

Only one thing occasionally relieved the pressure on me during these war years. Ruth's cousin Morrie Unger, the crazy painter, was living in New York now—he couldn't go back to Paris on account of the Nazis—and Ruth liked to take him to the ballet from time to time. The poor fellow could never have bought the seats on his own. On those ballet nights I mostly went to the East Side Bridge, Whist, and Pinochle Club for a gin game. I was grateful for the opportunity.

So I'll move on to another bad thing that happened during the war years. Though I suppose you couldn't actually blame the war for this.

One day, in October 1944, my sister Doris called me up and told me Papa was sick. This was an upsetting thing to hear, because Papa hadn't had a day's illness in his whole life. When he was a younger man he used to say he couldn't afford to get sick, who would look after the store? Doris also told me that he positively refused to go to a doctor. Only *mention* a doctor to him, and he closed his eyes and pretended he didn't hear. So *I* had to talk to him, of course—he wouldn't pay attention to anybody else.

I went crosstown right after work that evening—I gave up my before-dinner nap, that's how much it weighed on my mind. I found him, sure enough, in the usual chair, in the usual bad light, listening to one of his opera records. I said "Papa" a couple of times, but he wouldn't open his eyes. So I went across the room and lifted the needle off Caruso or whoever was making the noise. That made Papa look at me all right.

"I was in the neighborhood, I dropped in to visit," I said.

Naturally he wouldn't let himself look as if he was glad I came. "I can see that" was all he said.

"So—how are you?"

"I've been worse."

"Ruth sends her love. You'll be seeing her when you and Doris come for dinner next week."

"We come for dinner every week. You had to make a special trip this time to remind me?"

He never made it easy for you, did he? "We got a letter from Jeffrey yesterday," I said. "He gives you his best regards. They've got him running a typewriter in London. He says the bombing isn't so bad now."

"How do you have a good bombing?" Papa said.

Enough already, I thought. I wasn't going to stand there all night trading smart-aleck remarks with him. "Doris tells me you haven't been feeling so hot."

He didn't look a bit surprised to hear me bring up this subject. Obviously he knew all along what I was there for. "Did I complain to her?" he said.

"No, you didn't. She says you never talk about your health to her."

"Then she must be taking up mind reading in her old age."

"She knows you haven't been sleeping. She hears you moving around in your room, and going to the bathroom in the middle of the night."

"It sounds like *she's* the one who hasn't been sleeping."

"Also she says you hardly eat anything lately."

"I'm on a diet. I'm thinking of going into the movies."

What do you do with somebody that makes jokes when you want to talk about important matters? I pulled up a chair and sat close to him. "I know you don't like to make a fuss over your health, Papa. I'm exactly that way myself. But a man has to use a little common sense too. If you're feeling lousy, you should let a doctor look at you. He'll prescribe a pill, in no time you'll be on top of the world."

"There's a pill can do that? Why didn't you tell me about it years ago? I could've used it after the stock-market crash."

"Seriously, Papa. I want you to make an appointment with Irving Boroff, Ruth's brother. He's a good doctor, you've always liked him. Ruth'll send the car to take you down there and pick you up again. It'll be over with fast, and you'll have it off your mind. Now I'm not taking no for an answer."

"Who's saying no? I'm saying yes."

He brought this out in such a quiet voice that for a couple of seconds I didn't catch on to what he was saying. I felt silly—he was over seventy, but Papa could still make me feel silly. "You are? Well—good—that's using your head."

"He's a nice fellow, that Irving Boroff. It's a waste of time I should go to him, but I'm happy to throw a little business his way. It's all in the family."

"It's no waste of time. He'll be able to tell you—"

"Nothing I don't know already."

Again Papa's voice couldn't have been quieter. But this time that quietness made me stare at him, and there wasn't anything I could say.

Then he smiled. Very soft, you'd hardly know he was smiling at all. "It's all right, my boy," he said. "You shouldn't feel sorry. *I'm* not feeling sorry. I'm seventy-two years old. I've had a wife, four children. A business." He stopped for a second, and I could see the smile shaking a little. But then he went on. "So what am I hanging around for? Is this world such a lovely place nowadays a man should feel annoyed he has to get out of it?"

How do people act in such situations? You put on a "reassuring" tone of voice, you pretend to be optimistic. Nobody is ever fooled by it, but you do it anyway. "Oh come on, Papa, you're not going to—"

He wasn't even listening. He just went on talking, riding right over my words, only now it seemed to me he wasn't talking to me, he was talking to himself. "The truth is, I can't make heads or tails out of this world nowadays. The grandchildren come here—the little ones and the almost grown-up ones—they talk and they talk, I don't know what they're saying, it's like a foreign language."

"I can't figure out the younger generation either."

"It's not the grandchildren only. *Everybody* nowadays sounds to me like a foreign language—even my old friends, they're exactly my age. So I don't listen to people anymore. I listen only to my records, the opera. In between to the voice inside my head. There's one question it keeps asking me."

"What question, Papa?"

He looked up at me, and now he wasn't talking to himself anymore. His eyes were staring straight into my face—shining, like two little knives. "Why did I lose the store? Why was I forced, for fourteen years, to live off my son's charity?"

"I've never looked on it as—"

"I'll tell you why." Papa's voice got no louder, but somehow it got stronger. "I finally figured out the answer. I got what I deserved. It's a punishment from God."

"You never *did* anything to God!"

"I turned my back on Him. At the age of sixteen, when I was studying to be a rabbi—I turned away from serving Him, I ran to this crazy country and sold cheap necklaces to silly women. Could God allow such a thing to happen?"

He was talking foolishness, the way old people do. So why was I letting it get to me? Why was I raising my voice to answer him? "You built up a good honest business! You sold people what they wanted! You didn't do anybody any harm!"

"I tickled their vanity. I turned my back on God so I should be a vanity tickler. Why did I leave? Why didn't I stay where I belonged, and do with my life what God and my father wanted I should do?"

My voice was getting hoarse now, I could feel it in my throat.

"If you *had* stayed in the old country, where would the two of us be right now? Inside a concentration camp—dead!"

"What do you think I've been since the age of sixteen?" The strength seemed to fade out of him all at once. He leaned back in his chair and closed his eyes, he looked as if he was suddenly older. "I'm tired. I get tired quick these days. Put the stack of records back on. Then go away."

I got up and put on the records. "You won't forget about the doctor?" I said.

"Sure, sure," he said, without opening his eyes. "The doctor. *He'll* fix me up."

I turned my back on him, and while I was getting my coat out of the hall closet I could hear the music starting. That high voice, blasting out the Italian words—all my life, since I was a kid, I'd been listening to that voice, and I still didn't understand what the hell it was singing about.

It took Papa another nine, ten months to die. I was with him as much as possible—I couldn't neglect the business, could I? At the funeral there weren't many people, outside of the family. A man retires for fourteen years, nobody remembers if he's alive or dead. All through that funeral, incidentally, Ruth was giving sighs and groans and complaining about her latest ailments. She always talks about her ailments more than usual when somebody gets sick or dies. Like she has to keep up with the competition. It's a lucky thing Janet was at that funeral too, giving me sympathetic looks from time to time and keeping Ruth out of my hair.

My God, was I glad when that war finally ended! Maybe things will get better now, I said to myself. Maybe the world will turn into a nice place to live in.

Did I really, even for one minute, have such a thought—me, a grown-up man who was used to being logical and practical? Well, I found out fast enough that nothing ever changes.

So now I have to get to it—the worst night of my life. . . .

M O R R I S

. . . That war—I hate to remember it, I'm going to push through it as quickly as possible.

I was in Paris in 1939, when it broke out. A phony war, people said. Nothing bad could happen, the Germans couldn't possibly get past the Maginot Line. What was the Maginot Line? I had no idea, but it did sound reassuring.

Life went on pretty much as before, even into 1940. The luxury liners were still sailing across the Atlantic—didn't seem to be any reason why I shouldn't take my usual trip to America. I decided to go earlier this year, in April rather than October. Louie Hertzberg—doing nicely in the movies again now that he had switched from villainy to comedy—wrote that he was throwing a big party, on April 9, to celebrate the completion of his fiftieth picture. I ought to be there, the American economy was on the way up, people in Hollywood were buying art again.

Louise and I met for dinner the night before I sailed. She wouldn't see me off on the boat train in the morning. We never saw each other off on trips, that would be too much like husbands and wives. We ate at our favorite little place, the cheap one with no tablecloths. I looked across the table at her, suddenly I felt odd. There was something about her face tonight—deep furrows biting into it, one of those sad beggar women by Picasso. The blue period, when he still knew how to draw.

"The tripe is as good as ever," I said.

That was the kind of stupid conversation we made all through the meal. Squeezing it out. It was always like this before a long separation, there seemed to be nothing we could say.

She made me promise to take my heavy overcoat, because the Atlantic could be cold this time of year. She asked me how long I'd be in New York before I went out to the party in California, she asked me when I'd be back in New York, she asked me if the *Ile-de-France* was sailing on June 29 or June 30. I felt like screaming. I had answered these same questions a hundred times already. Our last night together in Paris, was this all we could find to talk about?

"How is Michel?" I asked. "Studying hard?"

"He's up till all hours of the night," she said. The boy was thirteen now. In May he would face another battery of examinations—in scientific subjects mostly, he wanted to be a doctor. The renewal of his scholarship was at stake. "I tell him he can't spend every minute at his books. He has to get some sleep, or he'll be groggy when the time comes. He says sleep is a luxury he won't be able to afford till after the examinations."

"He's a very serious boy."

"Too serious sometimes, if you ask me. I just wish he wouldn't torture himself."

"Aren't you pleased he wants to make something of himself?"

"I'm pleased—of course. But you know what it is, don't you? He sees his father lounging around the apartment, coming in late after he's been drinking—those crying fits, complaining how the world has mistreated him. The boy's afraid he'll turn out the same way. He thinks the seed is in him. So he has to fight against it harder than anyone else."

My throat was dry. I took a big gulp of wine. "If he has such a fear— Why should he go on having it? You could reassure him—" I couldn't finish. She was looking at me—intently, with such sadness. I lowered my eyes, went back to my eating.

She started telling me about her daughter. Mathilde was nineteen, taking courses as a secretary. There was a nice young man.

I listened, nodded, asked a question or two. I tried hard to be interested in her daughter. I had been trying for many years.

We finished our meal and left the restaurant. She couldn't come back to my place tonight. It was the middle of the week, her children wanted her home. They had complained bitterly when she told them she was sitting tonight for a sculptor who had to finish a rush job.

It came to me, as we walked to the Métro, what a complicated life she led. So many different things to balance: her time with her family, at work, with me. When did she ever have a chance to be alone? I would have gone crazy if I never had a chance to be alone. Almost constantly she must be tired, harried, making plans, wondering if everything was going to collapse on her. Yet who ever heard her complain, lose her temper, express discouragement? Who ever saw her when she wasn't joking, laughing, enjoying a nice bit of gossip, being gentle and tender? She's a heroic woman, I thought. Heroism isn't jumping from airplanes, climbing mountains, leading troops into battle. Heroism is going along from day to day, no matter what.

In the Métro she went through to her platform, I stood at the other side of the barrier. It's only an iron bar, we could easily talk across it. "I want you to have a nice trip," she said. "And be sure to write twice a week. None of your skimpy little notes either. Long letters full of all the funny things your American friends and relations are doing."

"Long letters, I promise."

The train was coming. She reached across the barrier to me. "I love you, my poor Maurice," she said.

"I love you too," I said. "I've always—"

The train roared into the station, drowning out my words. She had to rush off if she didn't want to miss it. Then it roared out again. I watched it, swallowed up in the tunnel. Nothing left but black parallel lines, stretching into darkness.

I sailed for New York the next day. All through the voyage one question was in my mind: did she hear those last words I said to her? How many times I've asked myself that, in these thirty years! How many times I've hoped with all my heart that the answer is yes!

The ship arrived in New York. The weather was fine. I was rather pleased to see my old hometown, those giant silver boxes shimmering in the sun. No premonitions, as usual. I went to California, and on April 9, the night of Louie's party, the Nazis invaded Norway and Denmark. Nothing to worry about though, they couldn't get past the Maginot Line. A month later they invaded Holland and Belgium, they got past the Maginot Line. In June, they swarmed into Paris.

I was back in New York by then. The French Line notified me—the *Ile-de-France* had never left Le Havre. No more ships were crossing the Atlantic. I called the airlines. Plane service was ended. Overseas telephone, cables, even the mail—all that was ended too.

"But what am I going to do?" I said to the man at the French consulate. "My paintings, my furniture—everything I've got in the world. It's all in Paris."

He was a small man in his fifties. Eyes red. He looked exhausted.

"I'm sorry," he said. "My wife and children are there too. We'll all have to wait until the war is over."

I went out into the street. People must have thought I was drunk. They pushed past me, all moving in the opposite direction. Bright noon sun, exploding into their faces, shattering their faces into fragments of light. Prisoners in front of a firing squad, being blown to pieces. Large canvas by Manet. Saw it many times in the Louvre.

What was I going to do now? My life was over. . . .

It's amazing though—you cut off the frog's legs, they still go on kicking. I plunged myself into plans, became terribly practical. My businessmen relatives wouldn't have believed it.

I asked myself how I would get along in New York until the war was over. My prospects didn't really look too black. This trip to America had been quite successful so far, from a financial point of view. My best trip since 1929, in fact. I had sold almost all the pictures I had brought with me, prices were edging up to the pre-depression level. I had more money here in New York right now than I had in my Paris bank account. I could say good-bye to that account, of course.

Also I had family and friends here in New York. Abe Boroff was gone, Sadie was in a nursing home, going fast, but their children were here. There was Ruth, eager to help. There was her sister Janet, a successful businesswoman, just as eager though not so loud about it. There was their brother Irving, the doctor. If I had to save money, I'd be grateful to know a doctor who was also a blood relation. There was Celia Solomon, the fat one, poetry reciter—she was married to a new husband, seemed to be quite well off. There was my cousin the rabbi, just took over Temple Emanu-el, richest congregation in America. If every one of my relatives invited me for dinner once a month . . .

Best of all, Danny Glick was in New York. His teen-age show, off the air by now, had put him in demand. He did all kinds of parts. He had been in a Broadway play that closed in a few weeks, had married an actress and divorced her—those were his failures. Otherwise he had only successes. I knew he would take care of me.

I had to find a place to live. A difficult problem. Rents were high in New York, my whole income could be eaten up. I couldn't move into a bad neighborhood, like the one where my old attic used to be. In your twenties there are things you can take in your stride, you couldn't bear them in your forties. Danny found the perfect place for me—the Beau Geste Hotel on Fifty-Third Street, a block west of the Museum of Modern Art. Old-fashioned, a little run-down, large long windows, high ceilings. It catered to artists, actors, musicians. If you rented by the year the rates were very reasonable, considering they gave you heat, electricity, a telephone switchboard. I moved into a two-room suite, small bedroom and living room, southern exposure. I could paint there. Not ideal—I missed my skylight. Not impossible either.

Next I had to get in a whole new stock of painting supplies. Everything I owned was back in Paris. Would Madame Voisin keep it safe for me? What about the paintings I had left there? Some weren't finished yet. There was a little one, dancer at the bar in the background, vase of lilacs in the foreground. Study in purple against white—I couldn't get it out of my head, I would have given a lot to get my hands on it. No point trying to start it all over from memory, that never worked. Danny found a store for me that sold everything I needed at cut rate prices.

One thing worried me more than anything else at first. Would I never see the ballet again, until the war was over? If I couldn't have dancing, dancers, in my life, what would that do to my work? Turned out there was nothing to worry about. New York had plenty of ballet through the war years. Tickets a lot more expensive than in Paris. Ruth Glazer treated me to performances regularly. She loved the ballet—or thought she ought to—couldn't drag Saul to it if his life had depended on it. "A lot of pansies prancing around in tights," he said.

I didn't mind going to their apartment for dinner first. They had a good cook. I liked looking at the pictures they had bought from me through the years. Not the Spanish dancer, she went too far back, I ignored her. Smaller ones I still liked. Louise had been the model.

I made other friends in New York besides Danny. He introduced me to people he knew, painters, actors. We gathered late at night at the Fifty-Seventh Street Automat. Had coffee, sweet rolls, sometimes a sandwich—quite tasty, actually. We sat there for hours, argued about art. Those Automats were the only places in New York where they didn't make you leave the table after you'd finished what you ordered. If I shut my eyes, used my imagination . . .

I was in New York five years, close to five and a half. I worked hard. I got a lot of painting done. I went to see my Degas once or twice a month. My things didn't sell too badly, old Anton Kleinsinger was pleased. Critics never paid much attention though—critics only care about what's in fashion.

As the war years went on, I noticed a funny thing happening around me. People weren't talking as loudly and clearly as they used to. People had taken to mumbling, swallowing their words. Ballet orchestras used a lot of mutes on their instruments. Radio tubes were getting weaker, you had to turn the volume higher and higher.

I went to Ruth's brother Irving, the doctor. He sent me to a specialist—tested my hearing, shined a light up my ears, told me I was going deaf. It was happening slowly. It would take a long time—a little worse every year, nothing anybody could do about it. I ought to consider a hearing aid, he said. Some good ones were on the market.

I put that advice right out of my mind as soon as I left his office. Machines hooked up to my ears, plugging myself in everywhere I went. No, thank you, it wasn't worth the trouble.

"But you've got to take care of yourself!" Ruth told me.

Why? What was the point of taking care of myself? No word came through from Paris—not one, in all those years. What was happening to her—to them? What were those madmen, those Germans, doing to them? I tried every way I could to find out. Nothing helped. Silence. I started going to synagogue on Friday nights, the big Reform temple that Saul and Ruth belonged to. Dear God, I said, please let me see her again. Please let us meet again, in Paris, our city. Let us live together—man and wife. Let our son live with us too. The way it should have been years ago.

I was pretty sure praying wouldn't work. What harm could it do to try? So I prayed regularly.

Also I read the newspapers regularly, following the war news. The invasion of Normandie—they landed on the beach near Caen. I knew that beach well, as a matter of fact. Painted there one whole summer. Beautiful girls, beautiful sunsets, delicious seafood. I followed the Allied army inland, every inch. Bombardments, old fishing villages ripped to pieces by shells, terrible losses. I knew when they were close to Paris. Those suburbs by the Seine—boathouses, little inns overlooking the water. Louise and I stayed at one of those inns for a weekend years ago. Hard to think of bloodshed there.

First thing every morning I bought a newspaper at the stand in the lobby of my hotel, said a quick prayer, opened it up. Always expecting to see it in the headlines—Paris Is Free.

How odd the human mind is. This mind anyway. When it finally happened, I was completely surprised. The shock couldn't have been greater if it had been completely unexpected. I had to sit down, I would have fallen on my face in the lobby. The bellboy brought me a glass of water. I think I was crying.

I got to my feet again, hurried to my room, tried to call the French consulate. Free French, of course, de Gaulle's outfit. The line was busy, of course, hundreds of people must have been trying to get through. I took a cab down there. Terrible extravagance. I never rode in cabs, unless somebody else was paying.

The consulate was a madhouse. Had to fight my way to the desk. Finally I got the bad news. No ships or planes were scheduled, probably wouldn't be for a long time. Nobody could go back till the war was over, till the Germans were defeated once and for all. Still a long way to go. I should have expected that. Amazing how irrational you can get when you want something badly and suddenly there's hope.

I settled down to wait. Went about my life as usual. Acted as if there was nothing special on my mind. One thing I did try to do. Maybe letters could get through now. I wrote—I wrote many times. No answer. No way of knowing if my letters even got to her. She might have moved to a new address. She might not be in Paris anymore. Wouldn't she write to me though? The people at the consulate eased my mind a bit. They told me mail out of France was still as undependable as mail into France.

I waited. Finally it came. The Germans surrendered, that madman Hitler killed himself, the war was over. That part of the war. The Japanese were still fighting in the Pacific, people were still dying—that wasn't the part of the war that mattered to me. Still no ships, I was told. Only a few planes were flying again. Long waiting lists, couldn't get a flight for over five months. I made a reservation—I wasn't going to be choosy. It meant getting to Paris in the winter. Well, Paris could be beautiful then too. Bare silver trees in the Tuileries.

How was I going to live through those five months? I had lived through five years—those last months seemed to go on forever.

I spent my next to last night with Saul and Ruth. She hugged me when I left her apartment. "Oh Morrie, I'll miss you," she said. "Our lovely nights at the ballet!"

On my last night I had dinner with Danny. The Automat—it seemed appropriate. He could afford a lot better nowadays. He had a leading part in one of those radio shows that were on every day, continuous story, people suffering—soap operas. It astonished me when he told me what he was paid. He worked for fifteen minutes a day, didn't even have to memorize his lines.

I had talked to Danny about Louise through these war years. I didn't tell him everything. Nothing about Michel, nothing about what I intended to do as soon as I saw her again. He knew how much I *wanted* to see her again.

"You'll find her, I'm sure of that," he said. "The only question is—"

"What question?"

"When you find her—*what* will you find? What—" He turned his face away, the rest of his words were a blur in my ears.

"Excuse me?"

He faced me directly, talking louder and slower. "It's five years since you set eyes on her, even heard from her. That could've been a terrible five years for her. We don't have any conception of it, what people went through over there. It could've changed her a lot."

"Not really. Nothing could change her."

"Her feelings. About you. Do I have to spell it out, for God's sake? Why haven't you had a letter from her? Didn't it ever occur to you— in five years, a healthy attractive woman, she's going to meet other men? What they just went through over there, people would naturally want to hold on to each other." Thin dark face. Devil's eyebrows.

I wanted him to stop. He was the best friend I had in the world, his company had always meant a lot to me. Why was he saying these terrible things now, these stupid things? "You don't know anything about it!" I burst in on him. "It's always been your one big fault—you love to hear yourself talk, you'll say anything!"

He gave one of his angry sighs. "All right, all right, I'm sorry I opened my mouth. I was only trying to— You're such a naïve person, Morrie. You're still a baby, in some ways. Haven't you found out yet what happens to people when they expect too much in this life? Setting your heart on something, thinking it's going to work out the way you want it. Nothing ever works out the way you want it. Take my word for it, will you. You're looking at the man who was going to be the American John Gielgud. King Lear, Hamlet, Cyrano— So what am I doing? My mother goes blind, my sweetheart gets amnesia, I'm on trial for a murder I didn't commit—that's the career I set my heart on, for God's sake? The way to survive in this world is, get yourself braced for that kick in the ass."

I looked at him, feeling very sorry for him. I knew he was talking nonsense. He always had. Always playing a part.

The next day I took the plane to Paris. A long flight in those days. The plane stopped twice to refuel—Gander in Newfoundland, Shannon in Ireland. Flat gray expanses, nothing in sight but rocks. Like those pictures they took a few years ago of the moon. Then Paris was below us, we were circling down and down, roaring onto the runway. Paris was outside the plane, waiting for me. . . .

S A U L

. . . So now I have to get to it—the worst night of my life.

They let Jeffrey out of the army in early November 1945. One night, after he'd been home a week, he waited till Ruth went to bed, then he said he had something important to discuss with me.

It was a mild night for November. We bundled up, went out on the terrace, and sat in a couple of iron chairs and looked at the city way below. I lit up a cigar and offered him one, but he turned it down—he never developed a taste for cigars. Finally he started talking.

"It's nice and peaceful out here. Do you and Mother still give parties on this terrace?"

I could see the last thing in the world he was interested in was our parties. "Not so much anymore," I said. "The air in New York is too dirty these days. You leave a tray of food out here, in half an hour it's covered with a layer of soot."

"That's too bad. It's really nice out here." He stopped talking. He was taking a deep breath. Now it comes, whatever it is, I thought. "I wanted to tell you something, Dad. I'm afraid it's going to upset you."

"I'm a grown man. I've been upset before."

"When I go back to college in January, I've decided not to take a business course. I've decided to major in English. My idea is, later on I'll go to graduate school, get a Ph.D., a doctor's degree—"

Did it come as a surprise? Wasn't it what I always expected—from when he was a little kid, squirming at the baseball games, crying after I took him around the factory? "I know what's a Ph.D.," I said. "So what can you do with it once you've got it?"

"Well, you can get a teaching job. Teaching English lit in college."

"Teaching English lit. How much does it pay, a job like that?"

"Not much to start. After a while though, if you get promoted, become a full professor, you could end up making fifteen, twenty thousand a year."

"Fifteen, twenty thousand!" I gave a laugh. I didn't intend it to come out sarcastic, but that's how it came out. "You know how much *I* make in a year? You know how much money there is in the ladies' nightwear business? I wouldn't tell you—but fifteen, twenty thousand, in a *bad* year that's still less than my taxes!"

"I'm glad of it, Dad, but—"

"You're damned right you should be glad of it!" I could feel myself getting mad. I was waving my cigar in the air in front of me, the light at the end of it was making circles in the air like one of those bugs, fireflies. "You been living very nicely all your life on account of it—good clothes, a beautiful apartment, the best schools, camp in the summer. You think a man could provide that type of life for his son he works as a college professor? You'll get married someday, you'll have kids of your own. You're planning already, they aren't even born yet, to bring them up in a slum?"

"College professors don't usually live in slums—"

"I don't *care* where they live! I don't know anything about them, I never knew one personally in my whole life, and I never want to! All right, let me get this straight." I tried hard to pull my voice down—getting angry was stupidity. Did I want him to think he could get under my skin? "No more beating around the bush—what you're telling me is, after you finish college you don't intend to come with me into the business?"

"I wouldn't be any good as a businessman, Dad. I love books. The idea of talking to college kids about great literature, making them see what I see in it—I just can't think of a better way to spend my life. You wouldn't want me to be a lousy businessman when I could be a good teacher."

"You told me once—you were a little boy—that you wanted to be just like me. You said that was the way you ought to be."

He gave a little laugh, embarrassed. "I can remember that, Dad. I meant it too. But the point is—what if I *can't* be just like you? If you want to know the truth, business scares me."

"You're scared to make a lot of money?"

"Yes, I am. There's no *chance* of making a lot of money as a college professor, so I'll never have to expect it of myself."

"That I don't follow at all. You're a human being—you can't tell me you don't want to be a success."

"I think I might want it *too* much. If I tried for it and I didn't get it— It would be like when I was a kid, when you tried to teach me golf and gin rummy, remember? Those feelings I had that I couldn't do anything, that I wasn't worth a damn. I can't go through all that again. I just can't take the chance."

In his voice, when he said this, there was something that made the anger go out of me. It was shaking, his voice. It was like it used to be when he was a kid, just before he started crying. "He can't take the chance," I said, holding on to my sarcasm, but already my heart wasn't in it. "How can I believe it? All this talk about feelings, isn't it a fancy way to tell me I'm a money-grubber, an ignoramus, a pushcart peddler, and you can't wait to get away from my kind of life?"

"No, that's not what I think at all! You're a wonderful man. You've had the strength to stand up to the pressure. I've always admired you for that." He reached out his hand—for a second I thought he was going to touch me on the arm, maybe even grab hold of me. Thank God he pulled his hand back, the exact moment when I pulled my arm back.

"You're a liar," I said, but my voice sounded weak in my ears. "You're your mother's son. Did you tell her about this yet?"

"Not a word. I wouldn't tell anybody before *you*."

"Maybe so, maybe not. How do I know you didn't talk it over with her, and she coached you exactly what to say so you'd really make me feel good?"

"I *swear* I haven't told her! I've *never* been able to talk about things with Mother. You know what she's like. She gets so excited, she never listens to what you say to her."

I knew it all right, but this was the first hint I ever got that *he* knew it. I looked hard into his face. Was it possible to believe him? Did he actually feel like that, or was he just making a sucker out of me? My God, I *wanted* to believe him!

But that was foolishness, it wasn't practical, I shouldn't waste my time with questions that nobody could answer. "I don't see the point continuing this discussion," I said. I took a big puff from my cigar and let out the smoke slow and easy, forcing my nerves to calm down. Plenty of times this was how I handled myself in the heat of a business conference, and it turned out to make the difference between victory and defeat. "You're not going into the business. You're going to be an English teacher. You're getting a doctor's degree."

"I *am* sorry, Dad. I know what it means to you. But don't you see, I have to lead my own life."

I looked at him again. His face was very serious, and I said to myself: Where did I hear those words before? And all of a sudden—I never planned it that way—I was bursting out laughing. I was roaring, like the comedian in a musical comedy just made some terrific joke and I couldn't control myself and Ruth turned red and nudged me in the ribs.

Jeffrey was looking at me like I was out of my mind. He kept asking me what was funny, and finally, when I had enough control of myself to speak, I answered him. "I'm thinking about Papa—your grandfather. He must be laughing his head off in the grave. After all these years he's finally getting a doctor in the family."

And then the joke wasn't funny anymore. I stopped laughing as fast as I'd begun. I turned away from his face again. "Go to bed, will you. I want to be alone, and finish my cigar."

So the boy got up and said good-night, and he left me alone on the terrace. And I thought for a while about what had happened. What do other men do when something they wanted their whole lives they find out once and for all they can't have it? About other men I couldn't say. What *I* do is, I don't waste my time crying over spilled milk. I pick myself up and get myself involved in something else. Anybody who knows me will confirm it. I was never the type that makes a fuss. . . .

So I put out my cigar and went to my room, my intention being to go to sleep. Nothing more would have happened if only I could have carried out that intention. I would have had a good night's rest, and in the morning I would have had myself completely in hand. I would have been able to face Jeffrey at the breakfast table without a quiver, I would have gone down to my office and done business with my usual energy and efficiency. I would have come home and read the evening paper on the couch and had my dinner, and my appetite would have been as good as ever. After dinner I would have sat down with Ruth to listen to the radio—Jack Benny or one of those other crazy comedy shows—and I wouldn't have had any trouble laughing at the jokes.

That's what would have happened. Only I had lousy luck. Ruth was awake, she was lying in her bed. And since when, especially if something depended on it, was Ruth ever capable of keeping her mouth shut?

"You're going to bed already?" she said. "Don't you want to talk about it?"

"About what?" I said. Hoping, if I played dumb, maybe she would let the matter drop. Some hope!

"I woke up with a terrible thirst, and I went out to the kitchen for a glass of fruit juice, and I couldn't help hearing what you and Jeffie were saying on the terrace."

"You couldn't help shoving your ear against the wall, in other words."

"Oh Saul, don't talk to me like that! I want to *help* you—I'm so *sorry*—"

Deliberately, with malice in her heart, could she have picked a word that would get me more annoyed?

"Don't waste your energy being sorry for *me* please. I never asked anyone to be sorry for me, never in my whole life. And incidentally, you're also a liar, because you happen to be very happy about what he's doing."

"Happy? Who says so?"

"You're the big intellectual, aren't you? All your relatives are so cultured and artistic—rabbis and painters and poetry reciters! Don't tell me you're not overjoyed you're going to have a college professor in the family!"

"Well, of course I'm glad he's cultured and intellectual and so on. But when it comes to making a *living*! Margie Weisskopf has a son-in-law who teaches in a college, and she says it's terrible the way those young people have to live."

"My God, am I hearing right? You're actually admitting you care about such an unimportant thing like money?"

"*Please* don't get sarcastic—you know I can't stand being talked to in a sarcastic voice. I'm just as worried about our son as you are."

"*Our* son?" Something was breaking loose in me, I could hear myself getting louder. "He's *your* son! Who influenced him? Who put these crazy ideas into his head?"

Her face started puckering up, in the old familiar way. "Now it's my fault, is it? You always take it out on *me* when you have your heart set on something and you don't get it!"

"Who had whose heart set? I know he's a grown man, he can make his own decisions. I don't set my heart on things it isn't realistic I should want them."

"You're brokenhearted, and you know it! Oh Saul, why won't you ever let anybody sympathize with you?"

Maybe at that moment, if I had happened to have a gun in my hand, I would've killed her. "Save your sympathy, God damn it! I don't need it—you know where you can put it!"

"Oh well, if you're going to be *vulgar*—"

"Vulgar! What a surprise! How many years have I been hearing that word out of you? All right, I'm vulgar. I'm thankful for it if that's the opposite from you and your phony family."

"My family again! Can't you get over this terrible jealousy—"

"Jealousy! *I'm* jealous of that bunch of impractical phonies? Your brother Irving who's such a great doctor he could never afford a decent office, your cousin Morrie the painter who never learned how to paint a foot, your father with his nothing civil-service job! I'd think maybe it was bad blood, if it wasn't for your sister Janet."

I saw her turn white. "Oh yes, Janet! That model of perfection—I *knew* you'd get around to her eventually! *You're* sick of being called vulgar, I'm sick of being compared to Janet! You should've married her instead of me!"

"I've had the same idea plenty of times! Maybe I'd be a happy man today, maybe I wouldn't have twenty-five years of stupidity and uselessness and misery to look back on!"

I stopped talking suddenly—this time did I go too far? But that feeling was breaking loose in me again—to hell with it, I was saying what I wanted to say, I *couldn't* go too far!

"Twenty-five years of misery?" she said, her voice a lot lower than before. "That's what you look back on?"

"You heard me say it! When I think of what I was before, the hopes I had, the fun I used to get—oh my God, what have you done to my life?"

"What have *you* done to *my* life?" Her voice rose to a wail, and she sat up in bed. "I was a girl nineteen years old when you married me—"

"Twenty-one."

"It doesn't matter. I was a young girl with everything ahead of me. I fell in love with you, and all I ever wanted from you was a little love in return, a little bit of affection and tenderness and consideration for my feelings. But you don't have any human feelings in you. All you've ever cared about is making money!"

"And what do *you* care about? Twenty-five years ago, when I came along, if I didn't have money and good prospects what chance was there you'd even look at me twice?"

"And would *you* have looked at *me* if I didn't come from a better background than you? You're always insulting my family, but it made you feel important to marry into it!"

"That's undoubtedly the stupidest remark you ever made!"

"You never took the slightest interest in me personally. What about our honeymoon? Niagara Falls—the most romantic place in the whole world—half the time you were on the long-distance phone talking to Oscar Kaplan. And you cut it short two days so you could get back to your office."

"So I could clinch that deal with Marshall Field's. *You* knew all about it, you were as anxious it should come through as I was. I notice you didn't complain when it did, you didn't turn down the mink coat I gave you."

"What was I *supposed* to do? I was a girl of nineteen, I was married to you less than a month, I was in love with you. You expected a mink coat to make me happy, was I supposed to throw it in your face? I would've traded a hundred mink coats for two or three nice sweet words from you. The night you gave it to me, I went into the bathroom so I could cry."

"You went into the bathroom so you could take a crap!"

She had her hands up to her ears now, her usual child-in-a-tantrum gesture. "He isn't saying it, I'm not hearing it! The doctor says this is what's causing my migraine headaches—"

"Stupidity and silliness, *that's* what's causing your so-called headaches!"

"Maybe I *am* stupid and silly, and I talk too much about my health and my family—but how did I *get* the way I am? What *else* could a person be if she's chained for her whole life to a cold fish?"

"Chained! Who's asking you to be chained? Anytime you want to throw away those chains, you're welcome, be my guest!"

"Watch out, Saul Glazer. One of these days I could take you up on that invitation!"

"One of these days? How about today? We'll both be better off. The best thing in the world for both of us would be a—"

The word was in my head, it was in my mouth—what stopped me from coming out with it? Damned if I know the answer. Suddenly I was staring at Ruth, noticing that she had a funny look on her face— a scared look.

"I have to get out of here," I said. "Before I lose my temper."

I started to the door, and then she was calling after me. "Where are you going?"

"Out—walking—getting some air—"

"When will you be home?"

"Who says I *will* be home?" And I walked through the door, slamming it behind me. . . .

Down the elevator, out to Park Avenue. Eleven o'clock, the beginning of the winter. Not too cold yet, but there weren't many people in the streets. I headed downtown, I didn't know where exactly. Chained together! She was right, for twenty-five years I was a prisoner on the chain gang. What a relief to break loose finally! Forty-seven isn't so old for a man, I had plenty of good years ahead of me. No reason why I shouldn't make the most of them.

And I knew how I was going to do it too! I damn well knew how!

There was a hotel on Sixtieth Street. I had a drink in the bar, then I made a phone call. Then I got a cab and had him take me up to Sixty-Eighth Street. Janet was still living on the third floor of that old brownstone house between Lexington and Third. I rang the bell and climbed the stairs, and she was waiting for me. She was ready, naturally, with a cup of coffee.

While I drank it, I told her about my fight with Ruth. I repeated to her every word we said to each other, not a single insult on either side did I leave out. I got a kind of satisfaction from going over the details—like you get sometimes from picking at a sore. "So I'm leaving her," I said. "I'm not going to live with her anymore."

"You're getting a divorce?"

It was the word I wouldn't say out loud to Ruth an hour earlier. I took it now without flinching. "I think it's about time, don't you?"

She started a speech about how Ruth and I shouldn't break up. She went through all the reasons people always come up with at times like this: we were together so long, we loved each other once and such feelings can never really die, we had so many memories together, et cetera et cetera. "The two of you had fights before," she said. "Why should this be any more serious?"

"We *never* had a fight like this one. She said things to me—I couldn't ever forget them."

"Maybe you said the same kind of things to her."

"Maybe so, but that only makes it more impossible we should get together again. What we said to each other was unforgivable."

"People who are close *always* say unforgivable things to each other. That's what marriage is all about. You say things, and then you forget them."

"This time never. Because it isn't only that I'm through with her. It's also that I see the truth now, what I *really* want from my life."

For a second or two she didn't make a comment on this. Then, very quiet and flat, "The truth is always a good thing to see," she said.

I pushed right on. "You put your finger on it once, my biggest fault. You told me I was afraid to make a fool of myself. I decided something, I announced my decision in public, I was afraid people would laugh at me if I admitted later on that I'd been wrong. And all the time, on account of this fear, I was losing out on life."

"Saul, I don't think you should—"

"All right, it took me much too long, but I'm finally getting smart. I won't stick to that old decision for dear life anymore, I'll admit I was wrong—I'll admit it gladly!" I was up from my chair, reaching out to her on the sofa. "For God's sake, Janet, what are we waiting for anyway? Why don't we finally—"

She was on her feet like a shot, almost knocking over her coffee. "Stop it, Saul—please!"

She was starting to back up, but I had no trouble catching her, taking hold of her by the arm. "How can I stop it? Don't you understand what I'm saying?"

"How many drinks did you have at your club tonight? Go home and sleep, or you'll feel terrible in the morning!"

"I'll feel wonderful in the morning if only you'll—"

"I won't! It isn't possible!" She gave me a push, and to my surprise I plopped back hard onto the sofa. Something was beginning to give a little flutter down in my stomach, like that first tiny suspicion that you're going to be sick. "It *is* possible!" I said, scrambling right back to my feet. "You feel the way I do—you always have. I can't be wrong about that!"

"Once upon a time maybe—like they say in the fairy tales."

There was a look on her face—a peculiar half-sad smile—but I didn't let myself think about it. "We nearly did it a few years ago, you remember? When I took you for lunch to that fancy French restaurant?"

"That was *many* years ago, Saul. If you *had* come out with it then— But that was *too* many years ago. Now it's much too late."

"Why late? We're not old people. Forty-seven is the prime of life."

"What do you think people would say about it? Our friends, our families—the ones that don't tell us we're out of our minds will cut us forever."

"We can afford to lose them, we both know too many people as it is!"

"And Ruth? Do you know what it would do to her? The hysterics we'd be putting her through—"

"I've had twenty-five years' experience of Ruth's hysterics. The only thing I'm sure of about them is that she always gets over them."

"Saul, Saul, where's that common sense you're so famous for? Tell me something. What do you and Ruth do at night, when you stay home? You listen to the radio, don't you?"

"Most of the time. Don't change the subject—"

"What shows do you like? The baseball games, the cops and robbers, the comedians?"

"That's about it. But what's it got to do with—"

"And Ruth—does *she* like those shows?"

"I suppose so. If she didn't she'd say so."

"Personally, I can't *stand* those shows. I like the plays, especially the romantic ones. And the ones about family problems and young people growing up and so on. Do you think you'll change your tastes and listen to what *I* like?"

I could see the trap she was setting for me—very tricky!—but I was damned if I'd fall into it. "There's no law against having two radio sets."

"What about having two apartments? Ruth will keep the penthouse, of course, so where will you and I live?"

"The city is full of penthouses. We'll get one that's even bigger and better."

"But I like my little brownstone. It's nice and cozy, there are trees right outside the window. I even like walking up two flights of stairs. I never could stand elevators, they make me woozy. I think you should move in here with me."

"Why, for God's sake? I *don't* like climbing stairs!"

"And then there's your car and chauffeur. If I had my choice, I'd never ride in such a big black car—it makes me feel like I'm in a hearse before my time."

"That's a pretty ridiculous feeling!"

"As for having a chauffeur, it embarrasses me, I'd rather walk. You'll have to get rid of him and do the driving yourself."

"I haven't driven a car in twenty-five years!"

"You'll have to learn how all over again."

"I'm *damned* if I'll—"

I broke off, seeing the I-told-you-so look on her face. Is anything in this world more aggravating than a *smart* woman?

"You see what I'm saying, Saul?" Her voice got softer. "We've both been doing things our own way for so long. If we tried to squeeze our two lives together, how long would it be before we were hating each other?"

"I couldn't hate you!"

"We've had such a nice friendship all these years. As if we weren't in-laws at all. Wouldn't it be foolish for us to spoil it?" Then she raised her voice again. "Besides, you don't really *want* to live with me."

"Who says I don't? Why not?"

"Because it's Ruth you want to live with. Nobody could possibly take her place."

"*That's* a damn fool thing to say!"

"Still, it's true. The two of you are perfectly suited to each other. You were lucky to find her when you were young."

"And I've been miserable with her ever since!"

"I didn't say you were happy with her. I said nobody could take her place. Now drink your coffee, it's getting cold."

That sad gentle smile of hers was going through me like a knife. It made me give a cry of pain. "I know what it is. You're afraid I wouldn't be loving and affectionate. There's a popular school of thought which says I'm a cold fish, all I care about in life is making money."

"*I* don't belong to that school of thought."

"If I lose you, do you know what it'll do to me? You're all I've got in the world!"

"You won't be losing me, for heaven's sake. We'll go on having our lunches together. We'll meet at family parties. Every Friday you and Ruth have me up for dinner—tomorrow's Friday, I'll be there the same as usual. Nothing will change between us."

"I want more than that! I want—" Suddenly I found myself pulling her close to me, and my face was pressing into her shoulder. "What am I going to do? How am I going to live?"

I was crying. That's a fact. Tears were running down my cheeks, sobs were coming out of me in great choking gulps.

And then I felt her hand stroking my back, and her voice, very soft, was in my ear. "The way you've always lived," she said. "On top. . . ."

It was almost one in the morning when I left Janet's place. I couldn't find a cab, so I started walking. In those days you could walk along the streets of New York late at night, you wouldn't automatically get mugged by some hoodlum teen-ager.

I walked, and there was a cold snap in the air, and it did me good. Common sense started coming back to me again.

What was the point, I asked myself, having insomnia on some lumpy hotel mattress when I had a comfortable bed of my own that I was paying rent for? And that rent wasn't peanuts either! You're going to make an important decision about your life, you don't make it on the spur of the moment, when you're in an emotional state. Was that how I did things in business? Should I suddenly start being unbusinesslike about my personal problems? What I had to do was think them through carefully—after a good night's sleep.

I was back at my building on Park Avenue. I went up to the apartment, and the front hallway was dark when I got inside. I thought maybe I could sneak into bed without waking up Ruth. I had a feeling I'd be able to think better if I didn't have to talk to her till the morning.

But she wasn't asleep. One lamp was on in the living room, and she was sitting in an easychair. Just sitting there, without even a book open next to her. Her eyes were red, with big heavy pouches under them, and I thought to myself, for the first time since we got married, My God, she's looking old!

She didn't get up when I came in. She said, "Are you hungry or something?"

"I don't think so," I said.

"I'm hungry," she said. Now she got to her feet. "Can I make you a sandwich? There's some of that fancy bologna you like."

"Any kosher pickles?"

"I got them fresh this morning."

"I probably won't eat it," I said, "but make me a sandwich."

"And a glass of something with it?"

"All right, I'll have a Coca-Cola."

"I'll have one too," she said. Then she gave a little laugh. "Eating at this time of night—with *my* stomach! I ought to have my head examined!" And she went into the kitchen.

And that was twenty-five years ago. . . .

M O R R I S

. . . Paris was outside the plane, waiting for me. Well, actually what was waiting for me was one small shabby hotel on the Left Bank. I remembered how it had been twenty-five years ago, my first night in Paris. The same kind of hotel, no improvement in a quarter of a century.

The same feelings inside me too. The strangeness and loneliness, the foreignness of it all. I walked around the neighborhood, recognized so many places, found I could still read the signs and understand what people were saying. I saw the beauty too: familiar pink light, lace-work buildings, chestnut trees stripped bare. I was frightened. The boy in his twenties—facing this strange new world—scared to death.

Louise's name wasn't in the phone book. Her husband's wasn't either. No Mathilde, no Michel. Well, I had expected this. Phone service must have been cut off for many people during the occupation. I started walking to the building where she used to live. Ten or twelve blocks from my hotel. My feet seemed to lead me in the right direction, show me when to make the right turns.

The building hadn't changed much. Old, weather-stained—black shutters on the windows, tall wooden doorway leading to the courtyard. Like a thousand other such apartment buildings in Paris. The concierge was a little old woman, wizened, like a nutshell. Couldn't be sure of her sex at first glance. Couldn't remember her from before the war. Then I realized there was no reason why I should. I had never been inside this building before. Walked Louise here a dozen times, never went inside with her.

"Yes? Can I do something for you?"

I asked the concierge if Louise and her family still lived there. She scratched her head over the name. "Oh yes," she said, "they moved out a year ago. Maybe a little longer. Right after the husband died. He went to the hospital, and he never came back."

My heart gave a little jump, I won't pretend it didn't. No pity was in me at all. Why should it be? He had never been anything to her but trouble.

I asked the concierge if she knew where they had gone. Scratched her head some more. There *was* an address, they had written it down on a piece of paper. Where had she put it anyway? She popped back into her little room. I heard her inside, opening and closing drawers, mumbling to herself. After a long time she came out again. A piece of paper was in her hand—crumpled, dirty. I smoothed it out, the address was there—on the Right Bank, far north. The handwriting wasn't Louise's. I knew that right away.

I went there by cab. A neighborhood I didn't know, a building much like the one I had just left, another old concierge—identical nutshell skin. I gave her the name, she gave a sigh. "They left a few months ago," she said. "The daughter got married. The boy went to live with her and her husband."

I couldn't understand that at all. It wasn't like Louise to let her son move away from her. No matter how hard she worked, she always had time for her son. I asked the concierge if she knew why the boy had gone to live with his sister.

"What else could he do?" she said. "He couldn't stay on here alone, poor thing. After the father walked out—"

"What's that? Excuse me, I'm a little hard of hearing."

She thrust her head closer to me, spoke louder. "The father—that man! One day he packs his clothes, takes all the money, and runs off. Just a note to say he isn't coming back. Any man who would do such a thing to his own flesh and blood—"

"Wait a minute, you must be confused. The father died a year ago, in the hospital. It's the mother who moved in here with—"

"No, no, you've got it the wrong way round," she said. "The mother died—she was sick a long time, she went to the hospital and died there. A month or two before they moved in here. Their old place was too big for them, they couldn't afford it once she was gone— What's the matter with you? Are you sick? Come in here, sit down."

I felt her grabbing hold of me, leading me into her little parlor, helping me into a chair. I can't remember much about it. Louise was dead, not her husband, I kept thinking. That stupid concierge back at her building. I cursed the old woman. As if she had been responsible for Louise's death.

I went back to my hotel. It was evening, dinnertime. I lay on my bed, never noticing if I was hungry. Yes, of course, this had to happen, I kept thinking. Five years ago, when we said good-bye at the Métro station, when she touched my hand and said "I love you!"—didn't I know right then that I'd never see her again? All these years since, while I was hoping and praying, didn't I know that everything was over? Black lines stretching into the darkness. Parallels never converge. It was the way things had to turn out for me. I wanted to be a great artist—I was a hack, an imitator of better men than myself. I wanted to marry the woman I loved—I waited too long, by the time I came to my senses it was too late. Of course—what else? Impractical and inept—what I always was, what I always would be.

I can remember these thoughts going through my head. What I forget is the pain. The human mind never remembers pain. Didn't I read that somewhere once? Otherwise we'd accumulate such a heavy load of it, life would become impossible. . . .

Three days passed before I was ready for what I had to do next. I went to the address of Louise's daughter. Another old building, near the Invalides. Another wizened concierge. Sent me to the second floor. I rang the bell, the door opened, Louise's face and my face stared at me across the threshold.

Difficult to keep from betraying the shock. I'm rather proud of myself, how calm I was. I told him I was an old client and friend of his mother. Just heard about her death, wanted to pay my respects.

He asked me to come in, offered me a seat on the sofa. An old horsehair sofa, probably dark red once, a pale ghost of it now. All the furniture seemed old, seemed to have given up hope. Like some old people.

His manner was stiff, cold. "My sister won't be home until lunchtime. She works in a store. My brother-in-law works in an office. I'm alone here, studying. You're welcome to wait, of course."

I was able to look at him more closely now. Eighteen he must be. A bit short for his age. Fuzz on his chin and cheeks—pale complexion, but that faint glow of red beneath it, you see it all the time in French boys. Wide eyes, glaring at me, not too friendly. And the nose, of course—long curving beak. It would thrust itself out more and more as he grew older, overbalancing his face. Who should know better than me?

"Your name is Michel, isn't it?" I asked.

"Yes." He winced. Insulted because I knew his name—at that age you resent any intrusion on your privacy. "Excuse me, I must get back to my books—"

"No, wait. Please let me disturb you one moment more. What happened to her, your mother? What was it like for her at the end?"

A scowl on his face, sharp edge to his voice. "She was in pain. That's what cancer does to people."

"How long— Was she ill for a long time?"

"A lot longer than she let on. She didn't go to a doctor till six months before. She was afraid she might have to stop working. In those days you were lucky to have a job. Once you lost it—"

"She was still working till the end? Sitting for her usual clients?"

"Artists?" The laugh that came out of him was grating. "There wasn't much room for artists, with the Germans here. She worked where she could get work. Bourget's, the department store—my sister is there now, she took over my mother's job. Ladies' scarves. The Germans bought plenty of them to send home to their *frauleins*. Now the Americans buy them."

His mouth snapped shut, his lips a thin gash of red against the pale skin. Why was he so bitter, so angry? Would he have such feelings if there had ever been a father—a real one—in his life?

"Before she died," I said, "I don't suppose— She never talked about me, did she? Mentioned me—in any connection?"

"Why should she do that?"

"No reason. I only wondered."

"What was your name again?"

I could hear the contempt in his voice. I told him my name.

He gave a little shrug. "Doesn't mean anything to *me*."

We stood and faced each other a moment. His eyes had a kind of challenge in them. Daring me to say the next word. He would wait me out, he would give me no help at all. "What about you?" I said. "What do you do? You're a student, didn't you say?"

"In the medical course, at the Sorbonne. I began this year."

"You're going to be a doctor? That would have made your mother very happy."

His scowl grew blacker than ever. "I don't see how you could know what would have made her happy."

What I wanted to do was run out of there. Something in me made me stay, even made me raise my voice to him. "I do know, young man," I said. "She talked about you often, when we were together. She wanted you to make something of yourself. She was only afraid you were overdoing it. Studying is important, she told me, but it shouldn't be everything in life." I stood up, shaking inside, but keeping up my firm manner. "Thank you for talking to me. I'll be going now. Get back to your books, by all means."

I started to the door. I heard his voice behind me—softer now, not exactly friendly, just a bit less sure of itself, more apologetic. "It's all right if you want to wait. I'm nervous today, that's all. I haven't been getting much sleep."

I wanted to tell him that she had worried about that too. I thought I'd better say nothing.

He took a couple of steps toward me. "Listen, you don't have to go. I'm sure my sister would like to see you."

He looked much younger all of a sudden. Eighteen years old—I remembered what it was like. That's the age when you're halfway in between. One minute you're strong, free, ready to fight the whole world. The next minute you're a child again, you're scared of the dark.

"No, I really can't stay. Thank you."

I held out my hand to him. He hesitated, then took it. I shook his hand longer than I needed to. This one handshake, it was all I would ever get from being a father.

"I hope we'll see each other again," I said. Such foolish things people say. . . .

It was November, late afternoon, when all this happened. Paris was cold. I shivered as I walked the streets, back to my hotel. It wasn't just me, I could see the people around me pulling up their coat collars, shoving their hands deep into their pockets. Where was I going to eat dinner tonight? I knew the answer while I was asking myself the question.

It was still there, down the little side street near the Sorbonne. The tables had tablecloths on them. The surly old waiters were gone, efficient middle-aged ladies in their place. I asked one of them, she told me the old owner had died, his sons had taken over, they were trying to attract a better clientele. They didn't serve tripe anymore.

After dinner, pulling my overcoat tightly around me, I went to the old café. The tables were inside, in the glass-walled veranda, where the cold couldn't get at the customers so easily. Not too many people there yet. The old table, our usual table, was empty. I sat there, ordered coffee, waited. The world strolled by on the street before me, the place got busy, the types who sat down around me were familiar—dressed a bit more shabbily than before the war, that was the only difference. I saw no faces I knew. I waited for an hour, two—nobody came.

I started back to my hotel. Even colder out now. I walked very slowly, my head down against the wind. Could I stay in Paris any longer, could I take up my life here again? It was all gone now, the Paris I had loved. I would never be anything but a stranger.

And what would I be in New York? Lots of family there, friends, clients, dealers, everyone speaking my language. Would New York feel any more like home to me? Had it ever?

You're a foreigner wherever you go, I told myself. You did this to yourself thirty years ago. Long before you went to Paris, you chose to be an exile. Freedom was what you wanted. From your family, your language, your country. You chose to keep moving forever even when you were sitting still. You made your bed, now you have to lie in it.

Paris, New York—what did it matter which one I lived in now? I might as well toss a coin. Leave it to chance—it couldn't do worse for me than I had done for myself. . . .

By the next morning I had decided how to go about it, which coin I was going to toss.

I still hadn't been around to my old building, my old studio. Very odd. My paintings, furniture, most of my other possessions. You'd think I would have been anxious to find out what had happened to them all. I decided to go over there now. If my paintings were gone, I would go too, I would leave Paris on the first plane I could get. If my paintings were still there, I would stay.

A crazy way to make a decision that would affect my whole future. It didn't seem crazy to me at the time. It seemed like the only logical thing to do. Let fate tell me what the last twenty-five years of my life had amounted to.

It was a gray day. I walked through the Luxembourg Gardens— empty flower beds, bare trees, no children sailing boats in the pond. Out of the park, down two blocks, and there it was, the doorway I knew so well. I stepped through, a high-pitched voice called out from the concierge's room. "Can I help you, monsieur?" She came waddling out, fat old woman, several chins, hair completely white.

She threw up her hands when she saw me. "Is it you, Monsieur Unger? You're alive—thank God, thank God!"

She grabbed me, hugged me, wept over me awhile. Then she took me by the hand, dragged me up the stairs. Same old stairs—the lights went out at every floor, we had to stumble for the switch. My old studio was waiting for me, she said. She cleaned it once a week, just three days ago she cleaned it. Nobody had lived in it all this time. Nobody had wanted it. Plenty of rooms in Paris during the occupation. Only the Germans could afford to pay rent. *They* didn't want anything they had to climb four flights to get. My furniture was still there. My paintings, my beautiful paintings—she had taken the liberty of packing them up, putting them away in the storeroom in the basement. It was warm and dry there, safe from the damp and the mice. Safe from the Germans too, worst pests of all. They never thought twice about stealing valuable works of art.

Well, it seemed as if I had tossed the coin.

The more I thought it over, the more sense it made. Yes, Paris was cold, strange, shutting me out. I would have to start all over again— no joke for a man who was almost fifty. But Paris was Louise's city. I had painted here. Some of those paintings had survived here, some- how. Anywhere else would be too far away from her.

I thought about the little picture I'd been working on when I left.

It must be down in that basement storeroom. Dancer at the bar, vase of lilacs in the foreground. I had an idea about those lilacs. I couldn't wait to try it out. Call me a hack, an imitator, would they? Wait till they saw those lilacs.

And that was twenty-five years ago. . . .

S A U L

. . . That was twenty-five years ago. I'm skipping fast over twenty-five years, because this whole damned afternoon is going to pot, and I want to bring myself up to these last few days, this craziness of Jeffrey's.

I'm seventy-two years old now, the same as Papa when he died. But one foot in the grave I definitely haven't got. My last check-up the doctor gave me a clean bill of health. The doctor, incidentally, isn't Ruth's brother Irving anymore. He retired, his son Artie took over the practice. It's nice to know there's *one* son in the world who went into his father's business.

My son is a professor of English literature at this little college in New Hampshire. They just gave him a promotion, that's what we're celebrating at the party tonight. He's moved into the highest salary bracket—which still doesn't put him in the caviar and Rolls-Royce class, believe me. He's an expert on William Shakespeare. Can you beat that—my son, the Shakespeare expert! What a kick Oscar would have got out of that—it's a shame he couldn't have seen it. Not only does Jeffrey teach classes in William Shakespeare, he also wrote a book about him. It was never exactly a best-seller though. It wasn't made into a movie with Paul Newman. I tried to read it once myself, couldn't make head or tail out of it. Will somebody tell me please, what's a phallic symbol?

Anyway, Jeffrey has given me something a lot more important than any book. I mean, naturally, my granddaughters, Cordelia age thirteen and Viola age eleven. Did you ever hear such meshuggeneh names for a couple of Jewish girls? But they're dolls, pretty and smart, and don't they know it. Jeffrey and Lois—she used to be Lois Feldman, what a surprise he married one of our own!—bring them to New York maybe twice a year.

My sister-in-law Janet? Still in the stockbroker business, though she must be getting close to retirement. Old man Hillman made her a partner fifteen years ago, before he died, so she must be minting money. You wouldn't know it the way she lives though. She's still in that old brownstone, climbing two flights. We still have lunch together, only maybe not so regularly as we used to.

And the other members of my family?

My sister Doris—don't ask! All right, her voice was always a little too loud, she had a tendency to be bossy—but what she has to live with now, is it really a fair punishment? If I treated my employees the way God treats some people, they'd shut me down with a strike in no time flat.

My sisters Goldie and Dodie—the Klutz Brothers died ten years ago, my sisters have been living together ever since. They get to look more like each other every day. And their crazy daughters are grown up now, with klutzy husbands of their own. Selma takes up a new religion every other week. And Estelle—people that know me are smart enough not to mention that idiotic bitch in my hearing!

And on Ruth's side of the family? Celia the blimp has run out of husbands, but never out of poems to recite. Nat Steinmetz, the rabbi, should have retired from Temple Emanu-el years ago. He gets the holidays mixed up in his head—right up there in front of the congregation he goes into Yom Kippur when he should be doing Purim.

And Ruth? She was seventy-one years old this July. Sixty-nine is what she admits to, but it's seventy-one—and if she puts up an argument, I've got her birth certificate in the safe-deposit box. I've never told her that, incidentally, because being Ruth she wouldn't stop nagging at me till she got her hands on it.

She looks every year of her age. Her face is all shriveled up with wrinkles, and her nose is suddenly bigger than it ever was before, like the beak on some big bird. Some people's looks improve when they get old. Janet, for instance, was no raving beauty as a girl, but everybody says she's a very attractive older woman. But Ruth definitely isn't in that category. As for her personality, the crazy things she does, the whining and the complaining, the imaginary illnesses, the bragging about her family, the phony baloney with art and music and so on—no changes there. It's my experience that what you are when you're young you go on being when you're old, only more so.

God knows I don't claim to be any exception to that rule. The life I'm leading now—how different is it from the life I've been leading since I first grew up and started out on my own? I'm down at the office every morning, nine o'clock sharp, and I don't leave till five. As a matter of fact, I'm working harder than I ever did, because business conditions have been so lousy lately—what with the shlock competition getting bigger, and the goddamned unions finally moving into my factory, and the headaches from the government. I don't travel much on the road anymore, but the buyers still come from out of town, and I show them a good time at nightclubs and theaters, though maybe I can't keep up with the champagne like I used to. If Oscar was around, *he* could keep up, I'll bet. Turning seventy wouldn't have put any dampers on Oscar. But me . . .

What's happening to me anyway, in my old age?

That's some question coming from a man like me. Since when am I the type that asks such a thing? A few days ago I wouldn't have, it wouldn't even have come into my head. Why am I doing it now? Sitting here with my mail piled up, going over my life in my head, like some kind of philosopher?

All right, those things Jeffrey said to me—last Saturday when he came to town—they got me a little aggravated at the time, but God knows it was nothing permanent.

He said he wanted to have lunch with me—by ourselves, none of our relations around—so we met in this little Italian place that he likes. Downtown in Greenwich Village. I used to go slumming there when I was his age! Wine with the meal, waiters smelling of garlic, very intellectual. I could tell right away he was nervous about something. He was talking a lot, and with that son of mine, that clam, talking means he's nervous. But it wasn't till we got to the dessert, some kind of Italian cake that tasted like an alcohol rub, that he came out with what was on his mind. Casual, like he was only making small talk.

"You know what they just did at our school, Dad? They lowered the mandatory retirement age. It used to be a professor had to retire at sixty-eight, but now it's sixty-five."

"In other words, they used to be stupid, and now they're even stupider."

"Oh, I don't know about that. It's not such a bad idea, when you come to think about it. A man works hard all his life, isn't he entitled to take it easy finally, lean back and enjoy himself?"

I gave a snort. When I hear foolishness, I snort—even if it's from college professors.

"Isn't he also entitled to go on working? Maybe that's the best thing for him?"

"Well, you know, Dad, lots of people don't *know* what's best for them."

He was fidgeting in his chair like a kid during the services in synagogue. I decided to put him out of his misery. "What are you trying to tell me—*I* should retire from business?"

"Well, you *are* over seventy, Dad."

"Two years over, to be exact."

"So why should you be any different from anybody else? Why shouldn't you start pampering yourself? Think what you could do with your time if you weren't working. You could play golf—more than once a week, I mean. Go to your card club more often. You know what a kick you get out of those gin games. Travel a little, go on cruises—you used to do that when you were younger—"

"You sound like your mother. She's been after me the last ten years, I should give up the business and buy a house in Palm Beach. All her friends are doing it, she's afraid it looks like I can't afford it." A suspicion suddenly popped into my head. "*She* didn't put you up to saying all this, did she?"

But he swore up and down that she didn't, and Jeffrey never lied to me. So I said, "So I don't know what's best for me, right? All right, tell me please. Am I hurting my health, going down to the office every day? Positively not. I told you what Artie Boroff said about me. Is business bad for my mental state, I can't take the pressure anymore? Foolishness! I love the pressure, I loved it since I was a kid, it's my meat and drink. Take it away from me, and *that's* when you'll hurt my mental state."

"But Dad, seventy-two years is seventy-two years. Even a man like you, who's bright and alert and in good health—well, isn't it inevitable you'd have to slow up a little? There are bound to be things you can't do anymore, problems you can't deal with, new ideas and developments you couldn't be expected to keep up with. I mean, you admit it yourself, the company hasn't been doing too well in the last few years—"

"That isn't just us, it's an industry-wide problem. These young girls nowadays don't buy our type of product as much as they used to. They think they'd be going against women's rights or something if they looked sexy in bed."

"But you know that isn't all there is to it. Your industry is changing too. There are new styles, merchandising methods, advertising techniques. But *you* won't have anything to do with them."

Then it came to me, like in the comic strips—an electric light bulb flashing over my head. "Wait a second, wait a second, since when do you know so much about the nightwear business? Could I give a lecture on William Shakespeare? You've been talking to Bob Katzenstein, my general manager!"

"Well . . . all right, yes, I ran into him in the lobby of my hotel when I was in Boston last month for the Shakespeare convention—"

"So it's all a plot, that's it! He filled you up with propaganda, now you're supposed to soften me up and make me come round!"

"That's not it at all. He told me some things I ought to know. I'm your son, I'm concerned about your welfare—"

"Welfare! I'm not on welfare yet! He's a bright young fellow, Bob Katzenstein, but there's still a thing or two he doesn't know, he hasn't got fifty years' experience to fall back on! I'll tell you about these new ideas he's pushing on me. Gimmicks, strictly gimmicks, the kind of crap the shlock houses go in for! So I tell him Je Suis Belle, Incorporated, isn't going to lower its standards. So he decides I'm a back number, a broken-down old model, he gets my own son to throw me away—"

"That's not what I meant at all!"

"All right!" I lifted my arm in the air, shaking my fist, and even while I was doing it I remembered Papa making the same gesture God knows how many years ago. "All right, you can tell Bob Katzenstein when you see him—"

"I'm not *going* to see him!"

"—you can tell him it was a good try, I admire a young fellow with determination, but my answer is the same it's always been. First of all, I'm not retiring. Second of all, as long as Je Suis Belle is my company, and I'm the sole owner and president, I'm running it my way. And third of all, it's going to *stand* for something, it isn't going to turn into another shlock house! And fourth of all—fourth of all— where the hell do you get off giving *me* advice about business? You never had to take responsibility for employees, fight the competition, figure out what the customers want. *Your* customers don't have any choice, they *have* to take what you're peddling! My God, I have to listen to this crap from a boy who told me once he was *scared* to go into business?"

He lowered his eyes at that. What else could he do? He knew I was right. He knew he'd been making a damn fool of himself. So I finished that Italian cake, even though I couldn't stand the taste of it, and ten minutes later I put Jeffrey in a cab and went up to my club for an afternoon of gin rummy. The argument was over. I made my point. I won.

So that was the end of that, right? Two parties disagree, they fight it out, one of them wins. That settles it, right?

So why am I sitting here at my desk, going over my life in my memory? Why do I hear a simple piece of news—Morris Unger is coming to the party tonight—and right away I'm asking myself foolish questions? Why can't I put them out of my head?

Should I sell the business, like Jeffrey wants me to do? It wouldn't bring anything like it would've brought ten years ago, but how much do I need? I've got plenty of savings and insurance, and Ruth is dying to move down South. I'll sell it before it's too late, before I run it into bankruptcy with my senility; and there's nothing left for Jeffrey and the girls. I'll sell it because there's no reason anymore to hold on to it. It's all turned sour on me now. On me, Saul Glazer, who used to be top of the industry, who used to have class!

Class—how many times in my life did I use that word? And also logical and practical! Cover-ups—lies—so I could go on closing my eyes to the truth about myself. Who says I was ever any of those things? Who says I was ever the top of anything? Maybe I was one of the dopes all along. Maybe something got away from me, something important. I turned my back on what Papa wanted for me, what God wanted for me. All along I was strictly shlock.

My God, it's after five. I have to go home, get ready for Ruth's party. That's the last thing I'm in the mood for tonight, a pack of hungry screaming relatives—and I still don't know the answer: what's the truth about my life?

M O R R I S

. . . that was twenty-five years ago. I'm skipping over twenty-five years because I must get to this trip to New York: the museum, the doctor, all the things that have happened to me. And then maybe I can understand why I can't open my sketchbook and start in on the swan.

They haven't been bad years really. I was right to stay in Paris—for once I made the right decision. I wasn't there a year—after that terrible beginning in 1945—when I was fitting in exactly as I had before, settling down to the same life.

I've done a lot of painting in these twenty-five years. I'm seventy-three, still at it. Painters last a long time, Titian was ninety-nine when he died. Has my work been getting better? Yes, of course, by my standards. Wouldn't satisfy a lot of critics, I know that. The kind who think a painter has to change his style completely every year, or he isn't "growing." Picasso—one year it's Neptunes with fishtails and long forks, the next year it's women with two noses. The garment industry view of art: can't be seen in the same dress two years in a row. *I'm* still painting what I've always painted—ballet girls, nudes. Beautiful things don't stop being beautiful.

I go on selling them too. Maybe not as much as I did in my very best years. Those years right after the war—whole new crop of American tourists coming over, people who made their money in the war, never bought pictures before in their lives. Loved my ballet girls. Tapered off after a while, of course. Lantin still handles me in Paris, Kleinsinger in New York. Well, young Lantin and young Kleinsinger. Amazing how many of my old clients are still loyal to me. The ones who are alive.

Louie Hertzberg's gone. Stayed on top to the end, regular role in a television series. Working in front of the camera when he had his heart attack. Ruth and Saul Glazer still buy my stuff too.

And I've seen things of mine in museums, on and off through the years. My little charcoal drawing in the Luxembourg Museum. My full-length portrait of Mrs. Newberry—first thing thousands of people have seen when they walked into her room at the Metropolitan Museum. I believe they've got something of mine in Russia. Never been to Russia actually.

I still take my trips to America. Not every year anymore. Every three or four years now. Not because I can't afford it—plenty of buyers to make it worth my while. Traveling isn't as easy for me as it used to be. At seventy-three you get tired. The luxury liners aren't what they were in the old days anyway. Terrible food in third class, no service to speak of.

My tastes are still simple though. Don't need much to keep me alive and happy. Still cooking for myself most of the time. If I eat out, it's at some cheap little restaurant in the neighborhood. Spending as little as ever on my clothes. Living in the same apartment— Madame Voisin passed away peacefully in her sleep ten years ago. Her married daughter has the job now, takes care of me very nicely. My relatives tell me I'm out of my mind. "Why do you want to go on climbing those stairs at your age?" Good for the leg muscles, I tell them.

My social life nowadays? Women—that's all over now, I'm afraid. Friendship, conversation—just as important as ever. The café is still there. Cafés never go away, in Paris. Thought my group was all gone after the war, disappeared off the face of the earth. Bit by bit they drifted back, came out of their holes, like mice after the cat's gone away. The ones who weren't dead. Some new faces joined us. Pretty soon we had our regular table again.

The café's bigger now. There's a dance band inside. Dreadful noise, hated it at first, I'm used to it now. I go there most nights, always somebody to pass the time with. The arguments about art don't change much.

Can't follow them as easily as I used to. This hearing of mine. Left ear's no good at all. Right ear's not too bad, if you talk straight into it, pronounce your words carefully. When I walk along the street with somebody, I ask him to stand on my right.

One more thing about my life nowadays. Louise's boy Michel. I kept track of him for a while. He didn't know I was doing it, of course. He became a doctor, married, left Paris—went down south somewhere. I never found out just where. Deliberately. It wasn't much good really, sneaking around in the background. Always the danger I couldn't keep myself there, my feelings would be too much for me. Better to stay away from temptation. When I happen to feel the need—for going back, that is, being with Louise awhile—I still have three or four of the pictures she sat for. I look at them, alone in my studio, till I don't feel that need anymore.

That brings me up to right now. Why I'm in New York on this nice November day. Not my regular trip to America. That was more than a year ago, never intended to come back so soon. Then the pains began—sharp shooting pains, up and down my arms. Very inconvenient when I was trying to work. I've always had this feeling about French doctors—they're fine for small ailments, for big ones only New York doctors will do. Hangover from my childhood, I suppose. I wrote to my cousin Irving in New York, got a letter back from his son. Irving is retired now, turned the practice over to his son. If you're planning to be in New York, the son wrote, I'll look you over.

Well, why not? What was keeping me from coming to New York? I let him know when I'd be here, asked him not to tell anybody. Not to tell my family. If it was something serious, there's nobody in my family I'd want to talk it over with. Nobody I feel close to. Nobody in New York I feel close to, now that Danny's gone.

No, I won't think about Danny. It was an accident, I've always been sure of that. Cold rainy night, ice on the road, car out of control.

So five days ago I arrived in New York. Sad blue light, same as ever. Rectangles everywhere you look. Paris is round, New York is a city of angles. Irving's son saw me the day after I arrived, specialist saw me the day after that. Sour little man, never a smile on his face. Proves how good he is, I suppose. This morning Irving's son broke it to me. Rheumatoid arthritis, they both agree on the diagnosis. Degenerative disease—it'll get worse and worse, finally cripple me for good, won't be able to uncurl my fingers. Nothing they can do about it, except pills for the pain. Five or six years they give me.

Is *that's* what's troubling me now? Odd really, but it isn't. I was ready for it—the moment I heard the verdict I decided it could be a lot worse. Considering some of the things I was expecting. A lot could happen in five or six years. They could find a cure for degenerative rheumatoid arthritis. I could drop dead from something completely different. Renoir had it at the end, didn't he? Went right on painting, strapped the brushes to his wrists.

I'm not going to think about it. More important things on my mind. My girl in blue, back home in Paris. That blotchy hair.

Was it the gallery this morning then? Rich woman—youngish, dyed blonde hair, looked at everything, didn't like anything. Hard brassy manner, might have been trying on dresses. Well, it's annoying, can't deny that. But typical—got used to her kind long ago. *That* wouldn't be making me relive my whole life.

Yesterday at the museum then? Metropolitan, went thei to see my Degas. I looked at her awhile—modest expression, heavy hips. Looked at other things too, had a salad for lunch, then went to Mrs. Newberry's rooms.

Stepped through the door. My God, she wasn't there. My full-length portrait of Mrs. Newberry, first thing you saw when you entered her room—something else was there instead. Nineteenth-century English landscape, boats in the mist. Very nice, I suppose, I was in no mood to appreciate it. Looked through the whole exhibit, every room, up and down the line. It wasn't anywhere.

They took it down to clean it, I thought. Every picture needs cleaning once in a while. Or to put a new frame on it. Something simple, to set off the flesh tones. Those old gilt frames were too overpowering. I asked the guard about it. He didn't know a thing. I went to the front desk, asked to see the curator of twentieth-century paintings. Of course he wasn't available—out of town, attending a conference somewhere, at the public's expense. The assistant curator was there, he'd be glad to see me.

Young fellow, black-rimmed glasses, pudgy, pasty faced. Looked as if he was made of cookie dough, they hadn't got around to baking him yet. Wet handshake. Soft purring little voice—any minute you expected him to start scratching. Long hair, turtleneck sweater. Museum curators dress like hoodlums nowadays.

I didn't tell him who I was, just asked him in a polite voice why Mrs. Newberry's portrait by Unger wasn't up in its usual place.

"Oh, we took that down months ago," he said.

I asked him why they took it down.

Little purring voice, pursed-up pudgy lips. "Well, we have to weed out the second-rate items sooner or later, don't we? A museum like this has to keep updating its standards constantly."

"When Mrs. Newberry gave you her collection, she specifically asked you to hang that portrait there—it was one of the conditions."

He laughed, soft pudgy little creases. "Good heavens, it's ages since she made that gift. Who remembers anymore what the conditions were?" His eyes narrowed—little pink white-mouse eyes. "I can't imagine who'd want to make a fuss. What's your interest, if I might ask? Are you a member of the family?"

I'm proud of myself really. Whatever I was feeling inside of me, I held it in, lifted my chin, spoke up in my iciest voice. Didn't realize before that I *had* an icy voice. "I'm a type *you* wouldn't be interested in. I'm an art lover." Walked away from him, head high. Never looked back. I could imagine his foolish mouth hanging open.

Is that why I'm so upset now? Why I can't even force myself to pick up my pencil—and that swan is coming around the corner too! I hope that isn't it. I hope I'm not finally letting them get to me—the curators, the critics, the gallery owners, the businessmen, the relatives I'll see at Saul Glazer's party tonight. . . .

Dear God, they haven't been right about me all these years, have they? I wanted to be an artist since I was a boy—nothing else I ever wanted. I've given up everything for it. Never enough money, never a country of my own, never a wife, children, a home. I didn't mind, not in the deepest part of me. It was worth it, because I'm an artist. And now it turns out I'm *not* an artist? A hack. An imitator. A second-rater.

What does that make me then? Seventy-three years of lying to myself—seventy-three years of being nothing at all. . . .

Good heavens, is it really so late? Hardly enough time to get ready for that party. Dreadful ordeal, but I'd better go. Otherwise I'll sit around the hotel all night, tormenting myself with that question: what's the truth about my life?

MEETING

It was seven-fifteen when Morris got to the party. Already the living room was packed and the noise level was high.

He barely had a chance to take a breath. Ruth led him over to Saul immediately; there was time for a quick handshake and an exchange of hellos, then somebody grabbed Morris by the arm and pulled him away. It was Ruth's brother Irving Boroff, who used to be Morris's doctor. He had a dirty joke to tell him. Irving had retired from his practice, and he moved very slowly, on account of his rheumatism, but he managed to keep up as conscientiously as ever with the latest dirty jokes.

As usual, Morris listened intently, one hand cupped to his ear, and tried very hard to laugh at the end of it. . . .

Saul was on his way to the bar, which had been set up in a corner of the living room—behind it was the colored. fellow who had been bartending at his parties for years—when his sisters Goldie and Dodie slid up next to him. Breathlessly, tripping over each other's words, they told him about the problem they were having with the plumbing in their little apartment on the West Side, and the landlord refused to do a thing. Would Saul call him up and give him a talking-to? Saul agreed. Every month or so they came to him with some complaint, and usually it didn't amount to anything, but how could he turn them down? He was the only man in the world they could depend on, their daughters having married such total washouts. And they looked so old and feeble these days. It was peculiar how fast they had both aged since the Klutz Brothers died. . . .

Morris was approached by this white-haired old man with a thin pale face, like something out of El Greco. It took Morris a moment to recognize the rabbi, Nathan Steinmetz. The rabbi asked him why they never saw him at synagogue on Friday nights anymore. His darling wife came regularly, so why not him? Morris didn't have the heart to explain that the rabbi was mixing him up with somebody else.

A woman came up to them—skinny, in her forties, with big shining eyes. Selma something—she was the daughter of one of Saul's sisters. She clutched at the rabbi's shoulder and told him she had just been converted to Christian Science and it was the first time in her life she felt truly at peace. The rabbi smiled, nodded, and told her how happy he was for her, and he hoped, now she was back in the congregation, that she would join the sisterhood. . . .

Saul saw that blimp Celia Solomon bearing down on him, but he couldn't dodge her in time.

"I'm going to recite after dinner," she said. "I didn't want to, but dear Ruth insisted. I *was* going to do 'The Boy Stood on the Burning Deck,' but I realized in the nick of time that it wouldn't do. Perfect for bar mitzvahs, but what's needed on this occasion is something with a scholarly academic twist to it, yet also dramatic and moving. Well, I finally came up with it. Jeffrey being a Shakespeare scholar, and all the generations being gathered together tonight, what could be more appropriate than Shakespeare's 'All the world's a stage'—that exquisite speech from *As You Like It,* you know?"

Saul was beginning to feel desperate. Then his sister-in-law Janet appeared out of nowhere, took the blimp by the arm, and led her off toward a waiter who was passing a tray of shrimp. The Marines to the rescue—you could always count on Janet! . . .

Morris, his feet a bit tired, sank into a chair. He found himself sitting next to an old lady with dark glasses. "Of course you don't remember me," she said, in a high sing-songy voice. "I'm Saul's sister Doris. You *don't* remember me, do you?"

What could he say? He tried to assure her that he remembered her very well, but she shook her head and said, "No, you don't. Why should you, I've been out of circulation for such a long time. Ten years I've had these cataracts on my eyes, I'm practically blind, a trained nurse lives with me, she had to bring me to this party. Nothing would've kept me away, no matter how much trouble it was. I had to celebrate this beautiful occasion with my brother, and if I pay for it tomorrow morning that's a sacrifice I'm more than glad to make—"

Morris jumped up and excused himself fast. . . .

Saul was just about to find Ruth and ask her whether she planned to starve her guests to death, when the maid announced dinner. The big rush to the dining room began. The spread on the table, which people were supposed to eat buffet style, looked pretty good to Saul. You had to hand it to Ruth—this kind of thing she still did as well as ever. People shouted compliments at Saul. "Still the best restaurant in town!" "Where did you get this turkey, it's the nectar of the gods!" "I haven't tasted cheesecake like this since before the war!"

It occurred to Saul that he might go up to Ruth and tell her what a good job she had done. Then he decided there was no point to it. . . .

Morris filled his plate, ate quickly, filled it again. Only when his appetite had finally subsided did he notice something that gave him a small shock. The picture he had sold to Saul and Ruth years ago, his Spanish dancer in red, wasn't hanging over the dining-room mantelpiece, the way it had been on all his past trips to New York. An odd-looking instrument of some sort—some kind of barometer, something that might have come off some old sailing ship—was hanging in its place. People did put the oddest things on their walls nowadays. He wondered if his dancer was out for cleaning or reframing. Or had Ruth simply got tired of it?

He hoped it wasn't that. He got up, looking around for Ruth, determined to put his mind at ease. . . .

Saul gave a start as Ruth rushed up to him and took hold of his arm. "Oh my God, I've made a terrible mistake!" she cried. "I forgot completely about Morris's picture—the Spanish dancer! You know how we always put it back in the dining room whenever he comes to town, and then take it down again when he leaves—because that imitation impressionist school really *doesn't* wear very well, does it? Well, I completely forgot to put it up again tonight! If I'd only known just a few days sooner that he was going to be here— Do you think Morrie will notice? Will his feelings be terribly hurt?"

Saul couldn't feel much sympathy. One year she *liked* the picture, the next year her friends started talking to her about "imitation impressionist schools" and she *didn't* like the picture! "You made your bed," he said, "you'll have to do your own lying in it!"

He walked away from her, and ended up face-to-face with his nephew Artie Boroff, Irving's boy. Right away Artie whipped out a snapshot of his new baby, his sixth. It was the talk of the family how Artie and his wife kept having babies. Well, Saul had said it at the time, hadn't he? What do you expect if you marry a gentile? . . .

Morris went into the living room but couldn't see Ruth anywhere. Then he saw her sister Janet. *She* would know where Ruth was. She was the sort of person who always knew everything. . . .

A voice blasted Saul's name, from somewhere behind him.

"Uncle Saul!"

My God, it was his niece Estelle, his sister Goldie's girl. As loud and pushy as ever, still didn't know how to keep her mouth shut. Fifteen years ago, at a party like this one—in this same room, in fact— she made one of her "cute" remarks, aimed right at him, which he had found snotty and offensive. Since then, though he had seen her plenty of times at family occasions, he hadn't spoken one single word to her unless he absolutely had to. But the nuisance was, she didn't know, or anyway she pretended she didn't, how much he hated her guts. She was always trying to make conversation with him, and he always had to run in the other direction.

"Uncle Saul, Uncle Saul!"

There she was, closing in on him. He turned on his heel and headed for the hallway. His intention was to hole up in the library, the little room off the hall where Ruth and he liked to sit when they were alone in the apartment and the living room seemed too big. Ruth called it the library because there was a shelf of books behind the TV set. . . .

Morris finally found Ruth.

"It's a funny thing," he said. "That Spanish dancer of mine—you used to keep it in the dining room, but it doesn't seem to be there now. Did anything happen to it? If the paint's been cracking or something like that—"

"Oh no, Morrie dear, it's in perfect condition. I moved it out of the dining room though—a year or so ago, since your last visit. It just couldn't be seen properly up there. We couldn't get close enough to really examine the brushstrokes, the workmanship. So we've got it in the library now—that little room across the hall, you know. Saul and I often go in there to look at it."

He wondered if she was telling the truth. After his experience at the museum yesterday . . . But he shook off this thought. There was no point upsetting himself. All he really wanted was to see her again, his Spanish dancer. To remind himself what she looked like.

He mumbled some excuse to Ruth and headed out to the hall, and then to the little room across from it. He opened the door, and found the room in darkness. He fumbled for the light switch, and when the light was on he went up to the picture hanging on the wall, over the television set. He stared at it for a while, until suddenly he realized that he wasn't alone in the room.

Saul Glazer was sitting in one of the leather armchairs, holding a glass in his hand.

———————

"Oh, I'm sorry. I didn't know you were in here. . . ."

"Don't mention it. Sit down, make yourself at home."

"Thank you."

"You had to escape from the hullabaloo too, did you?"

"Hullabaloo? Oh yes, it *is* noisy out there. The family is always so lively."

"Like a cage of tigers. I keep a bottle of extra special brandy in here, picked it up in France the last time I was there. That was ten years ago, but they told me it would age pretty good. So how about joining me?"

"Yes—yes, that would be very nice— Mmm. It *is* quite pleasant."

"Personally I'm not sure I can tell the difference. All I know is, I wouldn't waste this kind of quality stuff on that mob out there. Vulgarians, if you know what I mean."

"Excuse me? Aryans?"

"Never mind, it doesn't matter. So—Ruth got quite a shock, running into you this morning. Why didn't you let us know you were coming to town?"

"Well, as I told her, I came to see a specialist, I didn't want the family worrying about me."

"I'll tell you the truth, I didn't exactly believe that specialist story when I heard it first. I had a sneaking suspicion there was a different reason."

"What reason? Why should I—"

"You're positive you haven't got some little girl here in New York, some pretty little thing, you don't want to show her to us?"

"Saul, I assure you—good heavens, at my age—"

"What's age got to do with it? You're the same age as me, a year or two between us—and believe me, the old itch still comes over me from time to time. If I was an unmarried man like you, a free agent—"

"I'm afraid you must have a lot more stamina than I have. That sort of thing—all over for me long ago."

"I'm sorry to hear it. You keep yourself active in other ways, though, from what I hear. How's the art business?"

"Excuse me? Oh, the *art* business. It's very good actually—excellent."

"People still buy your stuff, do they?"

"Oh yes. Some things never go out of fashion. Beauty, grace, nice shapes and colors. I dropped into my gallery only this morning. Several people are interested in my latest things."

"That's good news. I know what being an artist can be like."

"Yes—well—how's *your* business, Saul? Are people still buying—er—your product?"

"Women are never going to stop buying nightwear. That's what makes the world go around, right? Je Suis Belle is still one of the top firms, making a profit *and* giving value for money, that's the only way to stay up there."

"Yes, I can see that."

"Some of these young people going into business nowadays don't go along with that philosophy. All they can think about are short-term profits, won't listen to what older, more experienced heads have to tell them. It's the influence of the shlock houses, in my opinion."

"The what houses?"

"Shlock, shlock. The ones that have moved into the industry. Sleazy methods, inferior material, no standards. That's the modern world for you."

"Yes, I'm afraid it is. A lot of this painting that gets so much attention nowadays—smears and squiggles, nobody seems to care about technique anymore. Well, you must be very proud of your son tonight."

"Jeffrey's doing all right. My son the college professor, would you believe it? Did you meet my granddaughters? They insisted on staying up, wanted to take a look at the guests. Bright kids—full of curiosity."

"Yes, I saw them briefly. Lovely girls, lovely. The tall one is built like a ballet dancer."

"Jeffrey and Lois are giving her ballet lessons, I think. I don't suppose she's serious about it though. In the way of a future career."

"If she *did* go in for it, I'm sure Ruth would be pleased. With her interest in art and culture."

"You can say that again. A ballet dancer in the family—that would be a great addition to her collection."

"Yes. Well . . ."

"Well . . ."

"So . . ."

"So . . . I noticed, when you came in here, Morrie, you were looking at that picture there, that Spanish dancing girl of yours."

"Oh yes, it's been so long since I've seen it."

"It's forty-seven years since you sold it to us—you remember?"

"Oh very well. Very well indeed."

"All these years, I've been meaning to ask you something about that picture. Somehow I never got around to it."

"Ask me what?"

"Her feet, Morrie. Are they or aren't they crooked?"

"Are they? Let me see. Yes, you're quite right, they *are*."

"So why did you do that, make those feet crooked?"

"Well, that's a question, isn't it? I'll just step a little closer to her—Why *did* I do that? There must have been *some* reason. I just can't seem to remember."

"You don't suppose—maybe it was a *mistake*?"

"A mistake? Could it have been? Why yes—you know, I do believe you're right, it *was* a mistake. Yes, it's coming back to me now. I intended to straighten out those feet, but then Ruth dropped in and saw the picture and wanted to buy it, so I just never got around to fixing it."

"Morrie—Morrie, my old friend—have some more brandy!"

"Why yes. It's very nice, isn't it? Thank you very much."

"And here's a toast—to the next time we meet. We should both stay healthy till then."

"Oh yes—I'll drink to that."

When the time came for Celia Solomon's recitation, Ruth commandeered everyone into the living room and made them sit down and be quiet. Saul and Morris had to take chairs at opposite sides of the room.

Celia Solomon, waving a long yellow shawl, told the family that all the world was a stage and the people in it merely players. She demonstrated this point by crying like a baby, sulking like a schoolgirl, fluttering her eyelashes like a lovesick teen-ager, brandishing an invisible sword and grimacing in a bloodthirsty manner like a soldier, rubbing her stomach like a hungry business tycoon, cackling and walking bent over like an old crone, finally lowering herself to the floor and playing dead. Several nephews, puffing and straining a bit, lifted her to her feet to acknowledge the applause.

Shortly afterward the party began to break up. Morris was among the first guests to leave. At the front door he kissed Ruth, but there was such a crush of people that he didn't have time to shake hands and say good-bye to Saul.

MOVING
AGAIN

M O R R I S

Lovely night, really. Soft golden glow in the sky—from the buildings and streetlights, not from the stars. It's been years since anybody in New York saw the stars. No touch of winter in the air yet. I'll walk down Park Avenue for a while. Why spend money on a cab when I've got a perfectly good pair of legs?

Poor old Saul. Looking so old all of a sudden. Stooped over. Circles around the eyes. Has he got a stomach ulcer? That's what businessmen get, don't they? Still goes down to his office every day. What on earth does he do there? Dull letters to read. Figures to add up. Customers to see. Outwitting, maneuvering, making money. It would drive me crazy, such a life.

And when he leaves that office at night, what's waiting for him at home? Ruth. Poor silly Ruth. Her bragging about her family. Her ignorant talk about art. Those pretty, delicate features, trim small-breasted figure—so beautiful once. And now . . . What *I* had—how much better!

What's the truth about my life?

The truth is, my girl in blue. Have to do something about her hair. To create a masterpiece for posterity? No, I won't worry my head about such nonsense. If I have or haven't created masterpieces. First-rater, second-rater, *any*-rater. What matters is, there's beauty in the world. I've seen it. Loved it. Tried to put it down on paper, on canvas. You have to try. Even if you're no good at all. Trying is what matters.

A touch of red maybe. Just over the left ear. Yes, of course—a glint of light through the window. And outside, the swan. Better go to the park tomorrow morning, catch up with that swan.

What a pleasure it'll be to get back to work!

I wonder if I'll ever see poor old Saul again.

S A U L

So it looks like I survived another one! Thank God it's over though. Everybody gone to bed, got the place to myself. Peace and quiet—no more war cries! One last cigar before I turn in. The last one is always the best.

Poor old Unger. Looks God-awful these days. Those pouches under his eyes, you could put your laundry in them. Deafer than ever too. And all that talk about people still buying his paintings, his stuff never goes out of fashion. Who does he think he's fooling? If he sells a couple a year, he's lucky. Thank God the old lady, what's-her-name, Mrs. Newberry, is supposed to have left him something. Was there anything going on between those two, any hanky-panky all those years ago? Probably not. If there ever *was* a woman in Unger's life!

Did the doctor actually give him a clean bill of health? He doesn't look so healthy to *me*. What's it like for the poor old kocker, for God's sake? All alone in the world, at a time like this. Sick, dying maybe, nobody to cheer him up, take care of him. Going home to some crummy little hotel room tonight—all by himself. You get on in years, things turn sour on you. What could be worse than being alone? What I've got, whatever it is, is better than that.

So what's the truth about my life?

The truth is, I've wasted enough time asking such questions. I'm in the negligee business, not the philosophy business. Which means no more of that foolishness about selling the company. What kind of a quitter would I be turning myself into? It's like a game—gin rummy, some game like that. The cards are running against you, but that doesn't mean you throw in your hand. Even if you're a lousy player—which damn it all, I'm *not*!—or if your opponent is God, and sooner or later, no matter how good you are, He's bound to schneider you.

Even so you have to fight for every point. Because otherwise what are you? You're Oscar jumping off his terrace. You're Papa getting lost in his opera records. No, God damn it, that type I'll never be!

So enough with the philosophy. I'll be at the office early tomorrow morning, I'll finish off that stack of mail. It's about time I got back to work.

I wonder if I'll ever see poor old Unger again.

James Yaffe was born in Chicago, Illinois, in 1927.
He graduated from Yale in 1948; three years later
he began his literary career with *Poor Cousin Evelyn
and Other Stories.* Since
then he has written seven novels,
among them *What's the Big Hurry?* and *Nothing but the
Night,* two plays, *The Deadly Game*
and (with Jerome Weidman) *The Ivory Tower,*
as well as two volumes of nonfiction.
He is Writer in Residence and
Professor of English at Colorado College,
and lives in Colorado Springs with his wife
and three children.